To Steve.

2012.

Charlie

A Jordan Wright Thriller

ENEMY AMONG US

RANDY REARDON

Copyright © 2011 Randy Reardon
All rights reserved.

ISBN: 1456508288
ISBN-13: 9781456508289
Library of Congress Control Number: 2011905422

What Readers are saying about Enemy Among Us;

ENEMY AMONG US by Randy Reardon is a solid read that should make the hairs on the back of your neck stand up because the plot the evil doers in this thriller are working sounds like something out of today's headlines. It's no stretch to imagine the madmen who fancy themselves the government of Iran doing despicable deeds in order to wreak devastation on The United States. Randy Reardon's story is well-plotted, has solid characters you can feel for and credible action and technique. In short, ENEMY AMONG US has everything a thriller needs to scare the heck out of a reader. As authors of eighty-two novels ourselves, we recommend ENEMY AMONG US.

Just finished this book, what a great read. I couldn't put it down. If you like Grisham, Baldacci, Patterson or Ludlum, this book is a must read!!!

I recommend this as a book that will frighten you!
Randy Reardon has created an interesting hero and solidly drawn subsidiary characters, all of whom reveal a depth of humanity. Most importantly, Reardon has hatched a complex plot that is scarily realistic, so much so that it will make you feel uncomfortable, because it could so easily be the headline on the seven o'clock news. In THE ENEMY AMONG US, the enemies of America concoct a convoluted plot that would never be expected and could not be guarded against, as it mines new depths of evil. The background detail -- setting in particular -- is very nicely laid out. This is a good, solid read you shouldn't miss.

Chapter One

✤ ✤ ✤

ITALY

"Forgive me father, for I have sinned," Jordan nodded toward the man, taking the seat offered. A moment of silence fell between them. Jordan looked at the wall and then at the Priest. "It has been six weeks since my last confession."

The Priest again nodded and Jordan realized the Priest while making eye contact was not necessarily engaged. Jordan couldn't blame him. It seemed it was a small parish, one of hundreds dotting the countryside of the Umbria region. Jordan wasn't sure why he had picked this church. It had more to do with his desire to get this over with rather than any spiritual calling. He knew what he was about to say would snap the Priest back to an attentive mode. It always had that impact.

"I confess to the using the Lord's name in vain," Jordan started and the priest acknowledged, "and I killed six men." Jordan thought the Priest was going to fall out of his chair and moved forward to catch him.

The Priest recovered and stared intently, not sure what to do. A man's instincts take over regardless of their devotion or occupation. The instinct was to flee a room you found yourself in with a newly confessed killer. But as in every other case, this Priest recovered, gained his composure and made eye contact with Jordan.

"My son, you have confessed to the greatest of sins, before I can grant you absolution, I must ask you what drove you to commit these acts?"

"It's my job," Jordan quietly replied.

The priest shifted in his seat. Jordan could see the perspiration appear on the man's brow.

"These men were sworn enemies of my country. If I hadn't killed them, they would have killed many, many others."

"I see, so you are a soldier?"

"Not really." Jordan could see the hesitation return to the priest. "I work for a government agency that supports anti-terrorism efforts throughout the world. We don't wait for the bad guys to come to us, we go to them."

"I see. Do you do this often?"

"Whenever I'm asked." Jordan sighed.

"We are often called upon to do things to protect others. Yours seems to have been an extreme version of that call. The men you killed were they Christians?"

"Not likely."

The Priest nodded. "Yours is not an easy confession to hear." Both men paused, which gave, which gave Jordan a chance to think about the events of the past day that led him to be in this room, within this church.

He had arrived at Leonardo Di Vinci airport on the overnight from Newark. Preferring not to stay on the large motorways he had exited the E-45 about an hour from the airport and plotted a route taking the SS3, passing through quaint villages until he spotted Trevi and felt the need to stop. Trevi, an ancient town situated on a sharply sloping hillside standing out in the flat plains of the surrounding countryside was visible from a great distance, rising from the earth like a sentinel and drawing you towards it like a siren of the sea. A walled city, with narrow streets and a large number of people milling about, Jordan quickly found the first car park and left his vehicle. He wandered for quite a while knowing what he had to do, but needing to find the right place.

Trevi was a city of churches, Jordan stopped at six before he came upon the Church of St. Emiliano. A plaque by the door stated that Emiliano was the first bishop and Patron Saint of the town as well as a martyr. He entered through the main door and saw the man he needed to speak to enter a room at the side of the church.

Jordan snapped back to focus in the room when he noticed the purple Biretta on the table next to the priest. The cap of a Bishop. "Oh great, what have I done now," he thought to himself. A Bishop may have a whole different idea of penance than a small parish priest.

Jordan noticed the man staring at him, staring at his cap.

"You're a Bishop?"

"Yes, my son I am."

"What are you doing here?"

"It's a long story, but it's where I've been assigned."

"I see. My guess is you didn't ask to be assigned here. Where were you before?"

"Rome, the Holy See."

"This is quite a change." Jordan stared at the Bishop.

"Politics are everywhere. I fought battles where men were not killed, but they were eliminated nonetheless. I bet on the wrong man and found myself in the position I had placed many others. Maybe we are more alike than you think young man. We both had to undertake tasks though unpleasant needed to be done to protect a greater good. I have no regrets for my action, and I don't believe you should either."

Jordan was taken aback. It wasn't the response he would have expected from any priest, particularly one that was a Bishop who used to work at the Vatican.

The Bishop continued, "our world has many enemies. Some we can see, others we can't. We have to battle both everyday. We are all soldiers in a cause. You must think of your duties and the greater good you bring about. Only when you doubt you are doing good should you question what you are doing. There seems to be something else troubling you."

Jordon nodded. "Yes Bishop, you are correct. The man I was ordered to find. A man called Tahir is very bad. He plans and finances terrorist actions around the globe. I found him and he is in custody, but he told me something that has me very disturbed. He told me there are enemy cells within the US that have been activated and are in the final stages of planning their attack."

The Bishop nodded. "Yours is a very hard job, my son. You carry a heavy burden. Remember there are those that will always be there for you. You should find solace with Saint Michael the Arch Angel and say his prayer daily. He will look after you. I know it may not be what you have come to expect. But tell me my son where are you headed?"

"I have a villa rented outside of Siena."

"You're far off track for Siena, even for someone on holiday."

"I'm stopping off in Assisi."

"I see. Paying tribute to St. Francis. A noble endeavor."

"He also gets me through the day."

"I'm sure he does. There is someone you should seek while you are there."

Oh no, Jordan thought to himself, can't I ever escape from him.

"Find a Father Marco, he would appreciate what you are going through. Though I've never gotten the full story from him, there seems to be some things in his background that are similar to yours."

Jordan held up his hand with his palm flat out. "You can stop there. I know Marco well. I do hope to see him."

"I see. I could ask why you don't confess to him, but I won't. But getting back to why you are here, pray the Act of Contrition with me and then I will absolve you of your sins. Pray a decade of the rosary and do start each day reciting the Prayer to St. Michael. It should give you comfort for what you are called on to do."

Jordan recited the Act of Contrition. Thanked the Bishop, turned and left the room, found a pew and did his penance.

When he finished, he left the Church, holding the door for a frail elderly women.

"Is the Bishop still taking confession?" She asked in Italian

"I think he is." He responded in the language he loved but felt he hadn't mastered. She seemed to understand.

"I've got a good one for him today. I'm sure it will be the best one he hears." She smiled and winked as she entered the Church.

He stifled a chuckle as he went to retrieve his car

Chapter Two

�֎ ✖ ✖

Mustafa Amadi grabbed the cell phone on the corner of the desk and flung it across the room, sending it directly into the second hand wall unit. On impact the back spun off, with the battery quickly falling to the floor. The rest of the unit took the full impact and fell in several splinters of plastic to the worn carpet.

He pushed back from the table, leaning back in his chair with his hands clenched in tight fists over his eyes.

"I cannot believe this. They are insane. They know nothing about how effective my team can be." He threw his fists up in the air still leaning back in the chair. He shifted his weight and it brought him forward as he scanned his translation of the note just received. What was it with these people?

Two days ago he received the message, coded in an email that had been routed through several servers around the world to disguise its origin. To anyone reading the message, it would seem to be a note from an aunt to a beloved nephew in another country. However upon decoding, Mustafa discovered his mentor had been killed, or in his mind assassinated. Tahir Alfani had been like a father to him. He had given him this assignment when many had felt he wasn't ready to lead such an important operation. He pleaded with Tahir to not undertake so many missions on his own, but to rely on others. A plead that was always met with laughter and being told to not worry, it was in Allah's hands.

Now he was gone, and when he pushed his leaders to let him activate his team as revenge, the response he just received was the time was not right. The time was never right for these fools. Now with Tahir gone, he was almost certain they would never act. They were weak. They were bureaucrats in a battle that needed decisive leadership.

Tahir had spent almost twenty years training his team and getting them legally immigrated to the U.S. and they had assimilated into their neighborhoods. With the funds he had been given he was able to set them up in various businesses. Beyond anyone's wildest dreams, he had actually been able to send more money back to the leaders in Iran then they had originally given. Capitalism was funding some of their violent activities and allowing them to grow their recruitment and training activities. But with all the success he wasn't able to convince them he and his team were ready to carry out their mission.

Now his biggest regret was sending the money back. They didn't know he and his team had generated such income from their endeavors. He wished he had kept it because it would have made him a very rich man. He could walk away from it all and get lost in this big country. Why not? If they weren't going to let them do what he had been trained for, then why not just go off and live the rest of his life. The families of the team would be fine. They all had jobs and if he no longer required most of their profits, then they would have a very nice life. For all they sacrificed, it would be a small reward because they could never return to Iran and their true families.

But Tahir's death would forced him to do something. No longer could he just sit there and do nothing. He would move forward on his own, but he didn't want his masters in Iran to get credit. He pulled open the center drawer of the table and fished through the unorganized papers and cards until he found what he wanted. It was a business card of a man who had approached Mustafa several months ago. He had wanted to form a partnership and had promised it would be very enriching for Mustafa. Mustafa had first rebuffed this man, because he was still a warrior for the jihad. But now with Tahir gone, martyrdom seemed like a vacant cause, but helping someone creates greater injury to this country while enriching himself, seemed more appealing.

He went over to the wall unit. The phone was beyond repair. He fished out the SIM card and went to the back bedroom. In the rear of the closet he opened a bin that had several unopened boxes of similar model cell phones. He quickly opened one and popped in the SIM card. He dialed the number.

"Yes." Came the response when the call was answered.

Mustafa thought it was the same man he had met. "This is Mustafa. Is this Mr. Medina?"

"Yes, to what do I owe the pleasure of your call? Have your circumstances changed?" Jerome Fernandez-Medina replied

"They have and I think there is an opportunity for us to do business."

"Fantastic, you will not be disappointed. Is your team ready and are you comfortable with the plan we laid out?"

"I am. It will work."

"Great. We will begin the work from our end immediately."

"We will be ready"

Mustafa heard the click on the other end.

"Allah Akbar." He shouted in his home. He had much work to do, but he now had the green light he always wanted.

Chapter Three

✠ ✠ ✠

Gleaming off the white granite of the cathedral, the bright sun was making it an even more impressive sight. Jordan had returned to Assisi, the place where it all had started. Driving up the narrow street, keeping his focus on the cathedral as it towered over the village, he was overcome with the sense of peace he found here. Finding a parking space on the street, he walked the remaining few blocks, continually looking at the imposing structure. Though he'd been here on numerous occasions, he was still in awe of the magnificence and simplicity of the church that lay before him.

He crossed the street and stopped in the middle of the plaza. He slowly turned himself completely around, taking it all in -- not just the grounds of the cathedral, but the city and the surrounding countryside. Though it wasn't his home, Jordan felt more comfortable here than anywhere else.

With the sun receding, he walked to the side of the church, entered through a door not marked, which lead to a stairway. He descended several flights and was soon in the lower undercroft, which housed the original church and the tomb of Saint Francis.

He'd not started out to be a fighter against terrorism. He'd grown up as a child of privilege. His father bought and sold manufacturing companies, usually able to buy on the cheap and sell at the top of their value. With his success, Jordan's dad became more consumed with building his business even larger. To achieve this, his dad was away from home often, and unable to help as Jordan saw his mother turn to alcohol to combat her loneliness. Eventually, the marriage failed and Jordan rarely saw his dad. His mother recovered from her alcoholism, but not before it had seriously compromised her health.

He spent each term at boarding school, then his mother and he would travel to Italy every summer. With all the sadness that had come into his life, these summer trips brought joy. They had come to Assisi together on their first summer visit and came back every year for the next seven. When he was here, he no longer hurt from the pain of his parents' divorce and his father's abandonment.

In his senior year, his mother passed away. Jordan was surprised to find his mother was as good at finance as his father had been. She'd used her divorce settlement for a series of shrewd investments, resulting in Jordan inheriting a substantial amount of wealth. He returned that summer, alone, and still felt the peace and calm of the past. It was on this visit that he met Father Marco. Marco, a Franciscan priest, had noticed Jordan and his mother on previous visits. This time, seeing the young man alone, he approached Jordan and they began a conversation.

Father Marco became a mentor to Jordan. He talked to Jordan about pursuing a life of service and not to just live off the money he'd been left. The priest was instrumental in Jordan's career choice, due to Father Marco's past. Jordan at first thought Marco was pushing him to pursue the priesthood; but, he later found that Marco had a different life before he joined the Order, with a past of espionage and efforts to undermine the enemy during the Cold War. For a portion of his life, Marco had been an operative of the CIA. As he got to know Jordan, the priest saw a lot of himself in the younger man, enough that he felt Jordan could be of value to his country, as Marco had been. He contacted a former colleague of his, who eventually recruited Jordan.

Jordan was brought out of his thoughts when Father Marco came and sat down. "How are you my son? It is so good to see you."

"I'm fine. I knew you would find me."

"Your last mission --it was a success."

Marco always amazed Jordan. A man of the cloth who still had enough connections that he always seemed to know what Jordan was doing. "Yes, it went well, but I'm troubled by something I was told by the man I was pursuing."

"Amadi has always been troubling. I'm glad you have taken care of him. The world is a better place."

Jordan looked at him. How could he know? Jordan had asked before and had never gotten anywhere, so he wasn't going to waste time now. He related to Marco the comments Tahir Amadi had made that his operatives were already in the U.S. "I need to find out if it's true. We've know there are cells, but he confirmed their activities."

"There is a man with whom you need to speak. Fortunately, he is close by. We were enemies at one time; but we have grown to be friends. The Cold War changed many things, including turning people who were supposed to kill you into those few people who truly understand what you did for most of your life. He lives in Siena. I'll contact him and have him meet you tomorrow. I know he can help. Stay at the Grand Hotel Continental and he'll find you." Marco rose, gave Jordan a blessing and walked out.

Jordan found his way out of the lower Church and found his car. Before getting in, he did the cursory check to make sure it hadn't been tampered with during his visit. He'd become a quick study of the techniques of the enemy and he knew, with his recent ability to dismantle several of their cells, he'd moved a couple notches up on their hit lists.

Satisfied nothing was amiss, he took one final look at the basilica, drove out of Assisi and headed toward his villa. By the end of the week he would be back home and into the fight again. He needed rest and he needed reconciliation. He was hoping to achieve both.

Chapter Four

※ ※ ※

IRAN – NINETEEN YEARS EARLIER

Following the Iranian Revolution in 1979 and the success of capturing the American Embassy with fifty-two hostages, the revolutionary council was surprised by the election of Ronald Regan in 1980. President Carter had been the ideal President for the Iranians, since he didn't exude confidence and leadership at the time his country needed both qualities most. His policies played right into the hands of the Iranians, who were able to keep the crisis on the front page of the world's newspapers for four hundred and forty four days; and, this elevated the Ayatollah Khomeini to status as a world leader. But Reagan was someone entirely different. He was a cowboy and, as predictable as Carter was, Regan seemed much less conventional in his approach and more prone to take more decisive action when he took office. The Revolutionary Council determined they had used the hostage crisis as well as they could and it would be best to release them at the beginning of Reagan's term.

Tahir Amadi would not let it rest. Not satisfied that they had inflicted enough damage and pain on the Great Satan, the United States, he convinced the ruling mullahs to form a new secret group, with their best minds in the areas of intelligence and military operations, charged with developing the next wave of action that would inflict the greatest damage on the U.S. While the Embassy takeover had been quickly put together as a mission, this team was told that the hundred-year revolution was just beginning for Iran and time was not as important as was striking a decisive blow.

A bold initiative was launched two years after the hostages had been returned, with the desire to take the fight to U.S. soil.

Amadi would lead the new initiative. At its simplest, the plan involved identifying Iranians and providing them the training necessary to ensure the success of their roles. They were provided few details of what they were going to be a part of, or what the ultimate goal would be.

Each had been approached in a straightforward manner by a representative of the government who had told them, as a matter of national security and the future of their country, it was imperative for them to travel to the capital. All had agreed, not realizing they would never return.

The world heard the tragic news of the hotel fire in the capital city in the middle of the night that had killed over three hundred people, many in town for a government conference. What the world did not know was that the dead bodies were those of tribesman who would never be missed by their families and could be used to cover up the real reason these people had disappeared.

Secretly removed from the hotel via an underground passageway and boarded onto busses prior to the fire, the people selected were all transported to a new compound, on a remote part of a military base. Here, they were given rooms and new clothing, since everything else they had was in the hotel. The following morning, they were brought into a large room and addressed by Amadi, a man they all knew but had never met before, a leader of the Revolution. A man everyone knew to fear.

Briefly, he spoke of the need for each of them to commit to a mission critical to the survival of their nation. He stated that no one would be returning to their families or would be able to have any contact with family or friends. The lights dimmed and a video played of the newscast of the fire. At the end, there was a scroll on the screen of all of the dead. Each individual in the room watched as his name scrolled across the screen.

"I'll not be a part of this," one man stated as he stood up in the audience. "I demand to be returned to my family and my business at once."

Amadi was somewhat taken aback and countered, "Why do you not want to serve your country? You should feel honored to have been chosen for this great role and opportunity to serve. You will be a hero."

"I do not want to serve this government." The man shouted back.

A gasp of fear escaped the lips of others in the room. While many were thinking the same thing the man was stating, they knew if it was said it in public one's fate was sealed.

Two men in dark suits came up behind the man who had been speaking.

"I'll give you one chance to change your mind and sit down. This type of outbreak will not be tolerated. The mission you are about to embark on is too critical and of the greatest importance. Will you join with your brethren?"

"I'll not! I demand to be returned to my village and my family."

"That is not possible because to them you are dead."

"I'll not participate in this!"

With barely a movement from the feared leader, one of the dark-suited men behind the protestor looped the long thin wire of a garrote around the protestor's neck, jerking it tightly. As the man gasped for air and began to lose color, the other dark-suited man grabbed the already dying man's head and, with a quick twist, snapped his neck, the sound of the bone breaking echoing across the room. The man slumped to the floor as his two killers stepped back.

It was eerily silent as two uniformed medical orderlies entered the room and quickly removed the body.

Amadi cleared his throat to get everyone's attention. "Please use this example as a lesson to you. Dissidence will at no time be tolerated. This program and your role are vital to the future success of our beloved country. I ask each of you to understand that your life as you once knew it is gone. You can only move forward with what we have planned for you. The families you have left behind will be taken care of and each will receive a substantial settlement from the tragedy at the hotel. You need not worry about them."

At that moment, he left the stage and a person that no one knew took the stage. He did not bother to introduce himself. Amongst themselves, they would later nickname him Ivan. It was clear he was not from their country, but rather from either Russia of one of the states of the Soviet Union. He would be their teacher and would define their future. He would pick their roles and would decide when they were ready and where they would go.

Chapter Five

Jordan was quickly approaching Siena. He knew it would be crowded today because it was the beginning of the first Il Palio, an event held twice each year, on July second and August sixteenth. Unlike anything Jordan had ever been to in his life, he'd stumbled upon it several years ago and tried to make sure his visits to Italy corresponded with one of the dates. Il Palio was part street festival and part horse race, which as a combination would only be possible in the ancient city of Siena. Jordan pulled off the roadway at a bus stop. He boarded the local bus for the journey into the ancient fortress city since Jordan knew parking was impossible on a regular day and only the bravest would attempt to park in the city during the Il Palio. Twenty-five thousand visitors would be in the city during the next two days.

As he waited for the bus, he was joined by others traveling into the city. He recalled the first time he visited Siena. People know Rome, Florence, Venice, Milan and Pisa, but many had not heard of Siena. In the heart of Tuscany, Siena was made up of seventeen "contrade" or wards. These neighborhoods were laid out during the Middle Ages and remained, more by their inhabitants' emotions and history than by any administrative or political function. Each contrade had a horse in the races, but only ten horses race on each day. Jordan had yet to figure out the politics of how it was decided which horses or contrade got to race on both dates; however, he'd heard enough to know the politics of contrade would make the politics of Washington look like kindergarten. The race was only one element of the events. To really enjoy Il Palio, one had to venture into the various contrades beginning the day before the race and become totally immersed in the event.

Officially, it would begin that evening, with each contrade hosting a dinner. Each contrade, as in most Italian cities, had its own Piazza or village square, which would be filled with long tables to accommodate the citizens and guests of the contrade. Jordan had been lucky enough on his prior visits to become friends with several Sienians and could always count on several invitations to dine with various contrades. And dine they did. Jordan had never seen so much food at one setting. The aromas, as he reached the center of the city, were incredible. He could smell the breads being baked, the tang of tomatoes being cooked for gravy and the strong odor of garlic. The combination was like nothing he had ever smelled. His mouth involuntarily began to water and his stomach began to growl. The crowds were pushing through the center of the city and it was quite difficult to get one's bearings and be able to head in the direction one wanted to go. Jordan knew, from past experience, it was sometimes best to go with the flow of the crowd, versus trying to move against it. He found he eventually got to where he wanted.

Jordan made his way to the Grand Hotel. If nothing else, Marco always knew the best hotels and restaurants. The hotel was a former seventeenth century palace, in the center of Siena and close to the Piazza Del Campo, where the horse race would be held.

"May I help you, sir?" asked the man at the reception desk, dressed in a white coat and black tie, blending with the opulence of the lobby.

Jordan was always bemused by the fact that, no matter how hard he tried to fit in, he was always quickly pegged as an American. "I believe I have a reservation. Jordan Wright."

"Ah, yes! We've have been expecting you. A friend of Father Marco's is always welcomed here."

The clerk handed him the room key along with an envelope. "You have a message. If there is anything else you need, please let us know."

After settling into his room, Jordan opened the note. It was from a man named Gerhardt, welcoming him to Siena and asking Jordan to meet him at one of the dinners planned that evening. Jordan stopped by the front desk on his way out and asked for a map. Quickly, he found the contrade where the meeting would take place. It took him almost twenty minutes to arrive, having to pass through several of the other contrades and their celebrations.

Walking through the neighborhood, Jordan was eventually approached by two men.

"Are you Mr. Wright?" The larger of the two asked.

Jordan nodded.

They turned and walked toward a large table. They hadn't said anything, but Jordan got the impression he was to follow. As he approached the table, he was shown to an empty seat next to an older man, who was in great physical shape.

"I'm Gerhardt.   Welcome Jordan and, I'm glad you could join my neighbors." Turning to the neighbors, Gerhardt put his arm around Jordan.   "Jordan is Marco's nephew.   He'll be one of us for the race tomorrow."   The table erupted with acknowledgements and welcomes.   Everyone seemed to know and have come under the charm of Father Marco.

Gerhardt leaned over and whispered to Jordan.   "Tonight we have fun and celebrate; tomorrow we will discuss business."

Jordan nodded.   "Sounds good to me.   I've been to Il Palio before, but never have been part of a contrade."

Everyone around Jordan began to talk about the horse they would have race tomorrow and their chances of winning.   Much of the discussion at dinner was the strategy the jockey should deploy.   It wasn't just about winning; it was just as important that your enemy lose.   The contrades each had a long history of alliances and enemies amongst the other contrades. Much had been lost to history and many had no idea why they are either aligned or opposed to another; but it was the way it had always been.   The citizens of the contrade, all who actually had a say in how their horse should run the race, would greatly debate over dinner on whether to go for the win or ensure their enemies' loss.   By the time the festival got underway, the horses had already run a series of trials, so the citizens had a good idea in regards to the strength of their horse and jockey.

As more food was served, the louder and more involved the debate became.   Jordan enjoyed playing the role of the observer, as he was thoroughly entertained by the back and forth discussions, everyone having his opinion and, more importantly, the opinions on others' opinions.   Jordan wasn't sure if any strategy were emerging that all would agree upon, but he'd come to discover there was a pecking order among the citizenry and, while everyone got their say, it was actually a few well-respected individuals who would decide the approach to be taken the following day.   Jordan had also discovered that, regardless of what they advocated tonight, tomorrow each individual would be telling everyone his strategy had been the one adopted.

Around midnight, Jordan finally made his way back to the hotel.   The city was still bustling, but his stomach was stuffed and he needed sleep. Opening the door to his room, he noticed the blinking red light on the phone. "Damn," he thought. Only one person would have known to look for him here. Max Bogle was just too good. Max, Jordan's boss, would only call if there were something brewing.

After he retrieved the message, Jordan decided to call back when he woke in the morning, prior to the beginning of the festivities. He stripped off his clothes and headed toward the shower. Steam enveloped the bathroom, relaxing him. He came out of shower dried off, and hit the bed. No sooner had he put his head on the pillow than he was sound asleep.

Chapter Six

Startled, Jordan woke up to his phone ringing. He took a quick moment to compose himself and then picked it up.

"Who is it?" Jordan demanded.

"Jordan. It's me, Max. Did you get my message last night?"

"Max, what's going on? I was going to call you back this morning, after I woke up."

"Sorry, Jordan. It can't wait. I need to see you right away. I'm coming to Italy. We need to meet tomorrow."

"What's going on, Max?"

"Jordan, we can't discuss this over the phone. Where will you be tomorrow?"

"At my usual place. Can we say ten o'clock? It's Il Palio today, in Siena"

"Oh, my gosh! Are you kidding? Well, lucky you that you can have fun today, because it won't be fun tomorrow, when we talk."

"Great, Max. I'll see you then."

"Have fun, Jordan." Max hung up.

He took his shower and went down to have breakfast. The hotel lobby was a bustle of activity. Excitement was everywhere with people loud and the lobby jammed, which made it a challenge for Jordan to maneuver himself across it to the lounge, where they served breakfast. He grabbed the last table by a window. It seemed he was the only one that was just now getting up, so he quickly filled his plate at the buffet and asked for a pot of coffee. People were everywhere in the street, wearing the colors and symbols of their respective contrade. He could pick out those that were from Tortoise and Wave, others from Owl, Snail and Giraffe. As he returned to his table, he found that Gerhardt had joined him.

He found himself quickly forgetting about the phone call from Max and seeing her tomorrow.

"Good morning, Gerhardt. Thank you again for dinner last night." Acting unsurprised by Gerhardt's appearance, Jordan sat down.

"Jordan, you are more than welcome. I was happy to be your host. Marco told me you were in need of some information. How can I help?

Jordan brought Gerhardt up to speed on the Pakistan operation and Tahir's comments. "Marco felt you might be able to fill in some of the blanks."

"I'll try my best. Marco may have told you I'm former Stasi. I was the number two in their clandestine operation when the wall came down and the Russians sold us out. Fortunately, I had friends in the Kremlin who gave me a heads up and I was able to be in Switzerland at the time. My wife was Swiss, but when she passed away, I wanted to be somewhere else. I came here on vacation and never left."

"Not a bad spot to live your life." They both laughed. "How did you connect with Marco?"

"Marco and I spent thirty years trying to recruit the same people, carrying out similar missions. We had seen each other many times. We knew who the other was and what we did. Spying is like any other business. You're competitors but, you know and respect one another. Sometimes, we won; other times, Marco did. But, we were always professional to one another. One day, I was walking down this street." Gerhardt pointed out the window. "Just a few blocks from here. And, I see this Priest approaching in his brown robes. The face is so familiar and then I recognize Marco. I thought he was retired, like me, but I assumed he must be on an assignment, to be dressed in that fashion. So I followed him. As I turned a corner where he'd gone, he grabbed me and pulled me into an alley. He'd seen me and thought maybe I was freelancing and was there to kill him. Once we got it all straightened out, we had a great laugh. We spent the rest of the day drinking and reminiscing. Two old colleagues, talking about people we had worked with over the years and wondering where they were now. No different than any two people. We're dear friends, now."

"That's a great story. I'm not sure I ever see myself sitting down with some of the folks on the other side, these days."

"It's a different world, today, Jordan. I don't envy you at all. Going up against men like you do, you have my blessings. I'm not sure I could do it. They are rotten. Men like Amadi play by no rules, like so many of his comrades. Elimination seems the only option."

"What about cells in the United States? I don't mean ones put in for the short term. I mean ones that might have been in place for years, just waiting to be activated."

"I think it is possible," Gerhardt responded after a moment. "I remember hearing about and seeing some documents out of Iran. They were disappointed they didn't get more out of holding the American hostages. It didn't cripple America, like they had hoped. They developed plans for a long term project and it was going to cost them a lot of money and more than ten years; but, I think they were moving ahead. It had to do with families and getting families into the States. I never saw the details or any status reports."

"So, you're not sure if they actually did it."

"No, but, I'm sure they started it. I'm just not sure they got people into the States. I think you're better off to assume they got some element in that could be activated."

"I agree Gerhardt."

There was much commotion on the streets.

"Jordan, we must go. It looks like Mass has let out and the race will be starting soon. Here are my contact numbers. I'll help in any way."

"Thank you. You've already been a great help."

They left the hotel and joined in with the throngs of people on the street.

Everyone was headed to the center of Siena. Unlike any horse race Jordan had seen, there was not a dedicated horse track in Siena, but rather the main Piazza del Campo in the town was transformed into the track. When Jordan had first walked into the Piazza for his first race, he thought his friends were pulling a fast one on him. No way could they race horses in this small area. On top of it all, over fifty thousand people were going to pack into the area to watch.

Jordan followed Gerhardt. "So, tell me what is our strategy for the race, to win or to make sure our enemy loses?"

"Ah, that is the question isn't it and, I'm not sure we know just yet. We will need to pay attention to our horse and jockey and see how the line up for the start of the race."

They started to climb up to their seats on one of the many balconies that surrounded the Piazza del Campo. Bleachers were placed on the balconies for the day, so as to accommodate as many people as possible for the race.

The attention went to the starting line. The Il Palio is run clockwise, versus counter clockwise, unlike most horse races Jordan had seen in the United States. Because of the small size of the venue and the quickness of the race -- about ninety seconds -- there was much bumping and jostling amongst the jockeys. The rules were such that the winner was the first horse that crossed the finish line, whether it had its rider or not. The course was narrow and more of a tri-oval than a circular course. Several of the turns were so tight that it would almost be impossible for every jockey to stay on his mount if most of the horses were running in a bunch as they entered the turn.

Jordan could hear the commotion of the crowd reach a crescendo as the horses began to arrive. Each contrade cheered as their horse entered the Piazza. As the horses moved closer to the starting rope, it looked, to the untrained eye, like a catastrophe waiting to happen. This race didn't have the organization of a Kentucky Derby, with marshals on horseback leading the racehorses from the paddock to the starting gate. There was no gate structure attached to a tractor, giving each horse a slot from which to start. At this race, there was a rope across the starting line and the horses moved up against the rope. To the virgin eye, it looked like utter chaos; but, as Jordan had come to learn, there was a great deal of tactical interplay underway, with the jockey and the horse. Depending on one's strategy, it was critical to be in the right position for the start of the race. The starting judge could delay the start for as long as the positioning was entertaining the crowds, for there was no countdown, or signal that the rope was going to be dropped. At a certain point, the judge decided to start the race. He would just let the rope go.

Switching between watching the horses and their jockeys' maneuver, and the judge holding the rope, Jordan tried to determine when the race would begin. The judge gave no indication of his intentions, as each jockey continued to attempt to put his horse in the best position, while at the same time trying to put enemies in a poorer position. Talking to one another, attempting to form alliances, the jockey would create partnerships for the race. Sometimes, they would bluff and make an arrangement they had no intention of keeping once the race began. Not only were the horses used as weapons, but so also were flying elbows, legs kicking and even the occasional whip lashing from one jockey against another. Several times, Jordan found himself flinching and moving backward, to avoid a blow he saw coming a jockey's way.

As the rope dropped, pandemonium erupted in the Piazza. Horses bolted onto the course like they had been shocked by prods. There was no announcer, not that anyone could hear one anyway, as the Piazza was walled in on every side by a 15th Century palazzo, becoming an echo chamber of disjointed sound, of cheers and screams. As they tore around the course, the horses showed none of the beauty of a thoroughbred race; but, in its own right, it was a sight to see.

As they moved into the turns, there was considerable bumping, as horses and jockeys collided with one another. Quickly, one jockey was off of his horse and rolling in the dirt of the track, while his horse continued with the race and was still a contender to win.

The horse from the contrade for which Jordan and Gerhardt cheered was in third place and part of a group of three that had distanced itself somewhat from the pack. This gave the trio some room to move and position themselves. As they moved into the second lap and the tightest turn, their contrade's jockey maneuvered his horse on the inside of the second horse, taking the turn intentionally wide, which forced the number two horse against the wall and gave that jockey no choice but to pull up and slow down, which allowed Jordan's and Gerhardt's contrade horse to move into second place. An erupting cheer thundered from those around Jordan and they pounded their feet on the bleachers and the whole balcony began to shake. For a moment, Jordan became somewhat concerned but, as his friends slapped him on the back, he joined in the cheers and decided not to worry about the stress loads on a 15th Century balcony holding ten times the amount of people for which it was intended.

Their horse closed in on the leaders as they entered the last lap. As they passed by, people leaped over the barriers and started running after the horses on the track. It was total mayhem. The horses were neck and neck, with no real space between them and two turns which remained before the finish. The noise in the piazza was thunderous. Jordan couldn't even hear the people next to him, albeit they were obviously shouting at the top of their lungs.

They barreled through the next to last turn, both horses were headed to the final turn and the finish line. What would the final strategy be?

Jordan could not guess. Both jockeys would have to make their move, as their horses seemed equal in speed and agility.

The horses entered the turn, the lead horse attempted to jam Jordan's contrades horse against the inside barrier, with the hope the crowd would spook the horse but, just as the opposing horse and rider closed in, the jockey on the horse from Jordan's adopted contrade quickly pulled back and to the left, sling shoting his horse around the leader and kept him reigned in tight, so the other horse found itself off balance and had to take short steps to regain its stride.

The horse of the contrade Jordan stood with rocketed across the finish line. Leaving the bleachers, Jordan and Gerhardt climbed down to the Piazza, to join the pressing throngs. Marching with the rest of the citizens of the contrade and their winning horse to the Church of Santa Maria in Provenzano, they proudly waved their banner and would spend the rest of the evening parading through Siena, while at the same time hosting the victory dinner for all citizens of Siena.

Chapter Seven

Leaving Siena after dinner, to return to his villa, Jordan's mind went back and forth from the grand events of the Il Palio to what Gerhardt had told him and, finally, thinking what was so important that Max needed to come see him. At least the day in Siena and being part of the contrade that won had helped him escape from the dread of what the next day might bring.

Rounding the last bend, his villa lay directly in front of him. Nothing spectacular, it was run down, not having been well-maintained and the furnishings were worn. The agent had shown him so many other choices within his price range that would have been more comfortable and given him, as the agent described, the true Tuscan experience but, Jordan had opted for this villa. It fit him. It was basic, it was comfortable and, when he moved in, he felt at home.

He entered the villa, finding it as he'd left it the other day. He grabbed a Peroni out of the refrigerator and took a seat in the old comfy chair in the living room. The cold beer tasted great as it was traveling down his throat. The long pull resulted in half the bottle being gone in his first gulp.

He scolded himself for not stopping and picking up a newspaper. One might have revealed some information about what was going on in the world that would have caused the pending visit. His spartan villa had no TV, radio or Internet access. Most of the time, Jordan was grateful to be off the grid and somewhat out of the loop on the happenings in the world but, now, he wished he could have some modicum of information, to prepare himself for what might be coming. After a second beer, which was consumed almost as quickly as the first, Jordan headed up to the bedroom.

While he had expected a restless sleep, he was surprised to find he'd slept through most of the night and it was almost five o'clock in the morning. Quickly, Jordan decided to shower and take a quick journey to Sant'Antimo and go to Mass. It was a twenty-minute ride from the villa to the Monastery but, it always seemed to Jordan to take him back five hundred years. Outside the small village lay the fields, church and monastery of an Order of Brothers. Every morning, at seven o'clock, they gathered in the comparatively large Church and chanted Mass. Though their congregants kept dwindling, Jordan was always impressed that, even with the smaller number and the increasing age of the remaining brothers, they were still able to fill the huge space of the church with the most incredible sound.

Though Jordan didn't understand Latin, he still felt the beauty of the experience. He found his favorite pew, to the left center of the altar, which allowed the acoustics of the Church to center right in that space. He would sit there and close his eyes and the most serene feelings would come over him. He felt as if he were floating, his mind becoming completely clear, devoid of all thought, except for the beauty of the sound that was enveloping him. It ended all too soon and Jordan found himself headed back to his car.

He was drove slowly home in anticipation that Max wouldn't arrive until noon at the earliest, given flight schedules and travel time from the airport. So, he stopped at a small restaurant for breakfast. He was able to find the previous day's Herald Tribune and scanned it to see if there were anything happening in the world that would explain the phone call and visit. He found nothing.

He slowed down, turning into the lane leading to his villa, noticing a different set of tire tracks on the dirt road. Possibly, the landlord had been by to check on him, as had been his practice every two to three days. Or, it could have been the local farmer who tended the olive groves surrounding the property and, on two occasions, left samples of his olive oil on Jordan's doorstep.

He rounded the last bend and he saw a car parked in front of the villa. He didn't recognize the car but, recognized the person standing next to it smiling at him. It was William Jendell, the co-leader from the Pakistan mission. How did they get here so fast, Jordan wondered as he parked next to the large Audi?

"Hey ya, Jordan!" William called, as he put out his hand. "Bet you're real glad to see me," he said with a shitty little grin on his face.

If William hadn't been so good at what he did, and gotten Jordan out of a few situations in the past, Jordan probably would have just hauled off and hit him.

"Hi, William. How's the leg." Jordan said restraining himself from taking any action. "You got here fast; I wasn't expecting you for another hour or so."

"Leg's healing. We brought a G-5 from DC," William said with a smile, his right hand simulating a plane flying fast. "Came directly into Florence. You can't beat it!"

"I guess not." Jordan stated. "Where's Max?"

"Inside, waiting for you."

"Hmm, I thought I locked that door?" Jordan focused on the door, mentally reviewing his actions earlier in the morning. He knew he'd locked it, but also knew it was a simple lock and would have been no challenge for William and/or Max.

"You did," smiled William.

Jordan walked into the house to find Max in the kitchen, standing in front of the open refrigerator, reaching deep into the shelves. "What in the hell are you doing in my refrigerator?" Jordan called, wanting to startle Max.

Max jumped.

Having the desired effect Max quickly turned around with the look of a teenager caught shoplifting. "I was going to cook up some breakfast for the three of us," Max stated.

"Allow me," Jordan said, as he pushed Max out of the way, reached into the refrigerator and grabbed the eggs, an onion, and some fresh ham he'd recently been given by the tenant farmer.

"I guess this must be important if you commandeered one of the boss's planes to get here so fast. I thought I had at least until noon to make the place presentable."

"There's nothing in this place to make presentable. You are the only person I know who goes on vacation and stays in a villa that no one else would ever, ever consider renting." Max ranted, touring the downstairs of the villa with widespread arms.

"I like it; it suits me just fine," Jordan declared as he pulled out a skillet and began cooking the ham. He grabbed a bowl from the shelf next to the sink and cracked the eggs to begin the omelet.

"Let me bring you up to speed on why I'm here and what we need you to do." Max began.

He silently chuckled to himself. Jordan always loved when he could get to Max. They had a love/hate relationship. He'd never met anyone quite like Max before. Smart, probably bordering on brilliant, but not brainy. Max was a strong leader, but not overbearing, and usually willing to listen to another's point of view. But, Max always had your back. A maverick, willing to get into someone's face if they were feeding too much BS in the process, Max had chewed enough people up and spit them out that most people within the Operations group knew not to mess with Max.

In another place, another time, Jordan probably could have fallen in love with Max. She was attractive, athletic of build, with shoulder length auburn hair, a killer smile and the personality to hold him in check when he needed to be. They had worked together for almost a decade, in all parts of the world and Jordan felt they had mutual respect for one another. There had been many a time when he thought he wanted more of a relationship with Max, but he'd never discussed it with her and never had he attempted anything romantic or sexual on any of the assignments when they had been together.

He didn't want the complication; he didn't want the complexity of balancing a romance with a working relationship. Jordan wasn't sure it could have a happy ending.

"Where did you go?" Max asked standing right in front of him.

"I went down to the old monastery where they chant Mass."

"No Jordan, just now, you were a million miles away, deep in thought about something."

"Oh, nothing. Just thinking. And, no I'm not going to tell you!"

With that, he pulled the ham from the skillet and cut it into three pieces and placed it on the plates. He removed the omelets and placed one next to each piece of ham. Grabbing the plates he walked over to the table.

He yelled for William to come in and join them. Max gave him a look.

"I really don't think anyone will attack us here. If they wanted me dead, you would have found me that way. Let's enjoy breakfast out on the terrace."

William came in and began to sit down. "Where's the coffee?"

Max laughed, "Jordan doesn't drink coffee and he doesn't offer to make it. My guess is you are out of luck to find any within the villa."

Jordan shrugged his shoulders and gave the "that's the way it is" look to William.

"All right, Max. What's going on? Why did you need to travel all the way over here to talk with me?"

"Something big is going on, we think."

"You think?" Jordan got ready to start his typical rant; but, before he could start, Max cut him off.

"Jordan -- just shut up and listen. I know we had promised to give you some time off and I hate like hell to have to interrupt your simple, devoted life here in Italy; but, you're needed. I need you. Let me walk you through what we have so far and then we can have the discussion on whether this was important enough to interrupt your sabbatical."

"I'm all ears."

"Several days ago, a man of middle eastern descent walked into the FBI office in Philadelphia. He asked for protection and began to tell an incredible story. Most of what he told us, we haven't been able to verify yet. However, it does fit with some other intelligence we have, including some specific hunches and insight provided by others."

"Hunches. You came over here on hunches?" Jordan started to get up from the table, ready to end the conversation.

"Jordan," Max said as she grabbed his arm and pulled him back into his seat. "They were your hunches. The thinking you have shared with us about long term cells in urban areas of the US."

"Really?" Jordan allowed his eyes to bore right into her's. He recalled the briefing he'd done eighteen months ago to a room full of CIA, DHS and FBI analysts. He'd outlined the scenarios in which immigrants could have been planted in the USA in the late eighties, to sow the seeds for terror cells to be used ten to twenty years later. As Jordan had speculated, these original immigrants might not be the terrorists. They would be model citizens, drawing no suspicion to them. However, their children would be raised to eventually take the role of launching terror attacks within America's borders.

On that day, almost every analyst had scoffed at the idea. They said it was impractical, couldn't be coordinated for the long term, the infrastructure needed would be too easy to identify and American intelligence and law enforcement would find such persons before they could do any harm. Jordan had almost quit that day. He felt everyone had their head in the sand and no one was willing to consider something that didn't fit into his or her view of how terrorists operated. It was the most frustrating thing in the world, to Jordan. Everyone was always underestimating the intelligence of the terrorist leadership. Now, he also had Gerhardt's validation that the theory had been utilized and more than likely been carried out.

"Jordan, can we get back to our discussion?'

"Huh, oh sure. I'm sorry"

"I know you were thinking about your presentation and the reception this idea received. So, yes, it looks like you were right, and that's why I'm here and that's why the Director gave us his plane to get here. It's not just me who wants you back to work on this; the Director demands it. Jordan. We were wrong. You were right. But, we need to stop it. Can we get into the details of what we know?"

"Sure. Tell me what you have, so far," Jordan stated with a quick shrug of his shoulders.

Max went on to explain how this individual made claims and provided information on how he'd been coerced by his government to leave his village to attend a meeting in the capital. During the middle of the week, they were quietly moved out of their hotel and taken to what seemed like a military base. They later came to discover the hotel they had been staying in had been destroyed by fire and each of them had been identified as a casualty of the blaze. In essence, they no longer existed. They then went through years of training, including English language classes, courses on American business, history and culture. They were paired up with a member of the opposite sex from within the program, and eventually given children to raise.

Over time, each of these "families" immigrated and, eventually settled in the Philadelphia area. They would socialize on a regular basis, to allow the children to get to know one another; and, over time, the children were indoctrinated into the beliefs in which their parents had been trained to instruct them and began to believe America was evil and they were those destined to right the wrongs of their people. The families were under the guidance of one man, who made all of the critical decisions. He would decide who would work where, the house each family would live in, what car they would drive. He also provided a monthly stipend to each family, in addition to the wages they were earning. He also assured that no one achieved a lifestyle that might give them too much freedom or bring undo attention to their family.

"So, why did he come in?" Jordan inquired, somewhat bored with the resuscitation of his own research.

"I'm getting to that."

Jordan moved his hands in a circular motion like a football referee wanting to move things along.

"He grew disillusioned when his wife was taken ill with cancer. She could have been cured with treatment available; but it would have been quite costly. The leader of the families would not agree to cover the cost of the procedures and medicines. He felt it would cause questions to be asked of how the family had the means to afford such treatment. The man was devastated he was not even allowed to use the savings his family had accumulated. So, he began to question his whole role in the operation. As you pointed out, Jordan, for some of these operatives, given a taste of America over time, they may grow more attached to the United States and begin to believe in the dream of the USA versus being soldiers of destruction for their former homeland."

She continued. "He knew he couldn't talk with anyone else in the group of families. He didn't believe anyone else was feeling the way he was and would be willing to risk escape. He knew the boy who had been placed as their son had bought into his future role and was actually being groomed as one of the leaders." Max paused to let Jordan absorb what she'd said. He nodded for her to continue.

"He agonized for weeks over what he should do. He received a call from the leader, stating he was going to take the children on a retreat, without the parents, during their next school break. This was not unusual and was happening more and more often, now that the children were older and the time was growing closer to when they would be activated. Our informant decided this was the time that he could disappear. It would be several days before he would be missed and he had an assistant in the store he owned, who was used to taking over when he'd go away.

"After the son left, our man took his car and drove over to New Jersey and took the PATCO train back into Philadelphia. After disembarking at Market Street, he headed to the Federal Building and showed up at the FBI."

"So, where is he now?" Jordan inquired

"Well, luckily one of the agents in Philly had been an analyst at the time of your presentation. When talking to this man, he couldn't believe how the man's story paralleled your presentation. He called a fellow agent, who was in the anti-terrorism squad, who had also been present during your discussion. Let me just say they were able to set off alarm bells. This man was quickly taken to DC by chopper, and he's now in a safe house in Virginia."

"So, what do you need from me?"

Max let out a big sigh. "You know, Jordan, you can have the attitude of 'if you would have just listened to me' or you can jump into what could be the biggest terrorism case in US history. The other fact I forgot to mention is that this wasn't the only group being trained at the same time. There could be others in the US or Europe, for all we know."

"I see," said Jordan.

"You know, there are times I could just slug you. You get so stubborn and on your high horse." Max began to shout. "This is just the beginning! We have nothing but this man. We haven't stopped anything and when they find out he's gone, they just might move their timetable up! We have to have our best minds on this and that means you!"

Jordan sighed, "Okay. Okay. What's the plan? You know I'm in."

"You need to come back with us. We'll head directly to D.C. You will have full access to this man. If we can get additional information out of him, we may be able to determine their targets and timeline. We just don't have enough yet and I'm afraid the FBI might be scaring this man into regretting he came forward. You have a way of getting through to people. They open up to you; for some reason, which I'll never understand, they seem to trust you."

Jordan smirked at her when she made her last comment. "Maybe because I treat them with respect and don't start with the threats right off the bat. Let me pack my things. I can be ready in ten minutes."

William offered to secure the house and limped around, closing the external shutters. Jordan was soon downstairs with his large duffle bag and was ready to head out the door.

"We'll have someone come out and take care of the car and landlord," Max stated as they piled into the car.

As they started out the drive, Jordan yelled, "Stop the car!" and bounded out the door and back to the house. He emerged a minute later, juggling five bottles of olive oil in his arms.

"This stuff is incredible; I can't leave it!" Jordan said as Max gave him an incredulous look. "Hey! I don't want to insult the farmer and set back Italian/American relations. Besides, I brought extra to share with the two of you."

"In that case, just get in the car," Max pleaded. "We've got a plane to catch."

Chapter Eight

✢ ✢ ✢

FBI SAFE HOUSE, TWENTY-SEVEN
MILES FROM WASHINGTON, D.C.

Akmed Aryanpur was alone in the room to which they had brought him after the meetings at what he believed was the FBI Headquarters in D.C. They had traveled twenty minutes from there to this house, and he'd no idea exactly where he was.

He was questioning his actions. Had he done the right thing? Akmed imagined he would have been treated more as a hero, but he felt like they didn't believe him and had hinted they thought he was some kind of agent sent, not to help, but rather to throw them off.

Maybe he should have gone with the other option he'd pondered and just disappeared; this was a big county. He could of headed West and found a place to start a new life. They probably would have looked for him for a while, but not forever. His son had grown to the point where Akmed was no longer the key influence, which was now being provided by Mustafa. They would be suspicious for a while and be on guard for surveillance, for anyone trying to infiltrate the group or approaching the children but, they would not find anything amiss and would soon go back to their normal routine.

His struggle had started several years ago, when he was allowed to buy his hardware store. He found much satisfaction and success in building his business. He was much more successful in the USA than he'd ever been in his old country. While he was only able to keep a portion of what he earned the payments were greatly in excess of what Mustafa had given him to purchase the business. It didn't take him long to figure out that, if he'd gotten a loan from the bank, it would have been paid off and he would have been enjoying a nice income. The family would not have to live above the store, but could have a real home with a yard, a house out in the suburbs. Aziz could be in a better school, enjoying a great education, which would allow him even greater success. But, fate would have it that he was going to be used for "the greater good" and his life would be destroyed in the mission he'd been raised to undertake.

As time had gone on, Akmed had come to find America not the evil, hate mongering land he'd been told it was, but, rather, truly a land of great opportunity.

When his wife became ill and the doctors laid out the only treatment plan that could possibly save her, he'd pleaded with Mustafa for assistance.

"They are treating you as a fool," Mustafa scolded him. "Do not listen to their lies. Her fate lays with Allah, not this doctor who only wishes to grow rich off of your pain and suffering. Our money is needed for our cause, which will rid the earth of this scum and show America for what it really is."

Akmed was beside himself. Where was the compassion that the Prophet Mohammed had taught? He ventured to the Public Library, the only place they were allowed to go outside of the community, without prior permission. There, they had Internet access and, while it was prohibited, Akmed always found a few minutes away from his family, to utilize it. He didn't use the pool of machines in the central area, but, rather, an obscure kiosk located on the third floor, back in a corner. He spent a lot of time researching the illness of his wife and he discovered that, while her prognosis was not good, the treatment the doctors had laid out had produced positive results in others. In addition he discovered she was a good candidate for this type of treatment.

Chapter Nine

❖ ❖ ❖

Jordan found traveling on the Gulftstream 500 to his satisfaction. He had a large leather covered chair in the middle of the plane. Max was in the back, on the phone, and William was up front, so Jordan had his privacy. The galley was stocked with all the food and drink anyone could want and the entertainment center had every movie or television series he could imagine. The flight went by too quickly for him.

As they approached Andrews, he re-hooked his seat belt and stowed the entertainment system. He raised the shade and looked out the window. They had just come across land and he searched for a landmark to tell him how close they were and what direction they were coming in from. He couldn't find anything that looked familiar and they still had considerable altitude; so, it was hard to pick something out on the ground.

Max had moved up to the seat beside him wearing a freshly pressed suit that spoke she was all business. "How was the flight?"

"I could get used to this. This is one nice perk, Max."

"Well, don't think I get to use this anytime I want. I should be thanking you; you're the reason I got the plane. They wanted you here as quickly as possible."

"Well, then you're welcome and I'll make sure I'm always remote when you need me, so you can pick me up in this baby"

"Don't go rock star on me, Jordan. This isn't about you; it's about the mission. We had to get you back, to get you involved. When we land, we hit the ground running. The clock is already ticking on this and we've got to figure out what is going on as quickly as we can."

"Okay -- okay. So, tell me what are we doing first?"

"When we land, we will be greeted by senior FBI and CIA terrorism experts who have been sifting through the evidence, so far. They will brief us as we drive out to the safe house where they are holding the man who came into the Philly office."

Jordan nodded. He hated these briefings, hearing interpretations from intelligence guys who had never been in the field running an operation. They always thought they had the answer, based on what had happened in the past. They didn't realize these terrorist groups didn't pay attention to the past and never did it the same way twice. For the bad guys, each mission was new and different; and, since most, if not all of them, would lose their lives in whatever action they had planned, there was no sharing after the fact. No debrief, no lessons learned, no after action report. When were we going to learn?

The pilot came on over the intercom and announced they were on final approach and would be on the ground in a couple of minutes. He also let them know their ride would be waiting for them on the tarmac.

After a forty minute ride from Andrews, Jordan felt the vehicle slow and begin to turn onto a long lane. He glanced out the side windows as they drove down, creating a cloud of dust behind them. He noticed the numerous cameras hidden in the trees and, as they got closer, the guards dressed as workmen in different areas of the property, ATVs close buy. No doubt the ATVs contained more firepower and deterrents than what most Humvees had in Afghanistan. No one was going to get into this place without a fight.

The Suburban pulled up to the main house and stopped. Everyone piled out and headed up the front steps to the porch. Stan Kershaw, the Acting Director of the FBI, greeted them at the door.

"Max, I see you have found our lost warrior." Stan stuck his hand out to Jordan. "How was Italy, my boy?" Stan drawled. A Texan pushing sixty, anyone ten years or more younger was automatically a "boy" or a "girl." Stan had been one of the first FBI agents assigned to investigate domestic terrorism. He'd been instrumental in bringing and getting convictions on McVeigh, Kaczynski, and the blind sheik and was at ground zero within twenty minutes of the first plane going into Tower Two and had almost lost his life when the second tower collapsed. Unfortunately, Stan's son, Lt. Tom Kershaw of the NYFD, wasn't so fortunate. He'd run past his father when Rescue 2, his unit, first arrived. His last words to his father had been. "It must be pretty bad if you're here before me!" They had their last laugh as Tom headed into the tower and Stan had yelled back, "Take care of yourself and your team, because I think it's worse than bad."

Stan had been instrumental in identifying the terrorists who committed the crime and linking them to Osama Bin Laden. He worked tirelessly, only leaving the investigative team to bury his son and to visit with his grandchildren and their mother. If he wasn't with them, he was working. His wife had passed away several years before and his other children were scattered throughout the United States. A bear of a man, the typical first impression Stan conveyed was that of someone who would make anyone feel intimidated and maybe even scared. As one came to know Stan, however, it was quickly realized that he had a big heart and found good in almost everyone, terrorists or anyone else who wanted to do harm to his country excluded.

Jordan and Stan had met several years ago on a case that could still not be discussed with anyone. At first, Jordan had resented Stan and wondered why he'd been paired with this man who stuck out like a sore thumb. Stan was loud, Stan liked to hug, and what really drove Jordan crazy was Stan liked to talk. He was non-stop and could always find something to yak about. It drove Jordan crazy. However, over time, he came to appreciate Stan's mind. It worked a lot like his -- maybe even better. Stan could connect the dots. Stan didn't need every thing filled in. He could make solid leaps based on the information available. What Jordan really came to appreciate about Stan was that Stan would act. He wouldn't break the rules but, would bend them to the point where they would almost break.

Because Stan had achieved so much and had been so instrumental in restoring the reputation of the Bureau, he was given leeway in how he approached and executed his cases.

Over time – and, over his constant objection -- he was brought into the Hoover Building in D.C. and into management of the Bureau. He didn't relish it at first; but, when Stan found he now had the ability to do away with the dumb rules and procedures, which had hampered him in the field, he jumped in with both feet. He quickly became the hero of the field agents and operatives who finally felt they had someone on the inside who understood how the field had changed. He was perceived as someone who knew the FBI was no longer primarily chasing bank robbers and kidnappers, and needed new tools, new rules and new capabilities to battle terrorism.

Stan was also well liked in Congress. He was straightforward and apolitical. He didn't care what party was in charge. He just kept pushing his agenda of more budget dollars and the right rules. Before long, he was the Assistant Director and, on the untimely death of Director Carl Hogan, Stan had been asked to move into the Director's office. The President and members of Congress, well as many of the Agents he knew, were pushing him to accept the position. Stan wasn't sure. He was at retirement age and been in the middle of this battle for so long -- maybe too long. He thought about retiring to his cottage at the lake and being twenty minutes away from his grandchildren. He was ready, and his retirement papers were completed and sitting in the draft file of his e-mail, just waiting for the "send" button to be pushed. He hadn't pushed it --yet.

"Well, Jordan here we go again." Stan slapped Jordan on his back. "I think we've got ourselves an interesting character upstairs, whom I'm sure you are dying to talk with. Let's go into the den and talk a little strategy before we jump in with our new friend Akmed."

Jordan put his arm around Stan and they crossed the porch to the front door. Stan entered first and Jordan noticed the doorframe was extremely wide and he heard buzzers and bells going off as he entered the foyer. Two guards approached. Jordan realized the thick frame hid a metal detector.

"You packing, son?" Stan inquired.

Jordan looked at him sheepishly and reached around to take the gun out of his holster. He held the gun by two fingers on the grip and handed it to one of the guards. "I don't leave home without it."

"We'll keep it until you leave Mr. Wright. You are safe here." The guard cleared the weapon, smiled and walked away.

Jordan, Stan and Max headed off to the den.

Chapter Ten

�֍ ✧ ✧

Akmed had gone to the window when he heard the cars pull up. He knew they were official vehicles, just like the one he had ridden in to come here.

The people exiting the vehicle were different from the others in the house. The young lady was quite attractive, but more casual in her style. The two men seemed to know each other. Why were they here? Did they not believe him? He would tell them anything. He would tell them everything he knew. It was over for him. Why would they not trust what he had to say?

He knew he was doing the right thing, but he had no idea what was going to happen next. His thoughts quickly drifted back to the day Aziz had been given to them to raise as their son.

Ivan entered the room and raised his hand to get their attention and ask them to remain quiet.

"Let me review with you the activities for the day," he began. "Today is a milestone in our journey to lead the revenge of our country against the infidels of the West. In appreciation of your hard work and dedication, our leader has granted us permission to take you to the National Park for a day of recreation. You have ten minutes to go to your apartments and gather anything you may want to take.

Please be on your assigned bus in ten minutes."

They all filed out and headed to their respective apartments.

As they entered their apartment, Akmed went to retrieve their coats.

Mahasin smiled back and went to the window. "Akmed! Come quickly. You must see this."

He joined her at the window and looked out. She grabbed his hand and held it tightly. "What do you think this means?"

Looking out, they saw busses lined up at the old dorms and the children being walked out and put on them.

Akmed shook his head. "I don't know."

He turned her away from the window and they walked to the door. They both looked back into the apartment, not sure what the day ahead held for them.

Upon arriving at a remote location within the Khab-o-Rochon, a 173,750 hectares wildlife refuge, Amadi stepped up on the platform and called them over and asked them all to sit as couples, but for each couple to find their own table. Everyone stole quick glances amongst themselves, wondering what was to happen. Rarely had they ever been separated solely as couples.

"Today," Amadi started, "we begin our last and final phase of training for our mission. To date, you all have made your country and our esteemed leader proud. You have continued to give us confidence that you are capable of taking on this divine mission and to carry it out successfully, which will guarantee for you a place with Allah."

"Who's this?" Akmed whispered, since he had not been attentive.

"He was just introduced. His name is Mustafa Alfani. He is going to be leading us for the next phase."

"Where did he come from?" Akmed wondered softly.

Mustafa began to speak and, initially Akmed had a hard time understanding him. Then he realized Mustafa was speaking English. While everyone had become fluent and much of their training in the classrooms was done only in English, this was the first time at the Park that English was spoken. It was a risk they probably didn't want to take; however, today seemed to be different.

"I understand you have all worked hard to ensure your success on our mission. It is now time to give you additional details and further explain your specific roles."

"We have for years wondered how best to strike back at the Imperial powers in the world who have continued to be non-believers in Allah, the heathen nations who harm our people and use their armies to inflict death on us and who use their political power to starve us and make it impossible for our people to have the medications they need to survive. Devils who take our resources for their own and consume more than their share of the world's goods."

Mustafa looked out at the couples, to ensure they were not only listening, but also supporting what he was saying. He was not disappointed.

Everyone was nodding in agreement and seemed engaged in his message. Akmed was nodding also, because he knew he had no choice. He was interested in hearing more about their mission.

"Our mission is to go directly to the heart of this beast and destroy it from within. We will live amongst the people we need to destroy. They will think of us as friends. They will join us for social occasions. We will celebrate their holidays. We will fool them into believing we're thankful to live in their homeland. Then, when they least expect it, we will attack them in a way they would never suspect. They will not only see death and destruction, we will destroy them psychologically, when they realize it was their neighbors, their friends who led these attacks."

"You are brave and you have been trained to fit into their world. Remember your training and you will ensure our success. The most important part of your mission begins today. For it is not you who will carry out the attack, but rather the child you will be raising." A murmur swept over the assembled couples. "Over the next twelve months, you will become a team of three. You are a couple, man and wife, and will now have a child to complete your family. Just think how no one would ever suspect families to be in their country to carry out the most important terrorist attack to ever occur. Allah be praised!"

"At the end of the next twelve months, you will be leaving here and heading to various points around the world. Then, you will be immigrating to the United States and will settle in the city of Philadelphia. You know from your history that Philadelphia is the birthplace of this evil country, where they declared their independence, where they wrote the profanity that is their wicked constitution and has allowed them to try to destroy us! But now, Allah be praised, we will destroy them!"

He read their looks and replied. "I know you have not been trained to be those who will directly carry out this mission. Your role is of even more importance. You will ensure the success of this mission by raising the child you are about to receive to believe in what we're doing while at the same time ensuring the child fits into the community in which you will be living."

"This mission is long in duration. You will live in Philadelphia among the infidel for several years before you will be called upon to act. You will raise your child into the teenage years and you must make the children above suspicion. The children need to be good students, need to be involved in the activities children their age do. You have been instructed in all of this and, by carrying out this role, you will ensure our success when the time comes for us to act."

Mustafa continued. "I know you must have many questions. The people who have joined me are the doctors who have been involved in selecting these children. We have studied your medical records and have attempted to find children who come close to matching you. Of course, it is not possible to exactly match. But, we think we have found children who will seem like they belong to your family and were born from you and your partner."

Akmed was thinking why go to all of this trouble -- the time, the training and now the children? This wasn't just some group trained to go bomb a building. This was a well planned and focused attempt to create havoc in the West. He wondered if the other teams they had started out with were hearing the same thing. No doubt, they were going to different cities, and potentially other western countries. This was bigger than he'd ever imagined and would change the world. He wasn't sure if it would be for the good or the bad, but it would be changed.

"In a few minutes, we will be bringing your child to you," one of the Doctors said, addressing the group. "These children have no recollection of their true parents. We removed them at about the time you first came to the compound. They have been raised in a separate facility and were recently brought to your old dorm complex. They have been raised in the belief they would be meeting their parents. That is what will happen today. From their standpoint, you are their parents. Some of them are aware of your absence and have been told you have been working with the government and were not in a position to have them with you. Today is a reunion, in their minds. Please avoid any indication this is your first time to know of them. We don't and they don't have expectation you have much information in regards to them and their lives so far."

Mustafa returned to the stage. "The rest of the day we will spend here at the Park. We suggest you take the time to move away from this area and the three of you spend time getting to know one another. It's not the time for many questions. Focus on the family being back together. Have fun with them. Start building your bond, because it will be critical, going forward that you become a family and can be viewed by others as a family."

More memories had returned to Akmed --

A knock at the door brought Akmed back to the present and the room to which the FBI had taken him.

Chapter Eleven

❖ ❖ ❖

Jordan, Max and Stan attempted to plot their strategy in the den of the safe house.

"Since we don't know the time frame, we really need to push him hard," Jordan offered.

"Yes, but we're on US soil, so it does tie our hands," Stan said, shrugging his shoulders.

"How motivated is he? Let's take a step back," Max interjected, as she rose from her chair. "He shows up and starts telling us this story. We quickly move him out of Philly and down here to this safe house. The guy hasn't uttered a word since. I think we've got to figure out if he is real or not. As much as what he has said so far is our worse nightmare, he hasn't really given any details. How do we know he isn't some nutcase that's taking us for a ride?"

"Or sent in to distract us, while the real incident unfolds," Stan added.

"That's why I think we have to go hard. I'm not talking about harming the guy. I just don't think we have time for the niceties. We need to get more information and we need to get it fast," Jordan insisted, beginning to get frustrated.

"You've got a point. I think we first need to find out if he's the real deal," Stan agreed. "But, if he's not, then we've got to believe he's been trained well enough to take us on a wild goose chase. He could tie us up in some big knots before we realize we're headed in the opposite direction of where we should be."

"Are any of the surveillance teams in place in Philly, yet?" Max wondered aloud.

"They took up their positions about ninety minutes ago; but, they haven't reported anything, nor have they visually identified the boy," Stan noted as he paced about the room. "We've got people on the street watching for…"

"Maybe we're making this harder than it needs to be," Jordan interrupted. "Let's assume this guy is on the up and up. He has bought into the American dream and is turning his back on this mission and what's left of his family. Let's play to that. I'll go up and talk to him, see if a new face brings out any new information, or at least if his story's consistent. Where are the notes from the earlier sessions?"

"I've got them right here," Stan said, handing Jordan a copy of the transcript. "There's not a lot there. As soon as they understood what he was talking about and how it aligned with your lecture, they got on the phone to DC and moved him here. He didn't say much on the ride down."

"Give me a few minutes to look this over; and, then, I want to have a crack at him."

"Okay, but I want Max with you," Stan ordered.

Jordan gave him his patented "Are you for real?" look. "I think I can handle it."

"No doubt you can, but I think one-on–one with you might put him in a position where he thinks he's about to get tortured. With Max there, I think it might give him the comfort it's just a conversation and not going to turn into something else."

Jordan chuckled. "If he only knew."

"Yeah, but he doesn't," Stan shot back.

Max just looked at them both. "I know how to control myself." Max, in the past, had led some of the toughest interrogations of suspected terrorists ever conducted. Her methods, including both mental and physical distress, were case studies taught by both the CIA and FBI. She'd conducted seminars with Mossad and MI6. She was a legend and proof a woman could be just as intimidating as a man, when it came to getting information.

"All right, here's what I want to do. There's a great little sandwich shop a few miles down the road that does the best cheese steak outside of Philly. Get three of them. If he's really been in Philly for as long as he says he has been, he's got to be partial to a good Philly cheese steak"

"We'll go in with the sandwiches and some Coca-Colas and just have a nice conversation. We'll see how he responds and if we can get anything more out of him. But, if by the time the sandwiches are done, we aren't any further along, we'll move to something a little more difficult."

Stan looked at them both.

"I think it will work," Max added supportively.

"Okay. It's your show, boy," Stan acknowledged.

"While we're waiting for the sandwiches, can I grab a shower and change of clothes?"

"Sure. You can go upstairs. You have a room at the end of the hall that has its own bath."

"How about you Max? Going to freshen up?" Jordan asked.

"I showered on the plane."

For the first time, Jordan noticed she was wearing a different outfit than what she'd worn when she came to the villa. He also realized she did look refreshed but, she always looked ready to enter the boardroom, even when they had been on missions for several days.

"You didn't tell me the plane had a shower. You mean I could have cleaned up before we landed?"

"You never asked," Max responded with a sheepish grin.

Jordan walked out to the room and they could hear him head up the steps.

Once he was sure Jordan was out of earshot, Stan looked at Max. "How do you think he's doing? Is he ready to jump back in?"

"Stan, I don't know. When we first arrived at his villa, I thought it was a lost cause. He just looked like he could have cared less.

"Yeah, what's that all about?" Stan shot into the conversation.

"I think it's about atonement. It's his way of dealing with all the ugly crap he's had to deal with. It's about finding that simple life away from all of this. It's the only place I've ever seen him relax. I can't explain it, Stan, but he looks like a different person there. William said he didn't even know him when he first saw him. He thought it was the caretaker. Oh, by the way. I did get you another bottle of the olive oil."

Stan nodded with a smile. He thought of the great meals his wife had made using the oil the last time Jordan had brought some back. He missed more than her cooking. He forced his mind back to the task at hand.

"But, is he ready. You haven't convinced me yet that he is."

"Sorry for getting side tracked. I thought he was going to tell me no and walk away. However, as I began to give him the details, I could sense he was becoming more engaged. His face changed. It was like he transformed back into the old Jordan, right in front of me. Stan, he got it. He realized it was everything he'd been talking about and no one would listen. Present company excluded," Max quickly added when she noted the change in Stan's facial expression. "We didn't have to force him to come with us. He came on his own."

"Okay, I get it," Stan nodded. "But, if I start to see him cracking, I'm pulling him out."

"That's fair. It would have been great to give him more time, but these things don't work that way and he knows it. I don't think he would have come if he didn't want to be in the game. Yes, he wants to prove the people wrong who told him he was full of shit. More important and why we have always admired Jordan, he wants to protect his country. He'll be as good as he always has been."

"I hope so. We need him more than ever, this time."

"He'll be there. He always steps up," Max started to leave. "I'm going to unpack and then check on the food. We'll start as soon as Jordan gets out of the shower.

After she'd changed into a more comfortable outfit of a long denim skirt and a long sleeve top, she headed back downstairs. She didn't want her appearance to be a distraction to the man they would be talking to. She'd found, if she somewhat followed their traditions, they tended to be more receptive. She'd also removed some of her makeup. Not that she wore a lot or needed to wear any, but again she wanted the man to feel as comfortable as he possibly could with a woman asking him questions.

As she went by Jordan's room, she knocked on the door. "I'll be in the kitchen. I'll wait for you there."

"Okay, I'll be there in about five," was the reply.

She headed down the long u-shaped staircase. This was a beautiful home. Too bad its purpose was no longer to raise a family. She could have been quite comfortable here. She entered the kitchen and found the bag with the sandwiches had arrived and was waiting on the counter. She grabbed a tray and grabbed drinks out of the refrigerator.

Jordan walked into the kitchen, grabbing on of the sandwiches and putting it under his nose. "I will never get tired of the smell of a great steak."

"How do you want to handle this?" Max inquired.

"I think we should use this first session to feel him out. Let's try to get him comfortable with us, but I also want to try to validate whether he's the real deal or not. When we're done eating, let's excuse ourselves to clean up and get more drinks and we can evaluate where we are."

"Sounds good."

They were at the door. "Are you ready?" Jordan inquired in a whisper. Max nodded affirmatively.

"Let's go meet Mr. Terrorist," Jordan turned and knocked on the door.

Chapter Tweleve

SOUTH PHILADELPHIA

Aziz opened the door.

It wasn't what he expected.

He wasn't sure what to do.

The weekend had been spent with Uncle Mustafa and his cousins. They had been in Southern New Jersey at a camp. It had been intense. He remembered several years ago when they first started having these trips without their parents. At first, they had been fun. Away from Mom and Dad and with only Uncle Mustafa to watch over them, there had been a lot of time to create mischief. At times, he would be the ringleader and come up with the idea, but get the others to do the deed. If they got caught, he would be somewhere else and not punished. But, he would also make sure he spent time with those he'd sent who got caught, not only telling them he was sorry, but also to give advice on what they could do not to get caught next time.

In actuality, Uncle Mustafa had been aware of the role Aziz had played and was impressed with his natural abilities to lead others. It would come in handy as they further prepared for their mission. One afternoon, Mustafa pulled Aziz aside and they went for a walk together in the woods. Mustafa told Aziz about what he'd observed and how impressed he was with his leadership ability and his ways of convincing others to follow him. His uncle encouraged him to play a larger role with all of his cousins.

Looking around the apartment, he wasn't sure what to do.

"Father? Are you here?" he called out.

He heard no reply. He put his pack down on the chair and hurriedly searched the entire apartment. He was aware of spouses who took their own lives after losing a wife or husband. He knew his parents cared about each other. They respected one another. He wasn't sure how much they were in love but, in talking with his cousins, his parents seemed to be in more love with each other than some of his aunts and uncles.

He decided to go downstairs to the family's store, to see if his father was at work. He doubted it but, it was the only other place he knew to check. Aziz headed down the backstairs of the apartment, which led directly into the store. As he got to the landing, he reached for the knob of the old beaten up door and found it locked.

He knocked and knocked again.

"Father? It's Aziz. I'm home," he called through the door.

There was no response.

He turned and bounded back up the stairs to the apartment. In the kitchen on the hook, he found the key to the door. Aziz headed back down and inserted the key into the lock. His mother had been on his father for months to change this lock. The key stuck and it was hard to turn the tumbler. Aziz stood there, jiggling the key, attempting to get it to turn and unlock the door. Finally, with his fingers and hands turning red from the pressure he was exerting, he felt the lock give.

He sighed and turned the knob. As he entered the store, it was completely dark, expect for a bit of sunlight coming in through the front windows. He decided not to turn on the lights right away since his father, in the past, had yelled at him not to waste the electricity when the store was closed. His father would talk about how, when he was growing up, they never knew when they would have power, so it wasn't something to take for granted.

He moved about the store. As he crossed the aisles, he would look down each one to see if he could find his father. When Aziz got to the last aisle with still no sign of his father, he turned to the right and headed to the back of the store. He went behind the rear counter and through the doorway, which began the storage area for the shop. It was completely dark back there and he'd no choice but to turn on the light.

It took a minute for his eyes to adjust, but he soon started his search again. The backroom was filled with stacks of boxes and pallets. His father, whenever he could, would negotiate a substantial price break if he bought in quantity. Since they didn't sell anything perishable, he could store product. The back room displayed no rhyme or reason to anyone but his father, who could always go directly to anything he needed. Though the area was much smaller than the front of the store, it took longer to search.

He found no sign of his father.

The last place to look was the office. It would really be the last place he would be, since his father didn't like being there. He wanted to be out with the customers or in the back with his inventory. He hated the book-keeping and the paperwork that came with running your own business and he would never spend a Sunday in this room.

The office was on the other side of the backroom. It was built into a corner, out of scrap lumber and plywood his father had found around the neighborhood and gotten from neighbors when they remodeled. The office wasn't anything great but, it was functional. He pushed aside the door and peered in. His father wasn't there and it didn't seem like he'd been there in a while.

Aziz thought to check to see if the family's car was in the garage. The garage was behind the store, in a separate building, on the alley. Aziz unlocked the rear door of the store and looked out. He couldn't tell if the car were there or not.

He ventured out and walked back to the alley. He turned and saw that the garage door was down. His father tended to leave it up when he had the car. Aziz didn't have the key, so he peered into the window. The car was gone.

He wasn't sure what to do. Maybe his father had just gone out for a while. Usually, he would leave a note, but since Aziz's mother passed away, his father seemed to not communicate as much and there had been other times when he'd left without letting him now.

Aziz headed back into the store and locked the door behind him. He went back to the office and closed it up and headed into the store itself. He made sure everything was back in place and then headed to the stairwell and closed the door behind him. He inserted the key and had as much of a challenge locking the door as he did getting it unlocked. At one point, he cursed and caught himself glancing over his shoulder, looking up the stairs, expecting his mother to be standing there with a disappointed look on her face.

He'd discussed it with Uncle Mustafa, who had assured him it was acceptable to mourn and he should miss his mother. Mustafa also instructed him on being strong and remembering his leadership role with his cous-ins. He should set an example on how to handle loss. Aziz tried his best to model the behavior his uncle wished him to have. He never showed his struggles when he was with his cousins.

Chapter Thirteen

FBI SAFE HOUSE

Akmed opened the door. Standing in front of him was the woman and one of the men he'd seen getting out of the car over an hour earlier. The man was carrying a tray of food.

"May we come in? My name is Maxine. You can call me Max."

Akmed was somewhat taken aback. He hadn't been expecting to be asked if they could come in. He'd anticipated they would just barge in and start asking him a series of questions.

He nodded and moved away from the door, so they could enter. They were differential to Akmed, acting like this was his house or, at least, his room, so different from how the other agents he'd met had been treating him since he first entered the FBI building.

They walked in and headed toward the middle of the room where there was a table. The man put down the tray and stuck his hand out.

"I'm Jordan," he said as he grabbed Akmed's hand in a friendly shake. "I know they are never as good as in Philly, but a place down the road here doesn't do too bad a job on a cheese steak. Hope you'll like it. It's not Geno's or Pat's, but it's as close as I've ever gotten outside of Philly." Geno's and Pat's were two well known rivals in the on-going Philly cheese steak wars. Located almost across the street from each other in South Philly, nothing could cause bigger arguments than a debate of who made the better Philly cheese steak.

"You are from Philly?" Akmed found himself asking.

"Born and raised. Try to get back to the neighborhood whenever I can. Still have aunts, uncles and cousins there."

Real ones, no doubt, thought Akmed, versus those I have in the city. As he took a seat at the table he grabbed a plate, just beginning to realize how famished he was. He'd refused earlier food and drink, fearing he might be poisoned; he didn't know whom to trust. This woman and man seemed different and he found himself not as suspicious and, besides, the sandwich did smell good. He unwrapped his as the other two did the same. He'd grabbed the plate that wasn't closest to him, so he would foil any attempt to poison him. He waited until the woman and man both took bites before he took his first, quickly followed by a second. The sandwich was good and the melted cheese and juice from the meat dribbled down his chin. He grabbed his napkin.

"Pretty good, huh?" Jordan chuckled as he noticed Akmed grabbing the nearby napkin,

Akmed smiled. He knew how he must look to them. "Yes, good. I'm partial to Tony Luke's but, this is quite good."

"Well here's a Coke to wash it down with," Akmed took the bottle Max handed to him and took a quick swig. It was ice cold and tasted great.

"Ah. Tony Luke's! You are a connoisseur. I'm more partial to his roasted pork, but my assumption would be you haven't had the pleasure." Tony Luke's was the new upstart in the sandwich scene and had gained a strong following and reputation.

Akmed didn't respond, but gave Jordan a rather sheepish look.

"We've all broken the rules at some point. Your secret is safe with us," Jordan stated with a big smile on his face, showing acknowledgement but not dissatisfaction.

"It was great," Akmed admitted with a smile.

"Well, we need to talk. Maxine and I work for the US Government. We aren't FBI or CIA. We're with a group you've never heard of and our job is to help other governments fight terrorism in the hope we prevent it from coming into our country. We know you've told the FBI your story and why you are here. But Akmed, we need you to tell us. Can you?"

Akmed nodded, "I'll start from the beginning."

Over the next ninety minutes, Akmed went through his story. Being taken from his family and how his death was faked and the extensive training that had started immediately, which later resulted in Mahasin and he being put together. He went in detail about the day Aziz came into their lives and the early years of them becoming a family. He recounted the last year in Iran and their move out of their home country.

Chapter Fourteen

✣ ✣ ✣

Mahasin and Akmed began to sense their time at the compound they had known for the past seven years was coming to an end. More and more of their days were being spent practicing mock interviews for asylum at the embassies they would be sent, filling out paper work for immigration and customs and, finally, practicing going through passport control at an airport. It was one of the most grueling aspects of the training and the instructors were ruthless in pointing out even the smallest mistake, since it was the most critical part of the mission and if they couldn't get out of Iraq and to the host country, then the past years had been for nothing. They had to do this and it had to be done right.

It wasn't until three days before they were to leave that they were told the initial country where they would be going. For Akmed and his family, it would be Denmark. This had been arranged through bribes paid on their behalf to staffers in the Danish Embassy in Tehran. As expected, their arrival in Denmark was uneventful. The family was taken to a small hostel for the night and was hosted by a local Iranian family for dinner.

In the morning, they left Copenhagen for the town of Odense, in central Denmark, on the Island of Fyn. It was known for being the childhood home of Hans Christian Andersen. The second floor of a converted home was rented for them at fifty-two Pjentedamsgade. Employment for Mahasin as a housekeeper had been arranged at the Hotel Ansgar near the Odense train station. Akmed would be hired at the port of Odense as an entry-level maintenance laborer. A neighbor who was Iranian would serve as a primary contact for them to their handlers in Iran and would also provide day care for Aziz.

After the first year, which had been a wonderful time, they received the first indication the mission would soon force them to enter the next chapter in their lives.

"They hired a new guy at work, today. He's Iranian. I think it's him." Akmed informed his wife over dinner.

Mahasin didn't need to hear anything else to know the next phase of their life in Denmark or, more realistically, the end of their life in Denmark was nearly upon them. She reached out to Akmed. "We knew it was only a matter of time. It's what we must do."

"I know. I was just hoping we could enjoy this part of our life a little longer"

The man, named Shamir, cornered Akmed during a break at work the next day. Loud enough for others to hear and with a finger poking in Akmed's chest, shouting, "I know who you are and what you did to my people! I'll get my revenge!"

"I don't know what you are talking about. I'm like you. I escaped from those people to live in peace," Akmed pleaded as he tried to get away.

Shamir kept his grip on him. "I'll expose you for what you are. You worked for the Ayatollahs you carried out their wishes. You killed my brothers and uncles."

With that, Shamir shoved Akmed against the wall and walked away. Several of Akmed's co-workers came over to help him. The attacks and verbal insults continued.

Akmed found himself sitting alone at breaks and lunch. Fewer and fewer of his colleagues would engage him in conversation and some had even refused to acknowledge him when they passed each other. It had begun with the Iranians, but the Danes soon sensed an issue among the Iranians concerning Akmed and knew best to stay clear and not take any side.

On a cold November morning, Akmed awoke and began his daily routine, starting with unrolling his prayer rug and facing Mecca. Then he made coffee for Mahasin. He cooked a breakfast of fried eggs and fresh fruit, and then he took a quick shower and dressed for work. He came back into the kitchen finding Mahasin drinking her coffee and gave her a quick kiss on the cheek, grabbed his lunch pail, headed down the stairs and opened the door to the outside. He was taken aback by what had happened to the door. Sometime during the night, someone had painted the word "traitor" in both Farsi and Danish, in red paint with an underlining in which the paint was allowed to run down the door to simulate blood dripping. As Akmed stared at the door, his eyes caught movement and he looked over to the street. People -- their neighbors -- were standing on the sidewalk, staring, commenting to one another. When Akmed turned and looked at them, they all looked away and continued on their way.

A white patrol car of the Danish Politi turned down the street with its blue light flashing. A second Politi unit had entered from the opposite end of the block and pulled up in front of Akmed's house. One of the officers got out of the car and began to talk to Akmed in Danish.

Akmed shook his head, indicating he didn't understand.

The officer began again in English. "Is this your home?"

Akmed nodded yes.

"What's happened and do you know who or why someone would do this to your door?"

"They think I'm someone else. They think I'm someone who killed members of their families. But, I have never done those things. I work at the port. My wife works at the Ansgar. We were accepted here as political refugees. I have suffered no differently than any of my neighbors. I despise those who lead my country today. I have never done anything in their name."

"I see," the officer nodded. "Let us take a report."

"With a crime like this and the accusations made, you will probably be summoned to the City Hall to talk to a case worker. They will need to verify your identification and ensure you haven't committed any crimes in your past. If the harassment continues and you have no connection to the crimes you are accused of, they can help you relocate."

"Within Denmark?" Akmed looked at the officer, a moment of hope filling him.

"It depends. Sometimes we find these things just travel with you if you stay in Denmark. We aren't that big of a country, where you can hide. These things seem to keep coming up with people even if they do move."

"I see," Akmed said, dejected.

The officer tore off a copy of the report and gave it to Akmed.

"Sorry this happened to you. Hopefully, it's a one time thing"

"I hope you are right." Akmed knew it wasn't a one-time thing, but it would escalate until Denmark was ready to be rid of them.

Akmed and Mahasin received a summons to appear at Town Hall. Located at S. Knud's Square, the Town Hall was an impressive structure of red brick, with the first construction done in the late nineteenth century, additions in 1936 and 1955 finished in red tile. While not only serving as the center for all municipal business, the civic leaders had also utilized its public spaces to house various works of art.

As they entered the building, Akmed went over to the directory and found the office for immigration was on the second floor, room two hundred thirty two. They passed by the elevator and went up the main staircase.

They entered the reception area and Akmed produced the letter they had received, handing it to the young lady who was seated at the desk. She quickly perused the letter and motioned for them to take a seat as she got up from the desk and headed down the hall.

An attractive woman came into the reception area. She walked over to Akmed and Mahasin and in greeted them in Danish.

"Hello, I'm Lise Hansen. I'll be your case worker."

Akmed and Mahasin replied in their stilted Danish.

"Please don't worry. We will conduct the meeting in English, if that is preferable to you."

"Thank you. That would be good for us, Miss Hansen."

"Please. You may call me Lise," she told them as she gestured for them to stand and follow her back to her office.

Lise was the perfect picture of a Danish female, tall, with striking blue eyes and brilliant blonde hair. One would have expected to see her on a tourism brochure, or at least living and working in Copenhagen. She was not at all what Akmed was expecting. He wasn't sure if that was going to work for them or against them.

She stopped in front of a door and turned around and, with her open hand pointing the way, allowed them to enter the office first.

"Please have a seat and make yourselves comfortable. Would you like some tea or a Coca-cola?"

"Water would be nice," Mahasin said as she took her seat at the conference table. Akmed shook his head, not wanting anything.

Lise quickly stepped out and returned with a bottle of water and a two glasses. "In case you change your mind," she offered, looking at Akmed as she put a glass in front of him.

"Let me begin by stating on behalf of the Danish government how sorry we are you have been faced with these actions against you and your family. It is the intent of our country to provide a safe and non-discriminatory environment for you. We know you suffered in Iran and we had hoped you would not have any issues here. With that said, I must review with you our process and what we will need to do to ensure we will not need to revoke your status."

Mahasin and Akmed, visibly nervous, nodded at Lise, but said nothing.

She continued, "We have done a preliminary review of your initial immigration documents, to again ascertain their accuracy versus the allegations that have been recently made against you. Fortunately, we found nothing to be out of order. I would like to schedule a follow up meeting in two weeks. In the meantime, here is my card; and, if anything else happens, please call the Politi and show them my card. Also, let me know if you have any other issues, or if you have any questions."

Akmed took the card and Lise stood. Both he and Mahasin stood and shook Lise's hand as it was offered. She walked them back to the reception area.

They said their goodbyes and Akmed and Mahasin walked back home.

Two weeks later, as soon as Aziz returned home from school, the family left the house. They walked over to the tourist area and strolled through the restored early Danish homes that included the childhood home of Hans Christian Andersen. The family had come here the first weekend they had arrived in Odense and had returned often. They had allowed Aziz to pick where they would eat dinner and, with no surprise, he picked his favorite *Den Gremme AEling*, which translated in English to *The Ugly Duckling*, a typical Danish Smorrebrod or buffet.

As they walked out of the restaurant, it had already grown dark, typical for this time of year in Denmark. It was one of the things that had taken them the longest to get used to, the long summer days with only three to four hours of darkness and the short winter days with only five to six hours of daylight.

A few blocks from their street, they began to pick up a scent of burning wood and thought of the many families who would be having a fire in their homes on a chilly evening such as this had become. Unfortunately, their upstairs home had no fireplace. As they began to cross over the last main road before entering their neighborhood, they stopped at the curb as two Fire Brigade units tore down the street, their blue lights twirling, and sirens shrieking in the cold night air. As the trucks passed, Akmed, Mahasin and Aziz followed their progress down the street, only to see them slow and turn into their neighborhood.

At the same instant, Akmed noticed billowing smoke arising from the vicinity of their home. They quickly rounded the block, only to see their home ablaze and the Fire Brigade just beginning to bring water to the flames. It was easy to tell it was too late. The second floor was completely engulfed and there was no way any of their possessions would survive. As they got as close as they could, Akmed put his arms around his wife and child and held them. This would be the end.

On the Monday after the fire, the three of them traveled from the Hotel Ansgar, which had graciously given them a room, to City Hall, to meet with Elizabeth Hansen.

Lise was waiting for them at the reception desk as they entered. She greeted them and led them to her office.

"I was so shocked to hear what had happened to your home. The Fire Brigade has confirmed it was arson. The Politi also found writing on the walls in the stairway, similar to what had been written on your door. It is definitely a hate crime and will be treated as such. The Politi have interviewed Mr. Shamir and have validated his alibi. At the present time, they have no further suspects and the investigation remains open."

"What is going to happen to us? We have no home, no where to go." Mahasin began to sob, her head lowered.

"I believe you will no longer be safe in Odense, and I question the ability for you to find a safe place to live anywhere else in Denmark. Our history with these incidents in the past has been that the Iranian community is well connected throughout our country and word tends to quickly spread and catch up with anyone we try to relocate within our borders."

Akmed interrupted. "So, what does that mean for us? You aren't going to send us back to Iran are you? We can't go back."

Lise raised her hand to calm Akmed. "No. No, we won't send you back to Iran. That is not even an option. We will need to work with another government that would provide sanctuary. What I need to ask you is if you have any relatives in any country you think might accept you?"

Akmed hid his feeling of relief. "I have an uncle and two brothers who have immigrated to the United States in the past three years."

While this wasn't anywhere close to the truth, any sort of records check would show these people were related and they had, indeed, entered and were living in the United States. Only a blood test would show that, in reality, they were not family.

"That could be helpful. Let me get you a form to fill out. Do you know their addresses, or at least what city they are in?"

"Yes. Philadelphia."

We will need to petition the U.S. Embassy here in the Denmark. Fortunately, I know the ICE Attaché at the Embassy in Copenhagen, so I can probably get the decision expedited. Akmed, I feel really good about this. I think it will happen. I'll let you know as soon as I hear anything else."

"Thank you Lise. You've been more than helpful."

As they left City Hall, Akmed leaned into Mahasin. "It is happening just like the instructors said it would," he told Mahasin.

Six weeks had gone by when a letter arrived at the hotel. Akmed waited until he got back to the room and was with Mahasin to open it. It was from Lise and it stated that the U.S. Government had completed its review of the request to immigrate to the United States and had issued its approval. They would need to present themselves to the Embassy in Copenhagen with this letter within the next ten days. Their travel documents and visa would be available to them at that time and they would have thirty days to arrive in the United States.

That evening, Akmed called the phone of Uncle Mustafa.

"Uncle, we have received all of our paperwork! We can come and be with you."

"That is excellent news! I'll wire you funds tomorrow, to cover your travel expenses. Two of your cousins have also recently been granted permission to come here. It seems soon the whole family will be back together."

"That is good news." A knot tightened in Akmed's stomach. Hearing others were arriving meant the mission was going forward. In the back of his mind, he'd hoped maybe the others would not be as successful and the mission would be called off. Then, they could just live in the United States as a family and put all of this behind them. It seemed such would not be the case.

"Did you hear what I said?" barked an impatient Mustafa.

"I'm sorry. There was static on the line. I couldn't make out what you said," Akmed blurted out, to cover his mind wandering.

"I said to call me when you have your travel arrangements, so we can meet you."

"Yes. Yes. I'll make the arrangements tomorrow and let you know."

"I look forward to it." And the line again went dead.

The next day, they didn't have Aziz go to school. They boarded an early train and headed to Copenhagen. The train ride took ninety minutes and traveled through the beautiful Danish countryside.

They arrived at the Embassy and they each had to be photographed and complete paperwork. After three hours they left the Embassy with their travel documents

Akmed went to the Danske Bank Branch across from Tivoli Garden and was able to pick up the funds Mustafa had wired to him. He found a travel agent a few streets over and was able to make their travel arrangements. There were seats available on a Continental flight in two weeks, which would take them to Newark airport. From there, they could board the Amtrak train that would take them directly to Philadelphia. With tickets in hand, Akmed rejoined Mahasin and Aziz and headed across the street to the Central Train Station, to return to Odense.

When departure day finally arrived, they walked the block to the station and boarded a train that would take them directly to the station at the Copenhagen airport. Upon their arrival they found the Continental counter and checked in.

Once boarded they quickly settled in for the six and a half hour flight. Before they knew it the pilot came on to announce their initial descent into the New York area. Akmed awoke and was thankful this part of the journey was over, but his nerves returned, knowing there was one big step ahead at the airport.

After the plane arrived at the gate, they grabbed their bags and made their way through the walkways to immigration. They had instructions on where they should go and Akmed had their documents ready. They found the right lane, which was much shorter than several of the others. An older man who took their papers without saying anything was sitting in the cubicle. The officer looked them over as he glanced at the paperwork. He looked at their passports and found the appropriate visa stamp in each. He then went to the computer and typed in information and swiped the passports through the optical reader. As he waited for the screen to come up, he again stared at each one of them. Akmed was beginning to feel more nervous. What if they had come all this way only to be turned back? He tried his best to make sure his nervousness didn't show. Finally, the officer turned his gaze back to the screen. He looked at the paper work and then to the screen, repeating the movement several times. Finally, he grabbed a big stamp and slammed it down on the papers. Akmed could feel himself jump. He knew everyone had to see it. The officer looked directly at him. "Sir." Akmed looked right at him. "Everything is in order. I welcome you and your family to the United States." The officer smiled at them as he handed the paperwork and passports back to Akmed.

Akmed wasn't sure he could move. Mahasin gave him a slight nudge to get him going. They took their bags and fell into line at Customs. They walked right through and gave the officer their card. They walked out of the international arrival areas and followed the signs to the train. They boarded the AirTrain and took it from the airside terminal to the Amtrak station at the edge of the airport.

Their train pulled into the station about fifteen minutes late. It took about sixty-five minutes to arrive at the Philadelphia station. They walked along the platform until they came to an escalator. They rode up into the huge Art Deco hall of the station. There, waiting for them, was Uncle Mustafa. They had made it to Philadelphia.

Chapter Fifteen

The following morning, Aziz awoke and prepared for school. Since his mother's death, it had been his responsibility to rise at his normal time and perform his routine. He left his room, dressed for school with his book bag packed. He was now used to fixing his own breakfast and headed to the kitchen. The door to his father's room was closed.

He thought he'd heard his father come home late last evening, or early this morning. He didn't want to have a confrontation, so he'd not gotten up to check. Now, he wasn't sure. His father would usually be up by this time, liked to have his morning coffee and read the Philadelphia Inquirer.

Aziz found no reason to disturb his father, so he ate his breakfast and cleaned up the kitchen. He grabbed his bag and headed down the front stairs, to the street, to begin his journey to school. As he exited the front door to the apartment, he saw Benny, his father's only employee, coming down the street to open the store.

"Hey Benny," Aziz called. "I thought you had Monday's off."

"Usually, but your father told me he needed to take some time off while you were gone."

"Really? Did he say where he was going?"

"No, but you know your father -- man of little words and he's never told me anything beyond what he thought I needed to know."

Aziz grinned at Benny. "Tell me about it. Did he even tell you when he would be back?"

"He told me I needed to open the store on Monday, so here I am. Other than that, he didn't say anything. My guess is he'll be here when you get home from school."

"We'll see." Aziz started to walk away. "Maybe I should call my Uncle Mustafa and let him know."

"Hey Aziz, I know it hasn't been easy on you or your Dad since your Mom died. Your Dad may just need some space and to get away from everything that reminds him of Mahasin. I wouldn't give your uncle a call yet. Let's see if he's not back today."

"Okay, Benny. I'll see you after school"

"Alright, have a good one. Oh, and Aziz! Study hard and mind your teachers," Benny said, imitating Akmed. For the first time Aziz broke out in a smile and then quickly held up the middle finger of his right hand with the back of his hand facing Benny.

"It's good to see you smile, kid!" Benny turned to unlock the store as Aziz headed down the sidewalk to school.

An agent was following Aziz to school and another undercover agent was working in the school as a temporary custodian.

Chapter Sixteen

❖ ❖ ❖

The Philadelphia Electric Company -- PECO as it was known in the area -- service truck parked across the street with two agents posing as utility workmen had picked up the conversation and been able to take a couple of photographs of the boy and the man he was talking with on the street.

They had watched the boy since the previous afternoon, when he'd been dropped off in a van filled with kids his age, an older man driving. The surveillance team at the rear of the building had noticed Aziz coming outside and peering into the garage and had noticed his concern when he discovered his father's car was gone.

Later, during the night, they had gotten approval for the warrant to place audio and video devices in the apartment. While they knew the boy was in the apartment, the insertion team was sufficiently skilled to enter, quickly install the devices and leave. Technology had advanced to the point that all of the devices were wireless and a quick RF burst about every two weeks recharged the batteries. The apartment was old and the floors had creaked as the team moved around. They became worried they would awaken Aziz, so they did not install the full complement of equipment but, felt they had installed enough to give them both visual and audio of what was happening in the apartment.

In the command center, everything was working well. They had picked up the audio when Aziz awoke and watched as he left his room and fixed his breakfast. It hadn't really been anything to let Washington know about but, this conversation on the street was a different story.

They now knew the father had indeed left suddenly without letting anyone know what he was doing. The son had been away with a group and even the employee in the store had no idea where Akmed had gone.

They downloaded a photo of Benny back to the command center to see if it would match anything in the database. Uncle Mustafa was the new person who piqued their interest but, they hadn't been totally set up and didn't have the camera operational when the van had dropped the boy off.

A photo of the driver would have been helpful and could have been the break they needed to figure out what was really transpiring.

During the day, they would set up the apartment they had just secured in the building across the street from the store. This would eliminate the need to be outside on the street in a neighborhood where everyone knew everyone else. They would also have perimeter cameras set up in the rear of the store so the team now there could be redeployed.

Chapter Seventeen

❖ ❖ ❖

FBI SAFE HOUSE

"Akmed, you have shared a great deal with us. How about we take a break?"

Jordan was pacing around the room as Max, seated at the table across from Akmed, took notes.

"Can we get you anything? Another Coke or some water?" Jordan asked.

"Water would be great. Could I go outside and get some air?"

"Sure. Sure. Let me get someone to go with you. You understand, we can't have you out there by yourself"

Jordan went to the door and opened it enough so he could stick his head out.

"Hey, William! You got a sec?" Jordan yelled loudly enough to be heard downstairs. After a moment, William appeared in the doorway.

"Akmed this is William, he would be more than happy to take you outside for a walk. Wouldn't you William?" Jordan shot William a grin.

"At your service. I was waiting for you to get me involved," William said sarcastically.

"All good things in time my friend."

"You'll have to excuse these two, Akmed. They are like two brothers"

"Yes, I have brothers. We do the same thing to one another."

"Are these your real brothers or your brothers in Philadelphia," Jordan quipped before thinking.

"Yes, I should clarify. My true brothers are still in Iran, as best I know. I miss them and the camaraderie we had. We were all still living in the same area and saw each other often."

"I'm sure you do." Max interjected, shooting Jordan a look that could only be interpreted as,"Don't be such an ass; this guy is helping us." Dismissing Jordan from the room, Max said, "Jordan why don't you get Akmed his water."

Max continued and turned to Akmed. "Thank you for everything you have shared so far, it has been helpful. We need to review the information and then we will have more questions and want to hear more in regards to the mission. William will be with you until you return to this room. If you need anything, just let him know. I'll see you a little later." Max got up from the table and walked out of the room and down the stairs.

William gave Akmed the once over. "Well. Shall we head outside?" "Yes," and Akmed walked to the door and followed William downstairs and they exited through the kitchen.

Max headed toward the library. Jordan was already there, in a conversation with Stan.

"I think he's on the up and up. We could spend a lot of time back tracking through all of this information, but I believe we would find it's all correct. I think he's the real deal. We've got a highly trained operative who is raising a terrorist and he's gotten the religion of capitalism in his blood and has decided what he was suppose to do isn't worth doing."

"I don't disagree, but I still think some validation of his story is needed. He could still be the diversion. Think about it," Stan said. "If they truly have been planning this for over ten years, they could have easily added an element of diversion, particularly if they are getting close to executing the mission." Stan had been listening to the entire conversation with Akmed in the library. He knew the details, but he wasn't as convinced as Jordan. "I don't think we have to cross all the t's and dot all the i's. I think we should pull his immigration papers and we can quickly talk to the attaché in Denmark and confirm an Elizabeth Hansen works for the Danish government. That won't take long, and we can still continue on our path. The team in Philly is settled in and thinks they had a visual on Mustafa. All the audio and video devices are functioning. I think we'll get more out of there today when the son comes home from school and finds his dad has still not returned."

"There's a problem." Max jumped into the conversation. "The father won't be home and the clerk in the store won't have seen him all day. I think the boy will call his Uncle to report his absence. We should run through some scenarios about what decisions they might make in regards to carrying out their mission."

"I don't get the feeling they are totally ready," Jordan said deliberately. "I think if they were close, the boy would have panicked yesterday. I'm not sure he knows he is there for a terrorist attack." As he spoke, Jordan was back to pacing around the room. "I think there is a safe premise, that the kids as sleepers haven't been activated yet. I think we have to focus on Mustafa and what he might do."

Stan shifted his weight and moved over toward the window. "I think you may be right. Mustafa is the unknown. We really don't know what resources he has at his disposal. If they are close to activation, he may not want to waste time on finding out what happened to Akmed. Maybe the death of the wife will provide enough cover. We have picked up comments he has been despondent and withdrawn since her death.

Max jumped in. "Yes, and as far as we know, he hasn't raised any alarm with Mustafa, Aziz or any of the other parents that he'd grown tired of their mission and wanted out."

"We have to tag Mustafa. If we can put him under surveillance, it'll be the key to understanding what the reaction will be and if they will continue to move forward. He may have no choice." Stan moved back behind the desk as he was talking, "He's not at the top. My bet is someone else is directing him. And that person we will probably never know."

Jordan stopped in his tracks and turned to face them both. "I think I need to get to Philly and take charge of the ground ops. We really need to get a handle on Mustafa. That's going to be the key. Max, you can continue the debrief with Akmed. He's totally cooperative we don't need two of us. William can be in there. I think they'll build a nice relationship." He pointed out the window where William was walking with Akmed. They seemed to be in some animated conversation, as both were gesturing with their hands and laughing.

"All right, get going. I'll arrange a plane to get you up there." Stan pulled out his cell and began to dial.

Max walked over to the window and knocked, getting William's attention. She gestured for him to bring Akmed back inside. It was time to get started on round two.

Chapter Eighteen

✤ ✤ ✤

SOUTH PHILLY

They had kept a watch on the store and Benny all day from the apartment across the street and it seemed nothing had taken place other than ordinary business. Frank Evans had arrived from D. C. on Max's orders and had taken charge of the team. Frank was a logistical expert who could bust through red tape and get an operation up and running in record time. They had gotten the report back about Benny and the man was as clean as they come. He seemed to be nothing more than an employee and, at this juncture, nothing pointed to him being involved in the plot.

The phone rang and one of the agents picked it up. "Okay, thanks, why don't you change and head back here? You can come in through the back. We're in 2-B." Agent John Lutz a solidly built man with a face that made him look twenty-five years younger than he was, turned to Frank. "That was Miguel at the school. He's posing as the substitute janitor. He said Aziz just left the school and is traveling alone. He is headed in this direction."

"Do we have anyone with him?" Frank moved toward the window and looked down the street.

"Yes, we have an agent, keeping about a block back. We aren't sure how extensive this network is in the neighborhood and if they have their own watchers. So, our guy's playing it low key. He'll probably only communicate if the boy changes direction or something happens."

"Good. That's playing it smart. The boy's our only link right now, so we can't spook him or anyone who might be watching him." Frank turned and spoke louder to address the half dozen agents in the apartment. "Listen up. We've got a strong indication this boy is a member of a cell, which is close to being activated, if it hasn't already. We lose him, we're back at square one. We've got to be smart and diligent. Let's not overplay our hand. At this point, I would rather error on the side of caution, versus sticking our necks out in haste and losing the only asset we have.

The interrogation of the father is continuing; but, so far, we have high confidence in every thing he has told us. Jordan is enroute here and should arrive by six o'clock. Let's just keep doing our best." There were affirmative nods around the room, as everyone returned to his work.

About fifteen minutes later, Aziz appeared, walking down the street. He'd headed straight home.

"Let's look alive. Subject is heading toward the building," the agent at the window turned and announced. "Our guy is about a block and a half back, with no signals." The signal was to have his coat zipped and a hat on his head if Aziz had been contacted during the trip or had anyone else following him. "I'll let you know if he goes to the store or directly to the apartment."

At that moment, the door opened and the agent who had been the janitor walked in. Miguel Scott looked more like a janitor than a Federal agent. Slightly balding and of thin build the overalls he now wore, seemed to fit him better than the suits he typically wore. Several of the agents acknowledged him. "Regular day at school nothing out of the ordinary. If anything, the kid is kind of a loner."

"He's headed to the apartment." Came the report from the agent following Aziz.

Chapter Nineteen

For Aziz, the end of school bell couldn't ring fast enough. He didn't really like school, and it wasn't the work; he carried a high grade point average and was in several honors classes. But, he loathed the social aspects. None of his cousins attended his school, and they were his friends and the people he wanted to do things with every day. There were few fellow students he could tolerate, other than his lab partner in physics. Jared was smart and wasn't caught up in all the drama that seemed to be what the other student's lives evolved around. Aziz hated the numerous cliques and the sense that you had to belong to one. He didn't want to be a jock, though he knew from pick up games in the neighborhood that he could play better than most of the varsity players.

Thinking about that brought him back to his parents. He'd been thinking all day about his father. Where could his father have gone and what was he up to that would make him leave. Aziz was confused. He knew the death of his mother had been hard on his father, as it had been on him. He had Uncle Mustafa to help him and they had grown closer after his mother's death. His father had his store.

Aziz crossed the last street before their apartment. He really hoped his father had returned. Aziz wasn't sure where to go first. Should he go up to the apartment, like he normally would, and drop his books off? And then go down to see his father and Benny? Or, should he go straight into the store, to see his father? He wasn't sure what he should do. As he got in front of the store, he decided the best thing to do would be to keep to his normal routine. He went to the door of the apartment and grabbed his key from his book bag.

Entering, everything seemed the same as it had been when he left that morning. He headed down the hall to his room and noticed the door to his father's room was still closed. He went to his room and dropped off his bag. He went back to the door at his father's room and slowly opened it. Fearing the worst, his father might have been in there and not able to call for help.

Aziz looked around and walked to the other side of the bed, but his father was not there. He backed out and closed the door.

Aziz went into the kitchen and grabbed a soda out of the refrigerator. He walked over to the door to the back stairway, opened it and went down to the door that would open into the store. He turned the knob, but the door was locked. This was not a good sign. If his father had returned, he would have gone through this door from the garage. Aziz found it hard to believe his father would be working and hadn't gone up to the apartment at some time during the day. Aziz walked back upstairs to get the key, returned and opened the door.

Benny was at the counter, helping a customer with some bolts and nuts. Aziz walked around, looking down the aisles. No sign of his father. He walked behind the counter, gave Benny a nod and walked into the back of the store. It was dark, indicating no one was back there working. So, Aziz continued to the makeshift office, but it too was dark. He turned around and headed back to the front of the store. Benny was just finishing with the customer.

"My father still hasn't come back?"

"No, Aziz. I haven't seen or heard from him. There have been several calls for him and I've taken messages; but, nothing out of the ordinary."

"I'm worried and a little scared. This isn't like him."

"No, it's not. But, your dad hasn't been himself since your mother passed away. It hit him hard. Sometimes, people deal with their grief in different ways. Your father may just need time to himself, but he didn't know how to tell you."

"Maybe, but since I was gone, I don't know how long he's been gone. I would have thought he either would of told you more or left me a note."

"I don't know what to tell you, Aziz. I'm sure he is fine" At that moment the bell hung over the front door of the store rang out, announcing the arrival of a customer. Benny turned away from Aziz and headed to the front of the counter.

"I'm going to go upstairs," Aziz called to Benny.

"Okay, Aziz. I'll come see you after I close up. Let's have dinner together."

Aziz walked over to the door and headed up the stairs. What should he do?

Chapter Twenty

❖ ❖ ❖

"I want to hear everyone's assessments," Frank called out as they finished replaying the conversation that had just taken place between Benny and Aziz.

"The kid's worried." Lutz called out. "The kid's beside himself, but Benny doesn't seem to be overly worried. Maybe he knows more than he's telling."

"If Aziz calls his uncle, that could cause a ripple effect, which we aren't yet ready to deal with." Philadelphia Police Detective Phil Johnson chimed in from behind his computer screen.

"I would concur. We need to contain this between these two. I think we've got to figure out how to keep this from spinning out of control." Frank interjected with his hand covering his chin. His pose of deep thought and taking in of the conversation.

"We've got the father, could we have him call the son. Tell him he's okay, but needed some time away and he'll be back soon." Lutz added.

Frank was taking it all in. "Are we absolutely sure there are no other taps in the store or apartment. I need complete assurance if we let the father contact the son, that the uncle won't become aware and this whole thing blows up."

"We scanned when we went in and picked up nothing. Everything was clean. I don't think they would have anything sophisticated enough for us not to pick it up." Lutz added.

"Okay, let me talk to Max and Stan." The officers gave Frank a quizzical look as they went back to work at their stations. No one knew who he was talking about but, then again, until three hours ago, they had never heard of Frank, either.

Frank headed to the back bedroom of the apartment. He'd commandeered this space when he first arrived, knowing he and Jordan would need space away from the others to think and plan strategy. It also had windows overlooking the store and the apartment, so they were able to key a visual

on what was happening outside. He placed the call to Stan, who asked Max
to join the conversation.

"I think the best thing would be for the father to call the son. We can
coach him on what to say to keep the kid calm." Max was leaning over the
desk talking into the conference phone.

"I agree we need to see if we can't buy some more time before he alerts
this uncle. Until we have a clearer idea of the bigger picture, I want more
time to observe." Stan looked at Max for support on what he'd just said.

"I agree with Stan." Max nodded to Stan as she spoke.

"When can we have Akmed ready?" Frank replied. He was a person of
action. Debating options for any length of time never seemed to make the
options any better. To him, it was decide and do.

"I think you should do it when Benny goes up to the apartment," Max
jumped in.

"Frank, when do we think that will happen?" Max stood up from the
desk and stretched her back.

"He said he would come up when he closed the store. Today, it's five-
thirty."

"That gives us ninety minutes. We need to get cracking here. Let's
reconnect at five fifteen" Stan looked at his watch as he spoke.

Everyone concurred.

"Akmed is with William. I'll go and get started with them." Max
turned to walk out of the room. The phones went silent as each person disconnected. Stan leaned back in his chair wondering how many more twists
and turns they would have to navigate before this came to an end.

Frank walked out of the bedroom, back to the large living area, where
the team was set up. "Listen, everyone. Here's what's going to happen in
ninety minutes."

Chapter Twenty-One

✤ ✤ ✤

FBI SAFE HOUSE

As Max went up the stairs she was trying to get her thoughts together as to how to present this to Akmed. They hadn't told him they were putting Aziz under surveillance. They hadn't told him they were going to bug the store and the apartment. He was a reasonable guy, but anything at this point could put him over the edge and make him shut down completely. She would have to be at her best to convince him they still had his and his son's best interests at heart in the action they needed to take.

She knocked on the door and slowly pushed it open. Akmed was seated at the table and William was over by the window, staring out into the surrounding woods. They were discussing baseball. Akmed seemed to be a genuine fan, with a strong knowledge of the game and rabid support of the Phillies. Max was glad William had found some common ground for their conversations. Akmed seemed relaxed and open with William but, Max couldn't waste the time to pull William out and brief him, so she would just need to start and hope William would pick up where she was going and be able to jump in with support.

"Well, if I could interrupt your conversation about the Boys of Summer, I've got some things we need to update and discuss." Max noticed Akmed's confusion as she spoke.

"Boys of Summer? I don't know that, what does it mean?" He had a puzzled look on his face.

William chuckled. "It's a term for baseball players. It's Max's way of trying to fit in with our conversation, but she knows nothing about baseball, Akmed. She couldn't even tell you in what city the Philadelphia Phillies play!" He shot a "gotcha" look at Max.

Akmed laughed. "Just like my wife. She could never understand the game. The Boys of Summer. I like that and I'll have to remember it -- Boys of Summer."

"Okay, you two; you've had your fun. Let me know when you're ready to listen."

William came over to the table and sat down. Akmed nodded to Max.

"Alright Akmed, we believe Aziz is worried about you. He seems quite concerned you haven't returned home yet. We have your store and apartment under surveillance."

"Do you have it bugged? How do you know this?"

"Yes, we do have listening devices in both places."

"You did not tell me this, I did not give you permission!" Akmed showed hostility for the first time.

William put his arm on Akmed's shoulder. "Akmed, we got a warrant from the court. It allows us to protect Aziz while you are with us. We also need to find out as much as we can about the mission and its timetable. We need to find Mustafa and isolate him. For now, the only physical location we have is yours and that's why we're there."

Akmed began to relax. He looked at Max. "So, what are you saying about my son."

"He's a strong boy, but he's worried. He went to school today, feeling you would be home when he returned. When he got home and you weren't there, his demeanor changed. He's frightened. Benny has been very good and supportive. When he closes the store this afternoon, he is going to go up and visit with Aziz."

"He's not planning on closing early is he? We usually do a nice business this part of the week in the last half hour or so," Akmed interrupted.

"Ah! Spoken like a true American Capitalist." William slapped Akmed on the back as he paid him the compliment. Akmed turned to William with a smile.

"I'm sorry. I don't mean to minimize Aziz's feelings. I worked hard to build my business and my customers count on me."

Max was smiling. "Akmed, we have no reason to believe Benny is closing early. We're certain he is going to go up after the regular closing time. We would like you to call the apartment during the time Benny is there and talk with Aziz. Reassure him you are well and just needed time for yourself. We can work up talking points for you, but it's critical what ever you say sounds normal and won't seem funny or cause further alarm in Aziz. He spoke of calling Mustafa to tell him. Frankly, at some point, we might want that to happen, but, at the present time, we're not ready for that to occur. Can you help us?"

"Yes. Yes, you are correct. Regardless of the situation, I need to let Aziz know I'm all right. I can and should make the call."

"That's great, Akmed. Let's do this, you and I'll practice the call." William got up and went to sit across from Akmed.

"Well, then -- I'll leave you two alone and come back when it's time to make the call." Max smiled at them both and turned to walk out.

After the door closed, Akmed looked at William. "William, were you kidding about her not knowing where the Phillies played?"

"Only a little bit, Akmed. She's a smart woman, but baseball is not her strongest area."

They both laughed, and then began to practice the call.

Chapter Twenty-Two

✤ ✤ ✤

SOUTH PHILADELPHIA

"Hello Aziz, it's me, your father. How are you?"

"Father, where are you!" Aziz was surprised it was his father. The caller ID was blocked and he almost hadn't answered. Benny had just come up from closing the store for the day and Aziz had just gotten him a soda and they were seated at the kitchen table. "I didn't know where you went."

"I'm sorry, my son. I needed to get away. I'm far from being over your mother's death. I miss her terribly."

"As do I, my father, but I need you, also."

"I understand and I love you, Aziz. Please don't be worried about me. I'll be home tomorrow."

"Why tomorrow? Why not now?"

"I need time. When I come back to you, I want to be able to support you and help you. I'm of no help to you with the way I have been. It is best not to say anything to anyone about this."

"Well.... I did talk to Benny. He's here with me now."

"Benny is fine. I trust him, but nothing should be said to anyone else. I'm glad Benny is with you. Let him know I'll be back tomorrow and I know I owe him a couple of days off."

"Oh, father, always thinking of everyone but yourself. We're going to have dinner together. He said he would stay until I go to bed."

"Ah, Benny is always there for us. Tell him I appreciate everything he is doing."

"You will be here tomorrow?" Aziz needed confirmation.

"Yes. By the time you get home from school, I'll be at the store."

"I can't wait to see you."

"And me you, my son." Akmed concluded the call, saying, "I love you Aziz."

Aziz, being in high school and not wanting to express affection in front of someone other than his family, said his final words. "I'll see you tomorrow."

"That sounded like it went well." Max crossed the room and went to Akmed's side.

"Yes, I think it did. He really wanted to know where I was, but I think when he found out I would be home tomorrow, where I was, isn't so important." Akmed turned to look at the man staring out the window. "Thank you, William. You did know how Aziz would respond."

"I've got a teenager at home and, in my line of work, I usually can't tell my family where I am but, when I can tell them I'll be home, nothing else seems to matter. You did great, Akmed. I can tell you love Aziz, regardless of whether he is truly your son."

Akmed nodded. "What do we need to do next?"

"We want to talk with you more about the possible target and the overall mission. We realize you haven't ever been told but, maybe, if we go through the things you have done with Aziz and the others, we might find something of interest or a pattern." Max smiled at Akmed, knowing this would be a slow and challenging process.

"I'll tell you whatever I can."

The door flew open with a bang and, Stan, out of breath from coming up the stairs, looked like the worst that could happen just occured. "I need you both downstairs, now!" He turned and walked out as quickly as he came in.

Max and William just looked at each other. If Stan was worked up, then something was happening and it wasn't good.

William turned to Akmed. "We should be right back. I'll send someone up to be with you. If you are hungry or need anything, he can get it for you."

"I'll be fine." Akmed realized they were gone before he'd even spoken.

Max and William flew down the stairs and into the situation room, which was remodeled out of the former home's family room. Filled with computers and sophisticated radio and satellite communications systems, along with a state of the art audio/video system, they found the room to be in state of organized chaos. Radio communication crackled over the speakers. She could recognize the voice belonging to Frank, but wasn't close enough to make out the actual words. It was obvious something was happening at Akmed's house in Philadelphia.

Stan saw them and waved them over to a video monitor. Neither Max nor William had been able to spend time in the situation room and weren't sure what they were seeing. Her facial expression caused Stan to speak in a low voice, so they could still hear the radio communication.

"This is a video feed from our command post across the street from Akmed's apartment and store. The van you see belongs to Mustafa. We think it's pure coincidence, but he pulled up just as Aziz was hanging up the phone."

"Could he have a bug in there?" William commented as he was bending over to take a closer look at the video.

"When we placed our devices in the apartment and store we did a sweep and nothing showed up. We've monitored from the command post and couldn't find a remote device being used. They either have really sophisticated equipment, or it's just happened to work out this way."

Max stared at the screen, trying to orient herself to what was going on so she could be of assistance. "It looks like he is still in the car?"

"He is and we don't know why. He's not on his cell. Aziz and Benny don't know he is here. Infrared shows he is the only one in the vehicle."

"Has he been in the neighborhood?"

"No, he didn't drive around back. The teams in the neighborhood tracked him directly here. Thank God we saw the van earlier."

"Maybe thank Allah." William smirked, he didn't take his eyes off the screen to see Stan's or Max's reaction.

Max stood up. "I guess we wait and see. The ball is in Uncle Mustafa's court."

"Someone needs to get to Jordan and get him up to speed. He could be walking into something different than what he expected."

"We've tried his cell. I sent a text to him to call in." Agent Lutz had turned back toward Max to answer her question.

The radio came alive with Frank's voice. "The driver's door to the van is opening and it looks like he is getting out."

Mustafa stepped out of the van and walked toward its rear. He looked up and seemed to stare right into the camera, which caused everyone to jerk back a little bit.

"That's really weird," Max blurted as she looked up at Stan.

"Frank? Anyway you are compromised?"

"No way! He can't see in and we've got all of our jammers in place and operational. Let's all relax. We haven't been made."

"Okay, let's see what happens." Stan had become calm, which was his trademark when things were getting stressful for no reason. "Do we have an extraction team ready if this goes bad?"

"In position Stan," was the quick reply from the radio. Stan knew Frank had it under control. He was by the book. He'd hoped Jordan would be there by now. While Frank would have everything in place and the team working efficiently, Jordan had the out of the box thinking needed when the best laid plans went awry. He wasn't much value in transit.

Chapter Twenty-Three

Mustafa walked around to the rear of the van. He opened the back and took out a package. He had hoped to get there before the store closed. Most evenings, Akmed would stay open past his posted closing time if people were around, but it seemed tonight he closed right on time. Mustafa stayed in the van and looked into the store to see if he could see either Akmed or Benny working with the hope he could just knock on the door of the store. He debated about whether he should go up to the apartment. He'd always tried to allow the people he was responsible for to feel where they lived were their own homes and not to feel like he could show up at anytime. On occasion, when he needed to visit, he would always call ahead. Though he'd never been denied a visit, and never considered he would be; but he didn't want to just show up. He really needed to get this package to Akmed and he knew if he didn't deliver it today, it would be next week before he would get back to the store.

So, with the package under his arm, he went to the apartment door. It had not latched completely from whoever went through it last, so Mustafa could go right into the foyer and walk up the stairway. When he got to the top, he rapped on the door.

The knock at the door startled Aziz and Benny. Benny looked at Aziz. "I thought I closed the door tight when I came up. Sorry"

"I'm not expecting anyone." Aziz moved toward the door. Since the downstairs door usually was latched and required a visitor to be buzzed in, the door at the top of the stairs didn't contain a peephole. Aziz couldn't tell who it was without opening the door.

"Who is it?" He called through the door.

"Aziz, it's you Uncle Mustafa. I have a package for your father."

Aziz froze. If his uncle came in, he would find his father wasn't here. He would have already known he wasn't in the store. If he told him he was running errands or with one of the other families he might decide to wait or call the family to see if his father were there. Aziz wasn't sure what to do.

"Aziz?" The voice from the other side of the door inquired. "Are you going to let your uncle in?"

Aziz quickly turned back to Benny. Benny shrugged his shoulder with a "what can you do" non-verbal.

"Yes, yes." Aziz called back and opened the door.

"I'm sorry to intrude without calling. I thought I would get here before the store closed. Oh, hello Benny. Anyway, I have this package for your father." Mustafa had been scanning the apartment since he entered. "Is your father here?"

"No he isn't," Aziz hoped his Uncle would just leave the package and go.

"When will he be back? I can wait." Mustafa noticed Benny was fixing dinner and only two plates were out. His demeanor changed. "Aziz, where is your father? Please tell me!"

Aziz hesitated and his panic showed. He didn't want to be in trouble with his uncle and he didn't want to get his father in trouble. He'd seen what had happened to others when they did something against Uncle Mustafa's wishes.

"I don't exactly know," Aziz sputtered, looking down at his feet.

"What do you mean you don't know? Benny, do you know where he is?"

Benny, who had always found Uncle Mustafa intimidating, quickly grunted a no.

Uncle Mustafa began to get agitated. "I need answers and I need them now. Where is Akmed? Where is your father?" His eyes moved back and forth between Aziz and Benny. Both felt the eyes boring right through them.

Aziz looked up at his Uncle. He was caught between total fear and afraid of what would happen to him. He loved his father, but his father hadn't been there for him lately. His uncle had been. Why did he protect his father? His father hadn't even left him a note that he would be gone. He'd learned much from his uncle and he had a great deal of respect for him.

"Uncle, I do not know where my father has gone. He was not here when I returned from my trip. He left no note."

His uncle interrupted him by raising his hand. "Benny, I would appreciate if you would leave us. I'll ensure Aziz has his dinner. We have a family issue we must discuss and it would not be appropriate for you to continue to be here."

Benny quickly left, his body showing his relief in being able to leave.

"Please, Aziz, let us sit and you can tell me everything." Aziz went into the living room with his uncle behind him. He sat down on the sofa and Mustafa sat in the chair directly across from him.

Aziz told his uncle everything that had occurred since his uncle had dropped him off -- how he'd looked for his father in the store and at his office, gone out and found the car gone from the garage, gone to school with the thought his father would be here upon his return. "After Benny closed the store, he came up here and we talked while he fixed us dinner. The phone rang and it was my father."

"He called?"

"Yes"

"From where?"

"He wouldn't tell me."

"What was the number?"

"It was blocked"

"What did he say?"

"He told me he was sorry he'd gone without letting me know. He was still upset about my mother's death and needed time for himself. He told me he would be back tomorrow when I got home from school."

"Did he say anything else?"

"No, nothing I can remember."

"And he gave you no idea where he was or how far away he was?"

"No, just that I shouldn't worry and he would be back tomorrow and that I shouldn't tell anyone he was gone."

Mustafa was surprised by Akmed's last statement. "Really? He told you not to tell anyone, including me."

"Yes, he said it was okay for Benny to know, but no one else."

"I see. You are a good boy, Aziz. You have grown into a fine young man. You know you are right to tell me this. It is important that you always tell me these things. Many good things are planned for you but, you must always remember to be honest."

"Yes, uncle"

"Aziz, here is some money. Why don't you go down the street and pick us up something to eat at the Indian restaurant. I'll stay here but, please hurry."

"Yes, uncle. I'll get you your favorite." Aziz grabbed his jacket and went out the door, leaving Mustafa still sitting in the chair.

Mustafa was perplexed. While Aziz might think his father's mourning and need to be alone was understandable, Mustafa knew the truth. Aziz's parents weren't man and wife. They didn't have the bonds of love of a traditional couple. None of the "parents" were that close to result in this level of mourning. Mustafa knew Akmed was upset that he wouldn't pay for the cancer treatments that would have undoubtedly saved Mahasin's life. But, the money was to fund the mission, not to cover medical expenses and, at this point, a parent was expendable. From Mustafa's perspective, he would be done with all of them and take the cousins into his own house but, that would raise too much suspicion. All the parents were becoming a challenge. They had tasted too much of the American life and had started to become beholden to the materialistic ways of this country.

He needed to find out where Akmed was and whom he'd been with. There would have to be a confrontation tomorrow. Mustafa would be here to meet Akmed when he returned, so he could get to the bottom of this quickly. He wasn't going to sacrifice the mission because of Akmed. The cousins were almost ready. He would move forward quickly if he'd no other choice.

Chapter Twenty-Four

❖ ❖ ❖

SOUTH PHILADELPHIA

Jordan hopped out of the cab, even before it came to a complete stop. Stan had arranged a military flight from D.C and Jordan had insisted on a cab and not a government sedan for transportation. The last thing he needed was the local gang scouts announcing "five-oh" and hollering "whoop-whoop" with his arrival. Things seemed to be unraveling and there was a need for a new plan. The variables had grown larger and more numerous than he liked and he wanted to get things reigned back in as quickly as possible.

He ducked down the alley behind the building housing the command center. He recognized the face of the man loitering in the alley. He couldn't recall his name, but they had worked together previously.

The sentry acknowledged Jordan with a slight tilt of the head that wouldn't have been picked up by anyone else, the man stooped over trash-can, acting like he was scrounging for food. As Jordan walked by, the man said softly, "Go down the second walkway, through the back door, up the rear stairs."

Jordan focused on the path to the rear of the building and turned left. The building was a typical Philadelphia row house. It seemed to have been fairly well maintained compared to others in the neighborhood. The paint was fresh and the yard and surroundings free of trash and litter. Jordan sprang up the steps to the rear door, entered and found the rear stairs. The building was incredibly quiet. As he got to the second landing, another man was standing at the top of the stairs. Dressed to fit in as a tenant, he eyed Jordan as Jordan hit the last step.

"You Jordan?"

"That's me."

"Second door on the right; it's mayhem in there now."

"No doubt. Thanks." Jordan headed down the hall and entered through the second door. The difference from the hallway to the apartment, command center, was like night to day. A dozen people were either at makeshift desks or huddled in groups of two or three. No one looked up when Jordan entered. He scoured the room for Frank when he came bounding around the corner.

"What's the update on Mustafa?"

Frank noticed Jordan and got a grin on his face. "About time you showed up. There's a bedroom down the hall I'm using as my office. Why don't you throw you stuff down there and I'll get you up to speed. It also overlooks Akmed's apartment."

Jordan nodded and, conscious of the rhythm in the room, moved down the hall. On his way, he ran into a Lieutenant he knew from the Philadelphia Police Department. They recognized each other at the same time. "Jim, it's been a while. I'm glad you're part of the team."

"Hey, Jordan! If I knew you were going to be a part of this, I would have turned and run the other way." They both laughed. Jim O'Keefe had been with the Philadelphia PD for thirty-one years. "It's good to see you."

"Yeah same here. I know you've had a tough year in Philly, with the officer killings." Jordan gave him a pat on the shoulder.

"Can you believe it? Five this year. You'd think we were in a war zone. It just makes no sense." O'Keefe lowered and shook his head.

"Any of them connected?"

"No. Just a bunch of two strikers who were trying to avoid their third." Jim was referring to the three strikes rule in criminal sentencing. Third convicted offense resulted in a mandatory prison sentence.

"Unbelievable. Hey, I'll catch up with you later." Jordan slapped Jim on the back. Jordan believed that things had connections, but they weren't always obvious but, to have five patrol officers killed in an eight-month time frame had a reason beyond just happening. When he had spare time, he loved to research such things for the sake of his own curiosity. Maybe, when this was over and he had some downtime, he would tackle the killings. He had many friends on the Philly force and in the DA's office, so he could probably get the reports and talk to people who investigated each of the incidents.

He found the room and threw his bag on the floor. He went over to the window and looked out. There was a diagram to the left of the window that identified the facade of the building across the street. Jordan could match which windows belonged to Akmed's apartment, which door led up to the apartment, as well as the store. He glanced back and forth until he was comfortable that he knew the layout.

Frank entered the room. "I'm glad you're here. We've got a good team here and all of the locals are cooperating, but they are all tactical. I need you to help with our strategy, which now is zero."

"Where's the boy?"

"He's in the apartment, in his room. He's reading, but should be going to sleep soon. He was pretty upset after his uncle left. He's struggling with his father's absence."

"Did he call someone to talk about it?" Jordan turned, alarm in his voice that another person was now involved and had this information.

"No. He talks to himself quite a lot. It's been helpful."

"Thank God for personality quirks. Where's Mustafa?"

"Home. We've got a team of watchers there both front and back of the house. There have been no visitors. We got a tech team on standby, ready to go in and wire the place if he leaves tonight. If he doesn't go out, they will go in first thing tomorrow as soon as he leaves."

"Any chance to do an outside tap now?"

"He's got two big dogs in the yard and they are barkers. We did a walk-by and, when our guys were a half a house off, the dogs started in and didn't stop until our guys were on the next block."

"What's the background check shown on Mustafa?"

"Nothing really. From Iran and been in USA for fifteen years. No problems, has a green card and is sponsored."

"By who? What does he do?"

"He's a manager for a cleaning service. They do offices -- even have some Federal contracts. We're doing a background on the company now. We should have it back in an hour."

"My guess is you haven't come up with anything pointing toward their mission's objective."

"No. We still come up empty. We're hoping when we get into his house we can get the names of the other family members. That might give us a clue. If Akmed is any indication, it seems only Mustafa knows and we aren't even sure that he isn't getting direction from elsewhere."

"No, I think he's the real deal. He may be waiting for the go signal, but I think he knows what they are going after. I want to listen to the tape of the boy's conversation with Mustafa. Who's got the tape?"

"Follow me." Frank led the way out of the bedroom and led Jordan down the hallway, into the family room. He walked him over to the back corner where several tape players were on the table with headphones. "Here you go. The tape is in the machine. Need anything else, just let me know."

With that, Jordan sat down, donned the headset and pressed play.

Chapter Twenty-Five

Jordan removed the headphones off and pressed the stop button on the tape player. He looked at his notepad. It contained many scribbles, thoughts and the beginnings of ideas, only to be scratched through and a new one begun but, by the end of the page, everything was scribbled over. He hadn't gotten anything out of the tapes, other than a concerned uncle spending time with his nephew. Mustafa was shrewd, didn't say anymore than he had to and he didn't overplay his hand. It was going to be critical to get into Mustafa's house. He hoped the man truly had a job, which would require him to be gone for a long period. Jordan was sure Mustafa would not leave things around for them to find so the team would have to be thorough and careful.

Jordan felt the need to talk with Frank and get updated. He wanted to ensure he was on site for the take down of Mustafa's house. He'd originally thought he would want to spend time in the apartment across the street, while Aziz was in school but, that would have to wait. He felt Mustafa's house could be the goldmine.

He shifted his focus from his thoughts to the people around him. There seemed to be a commotion in the room. Jordan turned to face the open room holding the command center when he saw her. He quickly turned away and, under his breath, said, "Shit. Why is she here?" But he knew it was really only a matter of time. She was the best the NSA had to offer and, his personal thoughts aside, this case needed her.

Kate Woolrich had driven up from D.C. after the Deputy Director assigned her to the case. She was the Agency's leading expert on foreign supported domestic terrorism. She strongly believed there were cells throughout the United States, as well as Europe and Asia, just awaiting a signal from abroad to go into action. She kept a bag of clothes packed in her government Suburban and was ready to respond to the newest threat or to track down any evidence which would support her theory.

Early on in her work, she'd crossed paths with Jordan. At first, she had found some of his theories and methods unorthodox. However, as she immersed herself into the same issues, she became ever more convinced he was onto something and might be able to crack the code on how to identify and track these groups and eliminate them prior to their activation.

"I learned more about what I'm up against and it has done nothing more than embolden me to eventually demonstrate to those fools that if you keep thinking about this as just another criminal investigation, they are always going to be able to carry out their attacks and we will continue to only be able to react to them. Sometimes, I'm not sure who is the bigger enemy -- the radical Islamic fundamentalists or the people who are paid to protect us. I choose not to be myopic about this. It's real and it needs to be stopped." Jordan had summarized in a briefing she had attended.

Kate recalled that as the moment she fell in love with Jordan Wright. She knew at the time the feeling wasn't reciprocated. Jordan was focused. He needed to prove he was right. She felt the best she could do at the moment was to support him. Hopefully, the love would come.

She was sure on the last case they'd worked she'd pushed a little too hard. They were in upstate New York, investigating a group of Libyan immigrants who had moved to the US prior to Qaddafi denouncing terrorism. The premise was that one of two things could be happening with this group. They could be going rogue, which means they were going to go ahead with their mission and not wait for a green light from their handlers in Libya or, there was always the possibility that Qaddafi was bluffing, to prevent future air strikes to his country and was still in control of the cell.

Jordan and Kate were the only two members of the team on the ground in New York, though they had substantial support assets in their respective headquarters to process all the data and information they were gathering. It had been a tough assignment but, it also gave them downtime together. Kate fondly recalled some great dinners -- not from the standpoint of food and atmosphere, since they were not near any gastronomic oasis but, rather, it was the conversation. She learned a lot about Jordan, where he'd grown up and the history of his family, along with the challenges of growing up in wealth and privilege, only to see it destroyed by his parents. It was so different from her Midwest upbringing in Ohio. Her parents both worked, her father at a local manufacturing plant making commercial food equipment, her mother a cook in the junior high school cafeteria. What they lacked in material wealth they made up in love and care for one another. Listening to Jordan made her appreciation of her parents deepen and, while she always couldn't wait to get out of the small town of her youth, she came to feel it would be where she would want to return, to raise her own family.

One night they observed the group leaving their compound and decided to attempt to infiltrate the house. They had a warrant and moved from their observation post as quickly as possible. They had notified the command center of the suspects' movement, but had felt it was better to take advantage of them all being gone, which was rare, versus following them to see where they were headed.

They did a quick reconnoiter of the house to ensure no one was present and also to double check there were no alarms or traps. Feeling confident that everything was how they thought it would be, they entered through the back door. The Libyans hadn't upgraded any of the locks, so getting into the farmhouse was accomplished with relative ease. Kate moved about the first floor as Jordan headed upstairs. They uncovered a treasure trove of information about the group and its makeup. They spent over an hour looking at and photographing documents and they were able to mirror the hard drives of the five computers they found.

Before they left, they headed to the basement and found a well-equipped chemical lab. It was hard to figure out exactly how the Libyans would utilize it, but it was obvious it could be used to create any number of explosive materials and, with the right hands and mind, some simple bio-weapons.

They felt they had pushed their time limit, so they headed out the door and back to their vehicle in the woods. Not long after they had packed their gear and begun the download of the information back to Washington, the headlights of a large SUV appeared. It stopped in front of the house and two men in overalls climbed out.

"If I didn't know better, I'd say it's one of ours." Kate chuckled as the men opened up the back and removed several large cases, which they carried into the house.

"We've never seen these guys before, but they sure seem to be on a mission." Jordan turned around and grabbed a larger pair of night vision binoculars off the back seat. They were too big to constantly use, but came in handy if he needed a higher level of detail. He scanned the vehicle. "It doesn't have any plates. It's definitely been customized with beefed up suspension, larger tires. No antennas, doesn't seemed to be armored."

After about forty-five minutes, the men emerged from the house and left in the vehicle.

"Should we follow them?" Kate looked over at Jordan. He nodded negatively and pointed toward the house. Kate returned her focus to the house and brought her binoculars back to her eyes.

Just then the whole area lit up as bright as a summer day as the house lifted off its foundation and exploded with a force that caused the complete destruction of the structure. Soon, pieces of wood and glass and other materials rained down on their car. Secondary explosions were coming from what was left of the basement.

"We'll go now!" Jordan shouted and he turned the key and threw the car into gear. The tires caught traction and the black Suburban jolted forward through the woods.

"Wow, that was close!" Kate shouted.

"Timing is everything." Jordan smiled as they came out of the woods and turned onto the paved road.

They proceeded to the hotel and called into their respective chains of command. The downloaded data seemed to indicate that this cell had put them on the market and had actually taken bids for their services. A name kept consistently popping up in the data. A man named Tahir. He seemed to be interested in engaging this group in some of his plans. Nothing seemed to have developed to a point of a specific target and mission but, it seemed this group had gone from being controlled by Libya to possibly being under Pakistani leadership. Tahir was a new name to both Kate and Jordan. That was not surprising as new names were coming up all the time. Terrorists were like cock roaches; the more you exterminated the more that seem to appear.

No one had any leads on the men who blew up the house. Maybe it was other Libyans who knew of the group's defection or it could have been Pakistani's who didn't want someone interfering on their turf. One step forward, two steps back.

The green light was given to take down the other sub cells identified through the data discovered as quickly as possible. Kate and Jordan were ordered to return to D.C. as soon as possible. Since it was Friday and it was going to take another twenty-four to forty eight hours for the specialists to pour through all of the data they had taken from the house, Jordan told them Kate and he would be there first thing Monday morning.

Chapter Twenty-Six

✤ ✤ ✤

UPPER MAKEFIELD TOWNSHIP, BUCKS COUNTY, PENNSYLVANIA

"So, you in any hurry to get back home?" Jordan looked at Kate, with anticipation.

Kate held her breath. "No, I've got nothing forcing me to get back. What did you have in mind?"

"Would you like to come to my place? Have a great dinner, real food, nice bottle of wine, spend the weekend combing through some antique shops."

"Sounds great and relaxing and, after what we've had to eat up here, I'm not sure I'll recognize real food." Kate felt her whole body tingle with anticipation. "How far away are we?"

"I think we can make it in about two and a half hours. The heart of Bucks County Pennsylvania is calling."

"Let me grab my bag and I'm ready to go."

They headed off and Kate soon found them leaving Interstate Eighty-Four and on rolling country roads. They went through small villages with the names of Upper Black Eddy and Carversville.

Jordan slowed the car and turned down an unpaved drive. In front of them was an electric gate. Jordan lowered his window and punched in a code. The gate slowly opened and they proceeded down the lane, with nothing in site.

"Oh, my gosh! You're a serial killer and you are going to dump my body where it will never be found."

"You've figured me out. It's the only way I can handle the stress of a Federal job."

They both laughed and Kate just about choked as they came around a bend and a beautiful stone farmhouse lay in front of them. A large front porch wrapped around the front of the obviously well restored three-story home.

"Wow," was all she could say. "Is this really yours?"

"Yes, my home away from home. I never get to spend as much time here as I like, but it's my paradise."

"It's right out of a home magazine. Are those your horses? My God how much are they paying you. I'm in the wrong agency."

Jordan laughed. "One of the few smart things my father ever did was to set up a trust for me. When he went bust, he couldn't touch what he put aside for me. So, it comes in handy for things like this. Let's get inside."

The inside was even more incredible than the outside. It was the most comfortable home she'd ever been in. Every room begged for you to come in and just drop into a chair. The kitchen was one step down from being in a five star restaurant. If Jordan asked, Kate would stay here with him forever.

"I want to take a quick walk around. Why don't you take your things upstairs? Pick any room except the one in the back on the far left. That would be mine. I should be back in about thirty minutes. Feel fee to take a shower. Kate, make yourself at home."

Kate headed up the stairs. She toured the three available rooms. Any of the three would have worked for her, but she fell in love with the bedroom at the front of the house. It contained a large canopy bed and, as she entered it was wrapped, in the warm golden sunlight of the afternoon. It also was ensuite, so she wouldn't have to go down the hall to use the bathroom. She unpacked the contents of her small bag and decided she would take a quick shower.

Out of the shower and into a comfortable pair of jeans and a cotton shirt, Kate headed back downstairs. "What a great place!" She thought to herself this was just another piece of the Jordan Wright puzzle she was trying to put together.

She walked around the downstairs, moving from room to room. All she could keep thinking was how perfect each room was and how everything flowed. Could Jordan really have done this himself? She entered the kitchen and looked out the windows, toward the barn. Jordan was talking to someone in the yard, a young male with work clothes on.

Jordan noticed Kate in the window and waved. She felt a little embarrassed that she'd been caught. She quickly waved backed and then moved away from the window and went back to the family room, plopped herself down into a comfy chair that seemed to envelope her and grabbed a couple of magazines from the table. She thumbed through them, most with articles about the area and restaurant reviews, when she heard the back door open and close.

"Kate?" Jordan was moving through the kitchen.

"In here, Jordan. Just making myself at home," Kate announced.

"Great," he entered the room and stood over her. "Found a room and the shower?"

"Yep. This is really a great place."

"Indeed it is. Kate, I need to ask you to keep this between us. I don't need a lot of crap from people and I definitely don't need the Inspector General investigating how I paid for this. I kind of like to keep my personal and professional lives separate."

"Jordan, you won't hear me say a word on one condition."

"And what might that be?" Jordan moved around to face her.

"You bring me back here every so often."

They both laughed. Jordan reached down and grabbed Kate's arms and pulled her from the chair. "Let me show you around. I'm pretty proud of this place."

He showed her the house and described the various places he'd found different antique pieces and then they headed outside. He took her into the barn and they climbed to the top of the hayloft and Jordan opened the access doors so they could look out at the rolling hills and, in the distance, see the Delaware River, dividing Pennsylvania and New Jersey.

"I've never been anywhere like this," Kate remarked, still staring out the door and looking at the incredible vistas.

"It has that effect on people. You can feel a million miles from anywhere. That's why I like it. There's no one else around. You won't believe how quiet it will be tonight."

"If there is no one else around, who was the man I saw you talking with?" Kate inquired.

"That would be Steve. He oversees this place when I'm not here. He has a cabin out in the woods. He is the true outdoorsman. Stocks me up with venison and wild turkey and he keeps this place in shape."

"Why would you ever leave?"

"Oh, you know. I have to save the world every now and then."

She turned and lightly punched him in the chest. They stood facing each other, not sure what to do next, both wanting to hold the other, but neither sure if that was what the other wanted. It was an awkward few seconds.

The silence was finally broken by Jordan. "You getting hungry?"

"Famished, but I'm not sure about venison and turkey." Kate said.

"How about some good old prime steer? I called Steve before we left and he headed to the market and stocked us up. Are you ready for a Chef Jordan meal?"

"How close is the nearest poison control center?" Kate looked up at Jordan with a smile.

"Well, you can always go hungry! Besides, you have to help. So, if we get sick it will be both of our faults," Jordan declared.

"Oh, Jordan! Always ready with the plausible deniability, whether at work or play," Kate teased.

They laughed as they headed out of the barn and back to the house. Together, they fixed an incredible dinner of filets, twice baked potatoes, sautéed spinach with garlic and onions and a tossed salad made from lettuce grown by Steve. It was one of the best dinners Kate had ever eaten. Part of it was the food, but more of it was the company.

After dinner, they went out to the back porch to watch the evening fade to darkness.

"You are an amazing man, Jordan Wright. Full of intrigue and mystery." Kate stated playfully.

"I'm an open book. People just don't take the chance to pick me up and leaf through the pages," Jordan shot back.

They both laughed. They spent the rest of the night on the porch. One bottle of wine turned into two. The conversation touched on everything -- work, mutual acquaintances, and even politics.

Kate glanced at her watch and realized it was after midnight, even though she thought it was no later than nine. She excused herself to turn-in. Jordan said goodnight, but decided to stay out for a bit longer.

Kate headed up to her room and got ready for bed. Her head was swimming, but she wasn't sure if it was from the wine or the conversation. She was truly amazed by Jordan. He wasn't just some macho terrorism operative. She was finding so many levels of who he was -- almost like pulling back a layer on an onion, only to uncover another with each one more of interest than the last. Oh, how she wished she could stay here and peel all the layers back.

When Jordan woke up, he could smell bacon being fried in the kitchen along with coffee being brewed. He wasn't used to having someone here that would also get up and cook. He grabbed his robe and headed down the backstairs that led directly to the kitchen from his bedroom. He opened the door at the bottom of the stairs, causing Kate to jump from the sink and away from the door.

"Sorry! Didn't mean to startle you," Jordan told Kate apologetically.

"You're lucky I left my gun in my room," Kate responded.

They both laughed and Kate returned to her cooking chores.

"This wasn't necessary, Kate."

"Well, I wanted to show my appreciation. I was up and hungry and my host was nowhere in sight, so I had to fend for myself," Kate said teasingly.

"Well, seems you're doing all right by yourself," Jordan responded, smiling.

Kate got plates out of the cupboard and scooped scrambled eggs, bacon and toast onto each plate. Jordan had taken a seat at the kitchen table. He dug in as soon as the plate was down.

"Kate, this is great. I would have never realized you could cook like this."

"Well, Mr. Wright, you aren't the only one able to surprise."

They left the house later that morning, for the trip back to Washington. They took their time making several stops at antiques shops along with a leisurely lunch at one of the taverns which could be found throughout the area. Any observer would have commented on the fun the young couple was having and would have guessed they were destined for the altar.

In much too short a time, Kate found herself saying goodbye to Jordan as he dropped her off at her apartment building. Memories of the past couple of days swirled in her head. She'd noticed, as they got closer to the District, Jordan changed. He was back to the Jordan on the mission. Their talked changed from wine, food, travel and antiques to a focus on the case. Who were those men that blew up the house? Who and where was Tahir? What happened to the Libyans?

Kate entered her apartment. It was dark and bland. She threw her bag down by her bedroom door and walked back to the kitchen. She grabbed a bottle of cold beer and before the door on the refrigerator closed, she caught it and pulled out another one. She headed back toward the bathroom and drew a bath, opened a beer and slowly slid her body into the hot water. She had one thought to ponder: Did Jordan harbor the same feelings for her that she had for him?

Chapter Twenty-Seven

✤ ✤ ✤

WASHINGTON, D.C.,
FOUR WEEKS AGO

Kate wasn't sure what the day would bring. She knew Jordan would be in every meeting she was in today. She knew he would be totally professional and she knew he didn't want people to know about his home in Pennsylvania or anything else they had discussed. She did, however, want to be focused on looking for other clues. Would he look at her differently, make some sort of gesture or subtle recognition?

They had their first debrief at eight o'clock. Jordan was already in the room when Kate arrived.

"Hey ya, Kate." Were the first words she heard as she came through the door. Surprisingly, they were from Jordan, who had the reputation of not always recognizing people when they came into a room with a response. She took this as a good sign.

The meetings were tough and while there was a lot of data and intelligence recovered from the house, most of it just reinforced things they already knew. There were no leads on the men in the Suburban who had planted the bombs. The Suburban had been found at Stewart Airport outside Newburgh, New York, in the parking lot. While not the busiest airport, it was the ideal airport to leave from. There was enough domestic service to get you to just about any city in the United States within two to three hours. It had a small TSA presence and, since nothing much happened there, the staffs of the airlines weren't that observant. Since neither Jordan nor Kate had gotten a good look at any of the men, no visuals were available to show.

Later in the afternoon, word came from the N.Y. State Police that the car had been found which the Libyans were driving when they left the house. Discovered in a warehouse area of Rochester, in an abandoned Kodak facility, word also came that the bodies of the Libyans had been found in one of the buildings, all executed.

At a break late in the afternoon, Jordan and Kate found themselves alone for the first time. Jordan approached Kate and, after looking around to ascertain they were truly alone, he bent over to her ear.

"If we get out of here at a decent time, do you want to go grab a bite to eat?"

Kate nodded yes, the less said, the better. His question had taken her by surprise, but now, she just wanted to get out of there and be back in that world with Jordan. She knew the rest of the day would just drag.

Stan came running down the hall. "Everyone back into the room now! We've got a break."

It took less than a minute for the room to fill.

"We've got a lead on Tahir. Tahir Amadi is a Pakistani national. He seems to be a brain for hire, helping less intelligent terrorist groups plot better actions to have a greater impact. We talked to the UK and Pakistan. They both believe Tahir has been involved in the subway bombings in London and the recent events in Spain. A cell they broke up in Denmark seemed also to be working with him. The Pakistani's have now asked for help. We're activating an Irregular Warfare Joint Operations Team under Jordan to assist them in bringing in Tahir. They have him isolated in Karachi, but have been unsuccessful in his capture. They keep missing him, and they are sure it is because someone is leaking Intel to him."

"When do we go?" Jordan didn't lift his head when he interrupted Stan. He was already in operation mode, beginning to list what he and his team would need.

"There's a C37-A being readied out at Andrews. You go as quickly as you can get out there." The C37 was the military version of the Gulfstream G-5. While the military version was stripped down compared to the corporate jet, it was still a great way to travel. To have secured it, this mission had to be of high priority and the top echelons of the Pentagon and State Department must have already been briefed.

Kate sighed to herself. There would be no dinner with Jordan tonight.

Chapter Twenty-Eight

✤ ✤ ✤

SOUTH PHILADELPHIA

Kate just stared at the back of his head. She hadn't heard from him since he left for Pakistan. She'd heard the mission had gone well and Tahir was in custody of the Pakistani ISS, but that was weeks ago and he hadn't even sent a text message. This was the part of Jordan she just hadn't been able to figure out.

She was also determined not to give up. One thing Kate Woolrich was known for was the fact that, once she set her mind to something, she didn't stop or let anything get in her way until she'd gotten it. Why should Jordan be any different?

She'd missed most of the introductions as she recalled the last time she had been with Jordan. She'd just nodded at individuals who had been pointed out to her by Frank. "Great," she thought to herself. "They just think I'm another stuck up Washington bitch, coming in to tell them how to do their jobs." Frank was looking at her, knowing that she was preoccupied. She grinned and turned. She had Jordan in her sights and she wanted to take the initiative. Nothing over the top, but she wanted him to know she was there and that they were going to be working together. More importantly, she needed to get his reaction. She needed to read his body language, to see if there was still interest. Or, did he consider her yesterday's news?

She walked over to the table where it looked like he'd been listening to some tapes.

"So, how's tonight for dinner?" Shy was never a trait attributed to Kate. She was always ready to put it right on the table.

"Kate, it's good to see you." Jordan stood up. "Fancy meeting you here."

"Yeah, last I heard you were off to Andrews to catch a flight."

"Ouch! You hit a bull's eye on that one." Jordan flashed back to his home, the dinner with Kate, the evening on the porch, his standing outside her bedroom door, trying to get up the courage to knock, but his courage never getting strong enough to put his hand into motion against the door.

He'd never met anyone like Kate. She excited him, scared him. She was something special and he just wished he could figure out the best way to approach her to begin a relationship. He was supposed to be the execution expert when it came to planning, but this time, he was stumped. "Dinner would be great but, unfortunately, I think it's going to be Chinese with twenty-five of our closest new friends." Jordan gestured around the room. "We've got a big one here Kate, with no real data on what the mission is and when it's going to happen. I'm glad you're here. We can really use your expertise."

"Is that the only reason you're glad I'm here?" Kate kept pushing.

"You are something, Miss Woolrich. I do want to have that dinner and, if not tonight, we'll make sure we get away for it tomorrow. Deal?" Jordan asked.

"Deal -- as long as no last minute flights come up." Kate was never one to stop a dig until she made her point.

"If they do, I'll take you with me. Has anyone briefed you yet?" Jordan so wanted to move the conversation to the case.

"Just the prelims. No real details. And what I got was several hours old." Kate told him.

"All right then, take a seat and I'll fill you in."

Chapter Twenty-Nine

❖ ❖ ❖

Mustafa awoke the next morning. He reached under his bed and retrieved his prayer mat. He unrolled it, placed it in the proper position facing Mecca and began his morning prayers. He was unsettled about Akmed and Aziz. He just wasn't sure what exactly was going on. Was Akmed struggling with Mahasin's death that he needed time away? He could understand it if they really had been man and wife. He'd been surprised that Akmed had even tried to save her life. At least he didn't know enough about the mission to compromise it if he were talking to anyone.

He was more comfortable with Aziz. While Aziz was concerned about his father, he was still dedicated to his uncle. Mustafa had worried he might need to place Aziz in a lesser role for the mission, which would have been a shame. Aziz had grown into a natural leader amongst his cousins. They respected him and did as he asked without questioning. To move him out of the role would have been a huge risk. Yes, Aziz would stay in his role.

Mustafa noticed the clock and would need to rush to ensure he arrived at work on time. The last thing he needed was to create issues at work. His job as a Shift Supervisor at the Brotherly Love Cleaning Service was a critical element to the mission. He'd worked hard over the past six years. Starting as a night janitor, he worked harder than anyone else. He surpassed all of the quality standards for his job and his performance evaluations were always excellent. He truly relished the feedback, "If only everyone here worked as hard as you do."

He eventually became the supervisor for the team, working at the Rohm and Haas Chemical Company Headquarters on Independence Mall in Philadelphia, always surpassing expectations. He was also in a position to hire and was able to place many of the people he needed for the mission into various roles. A year-and-a-half ago, he was again promoted. In his role as Shift Supervisor, he was now in charge of the day cleaning crews at the company's six clients in the Independence Mall area. He'd also made himself valuable to the business development team and had found cost savings that allowed their bids to be accepted by three more clients in the same area. He was given a substantial raise, plus bonus. His manager also assigned him a company van to use both during and after work. Mustafa would laugh to himself at how these American's thought everything could be fixed by money or material things. They had no idea what would be coming. They didn't realize that their star employee had the Brotherly Love Cleaning Company at the center of the plan to wreak havoc in Philadelphia. This company would never stand up to the scrutiny it would receive by the Feds when they discovered the role it played. It always gave Mustafa a big grin that his employers took as a sign that they once again had pleased their employee and that he wouldn't even think twice about leaving them. He finished dressing, thinking that any day now he would move his plan forward.

Mustafa left his house and jumped into the van. He stopped at the Wawa on his way to the office for a cup of coffee and an egg sandwich.

He headed to his office, which was housed in the basement of the Constitution Center, the most recent addition to Independence Mall and one of the newest clients. The General Manager hadn't been in favor of Brotherly Love Cleaning being chosen and had pushed for one of their competitors. Mustafa decided to work out of this facility so he could keep a close eye on things. He'd shifted his crews around so he had several of his best people working at this location. He made it a point to seek out the Operations Manager several times a day, to check in, and had scheduled a weekly walk through the building with the General Manager. Feedback he was getting from his boss was positive and Mustafa felt that he was building a positive relationship with the GM. He would spend most of his day here, but in the afternoon he would walk to his other locations and check in. They included Liberty Bell Center, Independence Hall, Rohm and Haas, the Independence Visitor's Center and the outside Mall area, which connected all of these buildings. During the day, he had a crew of sixty-five working for him.

Mustafa believed everything had fallen in place.

Chapter Thirty

�֎ ✖ ✖

As soon as the surveillance car notified the team that Mustafa had arrived at his place of work, the tactical team went into action. Agent Lutz walked up the alley to the back gate. Quickly checking his surroundings to make sure no one was watching, he rapped on the gate, alerting the dogs.

They dogs flew around from the front racing each other to the intruder at the gate. The agent raised his gun and fired at the first dog and then at the second. All that could be heard was the barely audible burp and then the low thud of the dogs falling to the ground. The tranquilizer would last four to five hours. By the time Mustafa returned, the dogs would be no worse for wear.

Lutz moved forward and retrieved the dart from each dog. If Mustafa returned unexpectedly, they had an antidote ready that would revive the dogs immediately.

"Dogs are down." He spoke into his headset mike.

"Everyone move in." The team leader replied.

Two Comcast Cable vans pulled up to the front of the house and four agents, disguised as installers, jumped out and went to the rear of the vans and grabbed large tool boxes and headed inside.

Another van pulled up in back of the house. This van included Jordan and Kate. While not dressed as installers, they moved rapidly to the back door, where Lutz just finished his inspection for tells on the back door before opening it.

He discovered a human hair stuck in the top hinge. He gently removed it, bagged it and taped the bag to the door. He then quickly utilized his lock pick set to open the door. They had anticipated no alarm and they were correct.

They moved in with Lutz, also dressed as an installer and moved to the front door. With a look out the window, he saw the agent on the other side who had affixed an envelope to the door and gave a thumbs up sign. Inside, the agent unlocked the door and opened it.

"Hey is Mustafa finally getting cable. I've told him for years he needed cable."

The four agents on the front porch turned around and saw a woman standing on the sidewalk near their vans, looking at them.

"Oh Christ!" Agent Reggie Smith whispered. "I'll take care of her,"

"Yep, he sure is." Smith pegged the lady as somewhere between forty and forty-five years old. She was dressed in an old tracksuit that did little to hide or flatter her robust figure.

"He must be getting the works, because when you boys come to my house, there's only one of you and he never looks as good as you boys do." The woman looked hard at each of the men.

"Well thanks, ma'am. We're actually using this installation to train some of our new guys. So, maybe next time you call, one of them will come out."

"If I knew I was going to get one of you, I'd go and break something," she laughed, teasing.

Smith smiled and laughed with her. "Well, we want our customers happy. But, I'll tell you what I'll do. Why don't you give me your address and when I get back to the office, I'll put in your file for them to call me if you have any problems."

"Well, I'm not sure you're the cutest one. Can you bring all of your boys out here and let me pick?" She laughed again.

"Well, I can't do that, but I'll tell you what next time you have a problem and you call, they'll call me and I'll round up all four of us and we'll come together. How's that for a deal?"

"Sounds good to me, I just live right down in the next block. Twenty-seven O three is my place. It's the third house in on the left." She pointed down the street.

"It sure is. Let me also get your name."

"Ms. Mirabelle Jones; but, my friends call me Belle."

"Okay, Ms. Jones, I'll put that note in the file."

"Honey, we're friends. You can call be Belle."

"Thanks, Belle. Oh, and one more thing. This installation is a surprise from his nieces and nephews so, if you could keep it quiet. They are going to come over with a new TV for him."

"Your secret is safe with me."

"Okay, Belle. I need to get in there and make sure my boys are getting the work done. It was a pleasure to talk with you."

"Honey, the pleasure was all Belle's." She turned and headed down the street.

The agent turned and headed up to the house. As he entered, the entire team stopped what they were doing and smiled at him.

"Did you get yourself a date for Saturday?" Jordan shot out to the agent.

Kate couldn't hold back. "If she's busy, I think my mother is available."

"Funny, funny -- I just saved us from the neighborhood gossip and all I get is grief. Don't we have work we should all be doing?"

The team refocused and, for the next five hours, they scoured the house. The house was a small, two bedrooms, built in the early fifties; and, it looked like it hadn't been updated. It was spartan with little furniture and any personal items that typically make a house a home. For the most part, the walls were bare with no pictures or artwork.

Half of the team went through every room, searching for any evidence that would identify the rest of the bad guys, the mission, and who the ultimate leaders were. The other half installed a series of audio and video devices, as well as planting bugs on the phones. The van in the alley contained a high speed-copying machine, so documents could be quickly duplicated and returned to their proper place.

By the time they left, they had duplicated over seven hundred and fifty pages, as well as mirrored the hard drive of the computer they found. They wrapped things up and did a final inspection of the house. Initially, as they entered they took a series of digital photographs, which they carefully reviewed in order to ensure they had placed everything back in its original position.

Once completed, the teams retreated from the house and replaced the tells in the doors and headed to the vans. The dogs were regaining consciousness, but still groggy and did not pose any threat to the team's exit.

"Good job, everyone." Jordan announced over the radio. "Base, we're returning; the house is secure."

Chapter Thirty-One

✤ ✤ ✤

When they reached the command post, Max and William had arrived with Akmed. A decision had still not been made on whether or not Akmed would return to the apartment that afternoon. Jordan wanted to delay the decision as long as possible, to give the team the opportunity to sift through all of the material they had found at Mustafa's apartment.

Kate had asked Frank, Max and Jordan to join her in the backroom, to share some intel her team had developed. They all headed down the hall, when Kate was finished. Jordan felt it would be a good time to come to a consensus on whether Akmed should return today. At present, Akmed was in the other bedroom, waiting for them. While he hadn't provided additional information in the last forty-eight hours, everything he'd told them had been validated.

Kate closed the door. "My team has been processing the forensic data from Akmed's apartment and Mustafa's house. We don't seem to be picking up any residue or signature data that would point to storage or manufacturer of weapons taking place at either location."

"Meaning what, exactly?" Max walked over to look out the window.

"If we think the attack in imminent, we have yet to find any stash of weapons and supplies. No bomb making supplies, nothing to restrain hostages, no communication systems. All of the standard things we have seen in the past. Jordan, remember the whole lab the Libyans had in New York?"

Jordan nodded.

"But, we haven't been in all of their locations. It could be stored at the other families, right?" Frank added.

"Could be, but, I just think if they're getting ready to move, we should have found evidence of something at Mustafa's. We've come up with nothing." Kate's frustration was beginning to show, while Jordan continued to just stare out the window.

"So let's go through the scenarios. We got a lot of brainpower in this room. Let's get in the heads of Mustafa and the families and figure it out." Max had now moved into position in the center of the room.

Frank jumped in. "Well, maybe our assumption they are getting ready to go isn't right. Maybe we can bring them down before anything happens."

"Okay. That could be one," Max agreed.

"We've missed a location. They could have a warehouse or another location where they are assembling everything." William contributed. William, Kate and Frank had created an informal circle around Max. Jordan remained off to the side, staring out the window.

"Possibly, Mustafa has access to something at the cleaning company which allows him to either store or make what they need. Maybe they aren't as far along and nothing has been brought in yet?" Kate contributed.

"Okay, guys. Enough chit chat. The answer is staring us in the face." Jordan said without turning around. "If I were planning an attack on a target in the United States and I needed to get my hands on chemicals, electronics, radios, guns and anything else I would need, you know what the best thing for me to have would be?"

"Yeah." Kate rolled her eyes at Frank and Max. "If you would have been listening to our conversation, we've gone over the list. A warehouse, possibly using the cleaning company, or if nothing else you've got it spread amongst all of these families or other..."

"Or..." Jordan cut her off. "You buy one of the fathers a hardware store. We're looking right at the supply depot. Think about it. The local hardware store can have everything a terrorist would need and no one would ask any questions why they were getting a certain shipment. The vendors would only care about getting paid. The trucking company just brings whatever they're supposed to bring.

"A hundred pounds of fertilizer being delivered to a house in a subdivision raises alarms. Being sent to a hardware store? Nobody would even question it. When the surveillance equipment was placed in the store, did anyone look in the back store room?"

Frank sighed. "We didn't have time. We got in as soon as we could, but we didn't know how long we would have. So, we just hung the equipment and got out."

"I get it. We need to get back in there as soon as possible. We need to focus on the storeroom and Akmed's office. Let's get Akmed in here. Max, I don't think he ever talked about what he might have ordered?" Jordan said.

"Nope -- and we didn't ask. I'll go get him. Let's see if he still comes through or if this is what he has been hiding."

Chapter Thirty-Two

Akmed sat in the chair with the five people surrounding him. He knew William the best as they had spent time together at the house and shared personal interests. Max had been kind to him, but had asked a lot of questions. The third one, whom he knew as Jordan, was nice, but intense, and seemed intelligent and would be a considerable adversary for Mustafa.

Akmed was happy the USA had someone who thought the way he knew Mustafa and his leaders thought. The other two, he did not know. The woman was attractive and seemed to be competitive with Max, but not about work. Somehow, he felt it had to do with Jordan. The other man seemed to be a peer of Jordan's.

"Akmed, I know we have asked you a lot of questions and we appreciate all of your help. We wanted to focus now on your business, the hardware store. How long have you owned it?" Jordan wanted to hurry through the preliminaries, so he could get to the heart of what really was going on across the street. But, he didn't want to panic Akmed and have him shut down.

"Almost five years. It has been a good business. I have enjoyed running the store. If this ever gets over with, I would like to have another one some day.

"I'm sure you are good at running the store. How did you get the money?"

"I had saved money from my other jobs and my wife and I both had received an inheritance"

Jordan shook his head. "I know that's what you are supposed to say, but you can tell us where the money really came from."

"Mustafa came to see me. He told me he was impressed with how well I was doing and thought it might be possible for me to have my own business. I got excited. He took me to the store and said he was thinking about having me buy it. I said to him that I didn't have that much money. He laughed and said not to worry about the money. He wanted to know if I thought I could run it. I told him I could and about eight weeks later he came by and told me the store was mine.

He took me to an attorney's office the next day and we signed the papers. He took me to the bank and gave me cashier's checks to deposit into my account, covering the cost of the store. He had documents from Iran, stating that Mahasin and I had inherited money."

"Then what happened?" Jordan was trying not to be impatient.

"I owned the store. I re-opened it. I bought one of those 'Under New Management' signs and hung it in the window. We were successful from the beginning. I remodeled the apartment upstairs and moved Mahasin and Aziz. I read many business books. Jack Welch, Michael Porter, Ram Charan. I learned how Americans did business and learned about listening to my customers and stocking the things they needed. By the end of the first year, we were doing well."

"What happened to the money? Who got it?" William had taken over the questioning. He'd picked up on where Jordan was headed and thought he could help, so it wouldn't come across like an interrogation.

"The money went to Mustafa."

"All of it?"

"Well, yes"

"Akmed, you can tell us. Did all of the money go to him?"

"No. He told me he couldn't believe how much money we were making; so, as the store made more, I started to keep some back. I figured out how to adjust the books so Mustafa or the other father, Jarill, who was an accountant and would audit the books, couldn't tell. I still have most of it, if I must give it to you."

"We don't want the money. You know what would have happened if Mustafa would have found out?" William suggested.

"Yes. He would have killed me. But, it was my success. I built it to what it was. We couldn't really use the money. We would go out to a nice dinner every so often. It's all in a brokerage account at Schwab."

"How did you pull that off?" Jordan asked, smiling.

"I saw Mr. Schwab on TV. He seemed honest. There was a branch in Center City I could get to and Mustafa did not understand these types of things. He would call around to banks, to ensure we didn't have separate accounts, but he would never have called a brokerage firm."

Frank was intrigued. "Did you invest?"

"Yes, mostly index funds and, I would also watch CNBC. I had some gold and muni bonds for diversification."

Jordan and William started laughing, eliciting a stern look from Max.

"Well, maybe when this is all done, you can give us some advice. By the way, how much is your account worth?" Jordan inquired.

"It's a little over six hundred and twenty-five thousand dollars." No one said a thing. Eyes met eyes around the room. Frank let out a whistle.

"Congratulations, Akmed! You're living the American dream. So, how involved was Mustafa in the store?" William asked.

"He rarely came in. He didn't care, as long as the money went to him."

"He never asked you to order anything or store anything?" Jordan inquired.

Akmed's expression changed. "Only recently, he would come in and walk around and then we would go to the back storeroom so Benny couldn't hear. He would ask me to order certain quantities of certain items. Sometimes, he would tell me to start carrying a product which I didn't have."

"For example?" Max asked.

"Ammonia nitrate. I have a small section for lawn and garden supplies and tools. As you can see, there aren't a lot of gardens and lush lawns around here. Most of it was for houseplants and there are a couple of community gardens in some of the vacant lots.

"But no one ever needed ammonia nitrate," Akmed lamented. "I ordered it and it sat there for a year. A month ago, he told me to order more. Now I've got close to two hundred pounds of that stuff and haven't sold any of it."

Jordan gave a curt nod to Kate and grinned.

If she could have she would have flipped him off.

"What else?" William asked.

"He's had me order heavy gauge wire. He told me to carry a certain type of appliance timer. They are good, but the price point is too high for my customers. So, again, they just sit there. He had me stock large PVC pipes. Not your irrigation grade, not that anyone needed it, but a more commercial grade. Tarps, lots of butane fuel, two way radios, police scanners, and, of course, guns."

"What kind of guns?"

"Semi-automatic pistols, shotguns, small assault rifles and lots of ammo. Getting the Federal Firearms License took some time. I know what a lot of this is for and most of it is in the storeroom. There are also other crates that were sent to the store that Mustafa told me not to open."

"Thanks Akmed. We need to get in there," William said.

"Akmed, I think it's time for you to go home. Frank, can you and Kate pull together a team to go into the store tonight. I've got a plan to get Akmed back and give us time to really go through the store room," Jordan told them.

"We're on it!" Kate called out as she and Frank bounded from the room.

Chapter Thirty-Three

❖ ❖ ❖

Agents had retrieved Akmed's car after he'd been moved to the safe house. It was returned to Akmed in a Center City parking garage, away from the neighborhood. It took him about ten minutes to pull into the alley behind the store and park the car in the garage.

Benny should have closed the store by now, so Akmed wasn't sure if he would be upstairs with Aziz or not.

Akmed entered the back door of the store. He'd been instructed not to lock it, so the team could get quickly inside to investigate further what was being kept in the storeroom. He walked through the back and into the store. He turned left and headed to the door leading to the stairway.

The door was locked, meaning Benny had probably not gone upstairs after work. So, he unlocked it and climbed the stairs. Hesitating as he came to the door leading into the apartment, Akmed wasn't sure he would be able to pull it off.

Slowly, he turned the knob on the door, not to make his entrance a surprise, but rather to prolong having to go in, knowing the agents were waiting to hear him inside and that they wanted him to keep Aziz busy while the team was downstairs. He pushed the door open and found the apartment to be quiet. At first he wasn't sure if Aziz were even there.

Walking through the kitchen and into the living room, he noticed there was a jacket thrown over the chair and a book bag, both belonged to Aziz. He then noticed the door was closed to Aziz's bedroom. Moving over to the door, he brought his hand up to rap on it, but his hand froze before it touched the wood. He took a deep breath and slowly exhaled. He pulled his hand back slightly and released it, letting it lightly rap against the door.

"Aziz? Aziz are you home?" his voice sounded as dry as it his throat felt.. It was barely a rasp. He coughed slightly, hoping it would produce the moisture he needed. Hearing no answer, he turned the knob and pushed the door open slightly.

"Hello father." The voice had come from behind him. He slowly turned and saw Aziz in the doorway at the front entrance to the apartment.

"Aziz. You are here." Akmed moved toward him, opening his arms.

"Yes, Benny had stopped up after closing the store and I just walked him out. I thought you said you were going to be here when I got back from school."

"I got delayed, had problems with the car."

"Again? Why don't you get a new one? The store is doing well."

"In time my son there is no hurry. I must apologize to you. I have been selfish and I should have never left you." They briefly embraced, as any typical father and teenage son would.

"Father, it is okay. I understand. Losing mom has been hard on all of us. I hope you are better."

"I am; but, I need to be here for you. Let's sit and talk. How is school?" Akmed and Aziz moved over to the living room. Aziz sat on the couch and Akmed took the closest chair.

"School is okay, but Uncle Mustafa told us that there are more important things we should be using our minds on. He has talked to us a lot about how we need to be sensitive to the wrongs our people have received. He believes and wants us to believe that we have the ability to change things."

"That may be true, but does he tell you what he wants you to do?"

"Not yet. But, he has asked us all to come to his house for the weekend and he said we won't be back for school next week."

"That's a long time. Is he taking you somewhere, or told you what you are going to be doing?"

"Father, you know my uncle. He never tells us more than we need to know. He'll tell us at the right time. He has been an inspiration, not only to me, but all of my cousins."

"Yes I know. He does keep things close. Are you hungry? Let me fix us some dinner and we can continue our conversation."

Chapter Thirty-Four

Jordan and Kate moved from the alley to the back door of the store. Jordan hoped that Akmed had remembered to leave the door unlocked. He grabbed the knob and slowly turned the handle. The latch released and he pushed the door open as cautiously as he could..

The storeroom was dark and packed full of merchandise. They entered hurriedly and closed the door, turning on tactical flashlights at low setting and shining the beams around the room, gaining a feel for its layout and contents. Jordan noticed the office area and nodded to Kate as she followed his gaze. They had decided she would begin in the office, going through the files and the computer, while Jordan would begin going through the boxes and crates.

Kate headed toward the office. She pulled out her lock pick set and had the door open in seconds. There were numerous files on the desk and an old HP desktop computer as well as two four drawer file cabinets and a fax machine. She sat down at the vintage Steelcase desk with an office chair that had to be over thirty years old. Every time she swiveled to the left, the chair made an annoying squeak.

Kate powered up the computer, and realized by its age that it would take several minutes to boot up so, she went through the files on the desk. She found mostly invoices and vendor information, but was impressed with how organized Akmed was with his business.

So far she found nothing of interest so she turned her attention to the computer as the screen came to life. She retrieved her mirroring device out of her bag and hooked it up to the appropriate port. She looked through the various files on the computer before she copied the hard drive, spending her time looking for any sort of paper trail.

Jordan headed to the part of the room where Akmed had told them he stored the supplies requested by Mustafa, Jordan quietly opened the boxes. He peered inside, and would move his hands around the box to see if anything else were in the box or if it concealed a false bottom or sides. So far, every box opened contained the same things.

One had a half-dozen Sig-Sauer P226 9mms. High end and expensive weaponry, the pistols had a fifteen round plus one capacity. The next box with a Sig Sauer logo contained three P556 machine pistols, which wasn't amateur stuff but top of the line. Mustafa was serious about whatever he was going to do and would have the firepower to back up his plans.

This would put them on parallel with most SWAT teams in the country from a weapons perspective. Considering his group would have the element of surprise and command of their location before authorities arrived, this was a critical piece of data.

The vast majority of times, SWAT teams went up against criminals who weren't well armed, nor had a good plan, let alone knew how to use a location to their advantage. The more he saw and learned of Mustafa, the more he was convinced that those elements giving the good guy side the usual advantage were not going to be present.

Jordan could disable the weapons by pulling the firing pins, but rationalized that Mustafa would not go into this mission without ensuring his his equipment was in perfect working order. Jordan moved on to the next set of boxes.

They contained the PVC pipe Akmed had told them about. The pieces were cut in various sizes and had connectors fitted to them so they could be pieced together. Jordan pulled several out of the boxes without being able to figure out how they were to be used. He placed them back in the box.

Moving to the next box, he found it contained book bags, just like the ones kids carried to school, only larger than most and of sturdier construction and materials. Jordan figured they would be used to carry everything the enemy personnel needed. He found three more boxes, all containing the same types of bags, for a total of eighteen.

Two more boxes contained a total of eleven two-way radios. Studying the radios and packing information in each box, Jordan was able to identify that five units in one box were on the same channel, while the other five from the second box were on a different frequency. The last radio had two channels covering both frequencies. Jordan copied down the two frequencies, and noted that the communications equipment again was top of the line with encryption capabilities.

The last set of boxes contained large sheets of opaque cloth with grommets sewn in. There were also pieces of string and quick ties to attach the material. Jordan hoped he might find some maps or photos or some information that would give him an idea of the location of the attack, all that Jordan found was an impressive arsenal, high tech radios, book bags and other items, the use for which he still wasn't sure.

As he continued around the storeroom, Jordan found additional boxes. One contained cable, wiring and timers, all obviously associated with explosive devices. He saw the bags of fertilizer, which Akmed had mentioned and Jordan thought again about how ingenious it was to buy a hardware store as a front.

Mustafa would be a formidable foe. Jordan moved around the storeroom for a second time to ensure he hadn't missed anything when Kate emerged from the office. Jordan glanced at his watch. They had been there for almost ninety minutes; there was no reason to push their luck any further.

"Did you get everything you need?" Jordan whispered as he came and stood beside Kate.

She nodded, "I don't think I've found anything that's going to crack this thing wide open; however. if you want to get into a good business, a hardware store just might be it. Akmed is doing fairly well for himself, even after he pays Mustafa his share. I have no doubt he's got the money he said he'd squirreled away in his account."

"Really? Well this hardware store might be for sale soon." They both smiled as they moved toward the rear exit door.

"I found everything Akmed said we would. They bought high-end weapons and radios. They've got everything they need to build bombs. There are a couple of things I haven't figured out yet. It's almost like they are planning two attacks and not just one."

"Interesting. I mirrored his computer and sent the data to my team. I'll check with them in about an hour, to see if anything turns up. The paperwork was mostly vendors, taxes, and bills. He runs a tight ship. Even the vendors from whom he bought the items you found are all legit. Even his Federal Firearms License book is perfect, an ATFE agent's dream. I found it in Akmed's safe. "

They slipped out the door and Jordan pulled it shut. They walked into the alley, turned left and walked to the street. They turned right, away from Akmed's and the command center. They would take the long way back to the apartment, so they wouldn't raise any suspicion.

"So how was Pakistan?" Kate decided to have the discussion she needed to have with Jordan. Plus, for their cover, they needed to look like a couple, not two people on a mission.

"Excuse me?" Jordan wasn't really ready for this.

"I just asked how Pakistan was. The last time I saw you, you were running to catch a plane. I didn't even get a postcard," Kate noted.

"Believe me, there was nothing to send a postcard of. It has to be one of my least favorite places. We went. We did our job. And, we got out." Jordan didn't want to be questioned – and, he realized he'd just sort-of paraphrased Julius Ceasar.

"Oh! So, you came right back home?" Kate kept pushing.

"No, Kate. I needed to get away for a while so, I went to Italy and I would still be there if it weren't for Max and William."

"Still. I didn't get a postcard and you can't tell me there was nothing to see in Italy." Kate looked at Jordan unwaveringly.

"I'm not much for writing. I really needed some time, Kate. It's been job after job. I needed some downtime. Anyway, I brought you some olive oil." Jordan quickly tried to count how many bottles he'd brought and how many he'd already given away, with the hope he still had one left.

"Thanks. Hey, I'm not saying you can't have your time -- and I can imagine how you would need it. I just would have liked to have heard from you. I really enjoyed the time at your house. I'm your friend, Jordan," Kate said softly.

"I know. I appreciate that. I had a great time, too." He stopped and grabbed her and pressed her lightly against the building. To anyone passing by, they would seem like a cute couple in an intimate moment of conversation.

"I had to think about us, too. I really like you, Kate. I think you and I could be really good together. I've always had a rule to not play where I work," Jordan continued.

"I understand."

Jordan put a finger to her lips to quiet her. "I'm thinking it might be a dumb rule. I just want to be sure. The last thing I want to do is to hurt you." Jordan hugged her. "I still want to do dinner. Not just get something to eat, but a real nice dinner, great food, great wine, ultimate chocolate for dessert."

Kate smiled. "I know a great place in Bucks County. I've only eaten there once, but it was one of the best weekends I've ever had. The best part was being able to go right up to bed and not have to drive anywhere."

Jordan laughed. "Well, maybe that's where we should go. First, we've just got to figure out what Mustafa is up to and put a stop to it. Then, we can plan our dinner."

Kate laughed. "Not like that should be hard to do."

They had turned a series of corners and had walked for several blocks. They found themselves back at the alley behind the command post. Kate felt relieved they'd had the conversation. Jordan was smiling, and she decided that had to be a good sign.

Chapter Thirty-Five

Aziz and Akmed finished their supper. They enjoyed the meal and both seemed happy to be back in each other's company. They cleaned the dishes together and then Aziz excused himself to do his homework in his room.

As he left the kitchen, the phone rang and Aziz went into the living room and picked it up. "Hello."

"Yes, Uncle Mustafa, it is good to hear your voice.

"Yes, my father is here. We just finished dinner.

"Yes. One moment." Aziz took the receiver from his ear and held it out to his father. "It's Uncle Mustafa. He wishes to speak with you."

Akmed hoped that he'd hidden his sudden anguish and apprehension from his son. He knew there would be a confrontation with Mustafa, but he'd hoped it wouldn't have been so soon. He walked out of the kitchen and reached for the receiver.

Aziz cupped his hand over the mouthpiece of the phone. "It will be okay, father. He isn't upset. It will be okay."

Akmed smiled at his son as he took the phone from Aziz and placed it to his ear. "Mustafa, it is good to hear from you. My sincerest apologizes for being away."

"I don't have time for that now. You and I'll talk later. It is important for me to get into your warehouse this evening. I need to pick up my boxes and I may need a few more things out of the store. Would this be a problem?"

Akmed knew he wasn't really concerned about it being a problem. "No. No. When will you be here?"

"Within the next half hour and, I'll have some men with me. We will come in through the alley. Please have the door unlocked, as well as the rear fence. Is that understood?"

"Yes. Yes. Not a problem. I'll be there to greet you."

"No, you won't. I only need you to do what I just asked. I'll require no other assistance. I ask that you and Aziz stay in your apartment, with the blinds closed and the lights on."

"Yes, Mustafa."

"Please, also tell Aziz that I want him to be ready to come with me, beginning tomorrow night. I'll pick him up after school."

"Yes, Mustafa. He'll be ready. How long will he be gone?"

"You weren't concerned with telling us how long you were to be gone. I don't see why you should be concerned with how long Aziz will be with me." It was clear Mustafa was frustrated and did not want to be questioned.

"You are right." Akmed heard the phone click from the other end. He hung it up and went to tell Aziz to prepare to be with his uncle. He'd hoped everything had been heard across the street. It seemed like events were going to take place fairly quickly.

Chapter Thirty-Six

❈ ❈ ❈

Jordan and Kate had been in the backroom of the apartment with William and Max, briefing them on the storeroom reconnaissance. Jordan was walking them through what his theories were regarding the small quantities of some items and larger supplies of others.

"I thinking there are going to be several teams focused on numerous targets. My guess would be that only the leaders will have guns and two-way radios. The rest of the team will be carrying the backpacks. There was nothing there to give us any insight into exact targets."

"We also know that money is not an issue," Kate began. "Going through the business records, it's obvious that Akmed runs a successful business. He has good cost controls and has negotiated favorable terms for buying his merchandise." Kate went on, explaining what she'd found in Akmed's office, focusing specifically on what had come from the computer's hard drive. "He has Mustafa believing he turns all of the profits over to him but, the reality is that Akmed keeps about twenty percent for himself. The eighty percent is a large enough sum that Mustafa would probably never question it. We figure they would have had in excess of three million dollars. We're also assuming that other members of the family have businesses with similar arrangements. Mustafa has no shortage of financial resources."

"That would explain the high quality of the guns and radios. They want for nothing, to pick up on Kate's point. We don't yet know what these other businesses might be so, in addition to providing cash, they might also be able to purchase other needed equipment and supplies. Think about it," Jordan said, sighing. "They never have to deal with anyone or any entity outside the family to get what they need in order to pull off their mission. Think about how many times we have gotten a break because of information originating from a sale, with some clerk or storeowner feeling that something just wasn't right and calling. We don't have that possibility. They have gone to the next level, becoming totally integrated."

Max stood up. "Their vulnerability is their size. There are a lot of people involved, beyond the kids, and there could be other parents like

Akmed, parents who want out. They see that what is going to take place could destroy everything they've worked for here."

"Yes, but do we have the time to find them and make a contact." Jordan was thinking as he spoke, causing him to pause. "I think things are going to move quickly. I really believe we're talking days, not weeks."

There was a knock at the door. One of the agents stuck his head in. "Mustafa is calling the apartment. Bounding out of the room, all four were trying to get through the door at once, with William and Jordan finally falling back to let Kate and Max go first. To someone not realizing the gravity of the situation facing them, it would have seemed humorous.

Everyone in the main room was situated around the speakers, hearing the voices of Mustafa and Aziz. Aziz was getting his father to the phone.

Jordan was processing the information as Akmed and Mustafa spoke. Twenty minutes did not give them a lot of time. Even knowing they had the alley and the back of the store under video surveillance, Jordan felt the need to have human assets in place, to gather additional information. Unfortunately, the alley and the back of the store didn't provide many observation points and someone couldn't just be hanging out in the area.

"Where's Mustafa now?" Jordan broke the silence of the room. Several stared at him as if he would be overheard on the call.

"He's at his house."

"Anyone with him?" Jordan continued.

"No. Mustafa came home from work and hasn't had any visitors."

"Well, we know he's only ten minutes away. So, if he leaves right after the call, he's got a stop to make before he comes here. Let's get the teams following Mustafa up to speed on this call and tell them we know he's coming here in the next half hour." Jordan ordered.

"On it!" one of the agents called as he moved to an unoccupied desk and pulled out a cell phone.

"Let's put our heads together on what the best approach would be to have surveillance in the alley. I know we have the cameras, but is there any way to have some eyes close by?" Jordan inquired.

There was a plat of survey, a map of the entire neighborhood. Similar to a blueprint, it showed all of the dwellings, both houses and outbuildings, in a several blocks radius of Akmed's store. Almost every home or building with property bordering the alley had a shed or garage with alley access. While several would provide adequate viewing posts, none had an easy, undetectable entrance.

Since timing would not allow them to gain permission from the owner, they needed to be able to sneak in, watch what happened and get back out unseen. It was unlikely any crime was going to be committed, so protecting the surveillance with a warrant was unnecessary.

Jordan was perplexed by one thing on the map. "What does the red "D" stand for?" He'd noticed several of the properties had a circled red "D."

One of the agents chuckled and several looked at each other. "It means there's a dog on the property. We've found that to be helpful in these situations."

Jordan laughed. "No shit. 'Once bitten, twice shy,' huh? Yeah, I would have liked to have had that information in the past. Nothing worse than jumping a fence or coming around the corner and you're facing a growling, snarling pooch."

"Yes, sir -- and I've got the bite marks to prove it," the same agent agreed. "Of course, if we need to gain access we have the same approach we used at Mustafa's."

Jordan nodded, looking once again at the map. "This garage here is two stories tall. If we could get someone upstairs with a camera, that would be a great observation point. I would also like a person at each end of the alley, just to monitor. They could station themselves here and here." Jordan pointed to sheds at the entrance to the alley from the two streets. "I don't anticipate the need for any action tonight. They're moving more or less legitimately purchased merchandise. But, just in case, let's have a tactical response on stand by a couple of blocks away."

Three agents stepped up to volunteer. Jordan gave each an assignment and they moved out.

"The surveillance team with Mustafa just called in. He left the house and is headed toward Center City."

"Okay, everyone! We're a go. Let's be sharp and see if we can't come up with several more pieces of the puzzle tonight." Jordan waved them out and on their way.

The agents who had volunteered for the various postings gathered up their gear and left, the remaining agents manning the various communication and computer stations. Max, Kate, William and Jordan went to the back room.

"With what we know from the call, Mustafa is gathering the supplies tonight and pulling the kids together tomorrow. I think we have to assume they are moving forward." Max started the conversation after closing the door.

Jordan jumped in. "I agree, but we still don't have any idea on what or where the target is."

"You don't think it's somewhere in Philly?"

"My gut tells me it is; but, in reality, in two-three hours they could be in New York, Baltimore or even D.C. I don't think we can take anything off the table at this point. Now that we know their funds are fairly substantial, he could put the kids on the train and be in the heart of Times Square in a little over ninety minutes. If you think about it, this is a great base to operate from."

"Location, location, location," William chimed in, reciting the real estate mantra. "I have to agree with Jordan. Think about dropping these kids in any major city. They carry out the attack and, if any of them survive, they can just blend in. If they're injured, they are taken to the hospitals and treated as a victim. No one's going to think of them as suspects, even if someone was close enough to see something. They probably aren't going to be in any condition to file a witness account."

"We've got to give them credit," Jordan observed. "This is well planned. I don't think we've ever come across a group with the resources to take this much time in planning and prep prior to execution."

"You know what it really is. It's patience," Max told them. "Most of these groups are so rabid, they can't wait to strike and, that's when they make mistakes. The patience this cell has displayed is what could allow it to pull off the biggest surprise we've known."

They all stared at each other; there was so much to do, but not enough information to do anything. Their hope would have to lie in the moving of the supplies, that it would get them somehow closer to understanding the target.

One of the agents stepped into the room. "Everyone is in place. Mustafa picked up three men and it looks like they're headed in this direction."

"Okay. We'll be out in a second. Thanks," Max nodded to the agent to shut the door. "This may be our opportunity. Let's not let anything get by us. The smallest detail might be the one that begins to pull this all together." Max led the way out of the room.

Chapter Thirty-Seven

Mustafa had jumped into his van, intent on what he must do, but still puzzled over Akmed. As he drove, he reviewed his conversation with Akmed for the tenth time or more and still couldn't tell if the man was a threat or not to the operation. On the phone, Akmed didn't seem any more nervous than usual. All the parents exhibited a level of nervousness around him and he used it to his advantage. None of them ever questioned him and they always responded to his demands. He felt it worked best that way, even though he'd never been instructed to be a threat to his people.

Akmed had seemed like himself – or, at least, like his recent self, since Mahasin had passed away. There wasn't anything Mustafa could put his finger on that made him feel he needed to eliminate Akmed, since getting rid of him could cause issues with Aziz. Aziz was too important to the mission and Mustafa could not afford to have him distracted by the death or disappearance of his father. Of all the children, Aziz was the best. He was a natural born leader and he could rally the other children to do almost anything and, even if they weren't totally successful in the task, Aziz would have inspired everyone to have done their best. In another place or time Aziz, would have been a leader in industry or politics. He would have had a bright and successful future -- but there were other plans for him. Aziz would achieve success but in that success, more than likely would come death and, that was the way it had to be. He would play a key role on the day of the mission and its success or failure would lie on how well Aziz carried out his part of the mission and how he would lead the others. Mustafa had all the confidence in the world about Aziz. A smile crossed his face as he thought about Aziz and the role the boy would play.

He'd driven through Center City, to an area knows as the "Northern Liberties." He would pick up the newest employees of the City of Brotherly Love Cleaning Service and they would go with him to Akmed's and help load up all of the supplies. He'd already asked one of the men to pick up an additional van from the local rental agency to also be used this night and over the next several days. After going around the block twice, he looked for any sign of a tail, Mustafa pulled to the curb, next to an old apartment building. While the golden sheen of lights glowed from several of the apartments, one could also peer inside and see that the units were old and poorly maintained. The Northern Liberties was one of those neighborhoods in transformation where many of the young professionals of Philly had moved into the area, followed by trendy nightclubs and restaurants. They would buy up the apartment buildings and old factories and turn them into condos at prices too high for the original residents, these people forced to leave the only neighborhood in which they had ever lived. Rumor had it that a Whole Foods Market would be building in the next block. Mustafa never understood the name. What was a whole food? It just seemed like a grocery store at which people were willing to pay more than necessary for the same products one could purchase at the local Acme. Americans, he thought, always willing to pay more just to pay more, they were never satisfied with what they had and always wanted more, while neglecting those who had less.

He saw two of the men exit the building and come down the stairs. They turned and headed toward the truck. One of them opened the side cargo door and both piled in. They seated themselves on the rugs Mustafa had placed on the van's floor. At the same moment, an almost identical van pulled up behind them. Mustafa recognized his third man as the driver and slipped his vehicle into gear, headed to Akmed's store.

Mustafa faulted himself for not having already secured two of the radios so he could be in communication with the other van. He hoped nothing would cause the driver to become separated from him in traffic. He knew the driver only had a rudimentary understanding of the streets of Philadelphia and Mustafa hadn't wanted to give them a map or written directions, in case the police stopped them. Mustafa would just have to place his fate in the hands of Allah that they would be able to stay together in the traffic. Mustafa was careful to time the traffic lights at the intersections they needed to pass through, so he'd instructed the other driver not to be right behind him, but rather remain a few cars back, with other vehicles between them, so it wouldn't be obvious they were in a caravan.

On several occasions, Mustafa stopped his vehicle as the light turned yellow, versus going quickly through, as the traffic around him did. This caused several of the cars behind them to honk their horns and, on one occasion, a car skidded to stop just inches from the rear bumper of the van.

Mustafa could see the woman in the car was upset and making obscene gestures through the windshield. Mustafa found the people of Philadelphia to lack patience. They were always in a hurry, and so critical of what went on in their city. If their beloved Eagles didn't win, they were instantly ready to fire the coach and the quarterback, only to love them the next week, when they had a big win. Mustafa just did not understand.

They were successful in their negotiation through the Center City traffic and soon pulled into the back alley behind the hardware store. The two vans were parked against the fence, attempting to keep the alley passable. They wouldn't be parked there long, but Mustafa didn't want to stop their loading in order to move the vans because another resident needed to get through to get in or out of the alley.

As the men jumped out, they opened the fence and found the door to the storeroom unlocked. They headed in and Mustafa found the switch for the lights. He quickly surveyed the room and found the area with the numerous boxes of their supplies. He directed the men there and assigned each one a certain box to take out to the vans, since Mustafa wanted certain boxes in a certain van, while ensuring everything was loaded that needed to go.

In less than an hour, the vans were loaded and headed back to the Northern Liberties. The second van contained the book bags, radios and some of the other items. Driving directly home, Mustafa had the guns and explosive materials in his van. He backed into the driveway, up against the garage door. He didn't want anyone to break in and steal the guns. He headed into the house to turn on the news, because he was interested in one particular news item.

Chapter Thirty-Eight

⁜ ⁜ ⁜

NORTHERN LIBERTIES
NEIGHBORHOOD OF
PHILADELPHIA

Sergeant Larry O'Meara rose from the table and grabbed the check. "Come on, rookie. Time to get back out there and ensure the safety of the citizens of Philadelphia. Tonight, dinner is on me." Heading to the cashier, he looked around. He'd been coming to this restaurant his entire eighteen and a half years on the force and, in two months, he would be eligible for retirement. He already had a job lined up, working at his brother-in-laws' sporting goods store in Montgomery County, and was counting the days when he would hang his gun and badge up for good. O'Meara had enjoyed his years as a cop and counted as his best friends the guys he'd gone with through the academy. But, he was ready to go. The last year was one worth forgetting. Five fellow officers getting gunned down had been enough -- more than enough. He was tired of coming home to his wife and knowing she'd been crying while he was gone. Several of his buddies were already off the force and seemed to be having the time of their lives. He was ready to join that club. But, first things first, he had this new rookie to train.

Sheila Brown hadn't always wanted to be a police officer. It was true that her Uncle and three cousins were on the force, but she never really saw herself in the blues. She'd married young and had three children. Then, her husband decided to move to Florida -- without his family -- and she found herself alone and in need of an income. Starting at Wal-Mart, she eventually became part of the store security team. That was where she met Larry, the responding officer on most occasions when she'd caught a shoplifter. She appreciated how Larry always kept the dignity of the person, even if they had committed the crime. He'd taken a liking to her and felt she was an ideal candidate to join the ranks of the blue line. Every time there was a new cadet class being formed, Larry dropped off the information, until finally he made her meet him for lunch and they filled out the application together.

She fell in love with the job. She excelled at the Academy and graduated second in her class. Larry put in a special request to be her training officer. Spending the last two and a half months together, she had learned more from Larry then she'd ever imagined -- not just about the job, but how best to do it. They took the time to meet people and get out of the car and know the folks in the community. Larry had become her mentor, and she dreaded the reality that, in two weeks, her training would be over and she would be reassigned. She also was disappointed that the man who had pushed her into this career would be leaving the force.

She got up from the table and pulled a few dollars out for a tip. She stopped to say goodbye to a few of the regulars she'd gotten to know along with the staff at the restaurant and followed Larry out the door.

Larry drove tonight and so she walked around to the passenger side. They had been given one of the new Dodge Chargers the department had introduced as patrol cars. They were the first cars where the interiors had been designed to accommodate all of the computer equipment officers carried with them. Being both roomy and fast, Larry loved it and liked to take it onto interstate ninety-five at least a couple of times each shift to really open it up.

"This could get me to sign up for another four years," Larry would always say when he got the chance to really show what the car would do. While Sheila wished it were true, she knew it wasn't.

They pulled out of the diner's parking lot and resumed their patrol. With the recent cut backs in the city's budget, they were one of only three cars on patrol in their district this night, when usually there would have been, at minimum, five. Sheila grabbed the radio and notified dispatch they had returned from dinner and were in their sector.

The next hour was routine. They had one traffic stop for a car with a broken taillight and Sheila had handled it. As they got back into the car, the radio squawked with the report of an armed robbery at a convenience store a few blocks from their location. Sheila responded to the dispatcher that they were in route and started to flip on the light bar and the siren.

Larry grabbed her hand. "Traffic's light and we're just a few blocks out. Best to go in quiet and not to panic whoever is in the store." There was a reassuring sound from the engine compartment as Larry urged the Dodge down the street. With all green lights and only one red – they coasted through it anyway -- they reached the "stop and rob," as Larry called the store. Larry took the cruiser around the corner and entered the side parking lot. Just as Larry and Sheila pulled up at the store, two suspects raced out of the store and jumped into a car that was backed into a space.

Before Larry could maneuver the police car to block them, the suspects' car shot out of the space, over the curb and slid into a turn and headed down the street. The convenience store clerk – Sheila recognized him – ran out of the store and shouted in Hindi-accented English, "Get them! They've got guns! Be careful!"

Larry punched the Charger's accelerator, and peeled out of the lot and onto the street, "Only job in the world where you get paid to break traffic laws!" Larry remarked as he flipped on the lights and siren.

"Unit 31-A in pursuit of armed robbery suspects driving dark blue late model Chevy Impala," Sheila began as she notified dispatch. She recited the license plate and, almost simultaneously, ran the plate through their on-board computer, to see if the vehicle had been reported stolen. Sheila gave their position and direction of pursuit. "Need backup. Over."

"No other units available in your sector at this time, A-31. Units being dispatched from adjoining districts, A-31. Over."

"We copy that, dispatch. A-31 Out."

Stealing a quick glance at each other, Larry and Sheila knew they were going to be alone on this one.

The suspects' dark blue Impala accelerated. Sheila felt herself pressed deeper into the seat and secured her seatbelt. Larry murmured, "Hang on, Rookie." The Impala started to turn, its rear end fishtailing, the driver's side front tire bounced over a curb as the vehicle turned onto a side street. "Shit! That driver's good," Larry snarled through clenched teeth. "Hold onto something!" Larry commanded as he tapped the Charger's brake pedal simultaneously with turning the all the way right.

"I'm gonna be sick!" Sheila announced to anyone interested as the Charger's rear end swung around and the front end was abruptly pointed better than ninety degrees in the other direction. Larry's foot was already pushing the accelerator to the floor as the Charger cleared the curb, swerved once and was back in the pursuit.

The Impala made another turn just like the last one and so did the Charger. "Girl, they are in trouble, these guys. Just ran a yellow light and failed to signal their intention before that turn. Hey! Look at that! They got a brake light out, too!"

"Larry!"

"These guys know the Northern Liberties as well as we do, Sheila. I don't think they're going to turn down some blind alley," The Impala cut diagonally across a grocery store parking lot, and nailed a shopping cart that created a firestorm of sparks as it crashed into a Cadillac. "Ouch," Larry noted. The supermarket was at the boundary of the residential and commercial area through which the chase had so far taken place, the Impala flew into an area of light industry, warehouses and small manufacturing firms.

"Whatever they've got under the hood must really be something, Larry," Sheila told him, raising her voice as the engine noise from the Impala and the response from the Charger started drowning her out. The Impala did another one of its fast turns and Sheila shouted, "I know – hang on!"

"You got it, Rookie!" Larry tapped, turned and punched, as tires squealed. Sheila thought to look down at the computer. The Impala was on a hotsheet. The Impala made still another lightning quick turn as Larry yelling, "One more time!" As the Charger nosed into the side street, Sheila braced her hands against the dashboard, Larry jammed on the brakes. The car they were pursuing had stopped directly in front of them, the car doors were open.

Sheila reached for the microphone to notify dispatch, her right hand reaching for her Glock as she saw Larry unlimbering his old .38 Special service revolver. It was only then that she looked up and through the windshield. Sheila didn't know a lot about firearms, but watched movies and newscasts enough to recognize assault rifles when they were pointed at her. Both assailants were out of the Impala and shooting into the Charger.

"Holy Shit! Get down, Sheila!" Larry yelled as bullets shattered the windshield. He heard a groan and saw the mike fall out of Shelia's hand as she fell back against the seat. Larry scrambled over the console and shoved Sheila to the floor. Sheila stared as the side of Larry's skull furthest from the window exploded in streaks of red and grey, then exploded again as part of Larry's face seemed to fall away. Shelia felt the full weight of Larry on top of her as the firing outside stopped. She knew she'd been hit and could feel the pain. She tried to speak, but couldn't. She saw the mike hanging by her and tried to grab it.

Sheila spat blood from her throat as she keyed the mike. As she listened to herself, her voice sounded odd, it made a gurgled sound. "Shots fired. Two officers down. Two officers down. Heavily armed suspects. Officers need assistance! Unit 31-A needs assistance!"

"State your location, 31-A. Over." The calm in the dispatcher's voice suddenly infuriated Sheila, and she thought for a moment. But, she couldn't remember. Her mind was a blank and her ears were still ringing from all of the gunfire.

She keyed the mike. "I don't know. We're several blocks from the last location I called in. We're in the warehouse district."

"Roger that. Units are in the area. Are you able to activate your siren? Over."

"Yes. Stand by." Sheila continued to turn the siren off and on for what seemed like an eternity.

Sensing someone was near, she wondered if the gunmen were coming back after hearing the siren and realizing they had left someone alive? She tried reaching for her Glock, but it was wedged under her.

"Larry? Sheila? Are you guys in there?" She knew the voice. It belonged to Bill Callahan, the other sergeant for the district. "Oh, my God, Larry! What happened?"

"I'm here, Bill, under Larry."

"I'm going to get you out, Sheila. The paramedics are here now."

She felt the car door open and the dome light came on. Bill pulled Larry out of the car and placed him on the sidewalk. Reaching in for her, he took out a knife to cut away the seatbelt and lifted her out. Paramedics were waiting with a stretcher and Bill placed her on it. A thin line of blood drooled from the left corner of her mouth.

"No. No, take care of Larry first. I think he's hurt worse than I am."

"Sheila, Larry's gone. We've got to take care of you." Bill Callahan got his first actual look at Sheila. He wondered if it had been smart to move her. She had several visible wounds. Both of her arms were bled from various spots and there was a wound to her neck. It didn't look good. "Get her to the hospital as quick as you can.

Sheila's last view of the scene was of more units arriving and the reflection of all the lights flashing off the buildings and the echo of the police radios.

"Bill! Get whoever did this to Larry. Make sure you get them." Shelia cried out.

Bill watched as they put her in the ambulance, then walked back to the bullet riddled police car. He spotted Larry's well-worn .38 Special revolver, much of the bluing rubbed off by years of carry. He picked it up. Weighing his dead friend's weapon in his hand, Bill rasped, "I'm going to get whoever did this to both of you."

Chapter Thirty-Nine

�֍ ✤ ✢

COMMAND CENTER ACROSS
FROM AKMED'S APARTMENT IN
SOUTH PHILADELPHIA

Surveillance personnel had gotten pictures of the other men with Mustafa, now being run through various databases for identification. The van had come back as a rental from the Able and Ready Rent-a-Car lot in the Northern Liberties. Since it wasn't part of a national or even regional chain, there was no database to access. The rental company was closed for the evening and Jordan cautioned against making an in-person inquiry, since it was important not to set off any more alarm bells.

Jordan, Kate, Max and William were in the middle of the debrief with the alley team when they heard a commotion, originating in the main room of the command center. All of them rushed into the main room. The faces of the agents there were ashen. All work had stopped.

"We just got a report of two officers down, needing assistance." Frank walked up to the group. "We don't have any more details."

Jordan and the others waited with the rest of the team. The radio traffic was fast and clipped. One of the officers tried to gather additional details and was on the phone with the precinct where the shooting occured.

With the last transmission, which Jordan couldn't make out, several of the officers threw things to the floor or hammered fists against tables or walls. Murmured obscenities rolled like a wave across the room. Frank looked at Jordan. "There's one cop dead at the scene and the other is being rushed to the hospital. It's going to be touch and go for her."

One of the officers, who had been on the phone, came over. "They were on patrol and got a call about a robbery at a convenience store. As they pulled up to the store, the suspect's car left and they pursued. About five minutes away, a witness says the perps stopped their car in the middle of the street. When the patrol car stopped behind it, the two bastard shits piled out with automatic weapons and they just fired into the patrol car. The officers didn't even have a chance to get out or get off a shot. The perps emptied their magazines, jumped back in and took off. The witness got a license plate and a good description of the car. It matches the plate and description one of the uniforms gave to dispatch when the pursuit began."

"Okay. Nothing tells us this is related, but I don't want to dismiss it as having no connection at all. I also realize the team needs to get a resolution on this, so let them have the time they need. Anything we can throw down to Washington to pick up, let's do it." Jordan had been in these situations before and he knew it was futile to try to pull the team back on task until this situation resolved itself. He understood the heightened emotions coming on the heels of the recent deaths of five other officers. He wanted to be respectful in an obvious way, because the respect was sincere.

Twenty minutes later, radio traffic reported that the killers' car had been found, the assault rifles left on the backseat, which made no sense. The weapons would later be determined stolen, since selective fire assault rifles weren't available in ordinary firearms stores because they required stringent special licensing procedures. The area was quickly cordoned off and all available units converged on the area. Two Bell Long Ranger Police helicopters were in the air, sweeping the area with high intensity LED searchlights. A short time later, one of the suspects was located in an alley behind a commercial warehouse. As officers approached, the suspect produced a small handgun, put the muzzle in his mouth and took his own life.

Officers searched the area and found a warehouse door had been jimmied and began a search. A body was found inside shot to death and the belief was it was the other suspect. A closer inspection of the weapon used by the suspect who had shot himself in front of the police revealed that three shots had been fired. The suspect inside the warehouse had been shot twice in the back of the head.

The phone rang and one of the agents picked it up. He didn't say a word in reply to whoever was on the line. He put the receiver back in its cradle.

"The other officer just passed away. She was just a rookie. Had some kids and no husband around. Shit."

Chapter Forty

✤ ✤ ✤

SOUTH PHILADELPHIA

Mustafa pulled into his driveway. The brakes squeaked as he brought the van to a halt. Aziz and three other boys were in the back of the truck. They were the oldest of the cousins and those that would be leaders for the mission. Tonight, he would be giving them details for the first time. If Allah willed it so, they would be not only ready to hear what he was about to tell them, but also excited by the opportunity this presented them. If they showed enthusiasm, then he would know that his work was complete. It would also ensure the mission would reach a successful conclusion. If any of them balked, he would have to make changes. He couldn't afford to have someone in a key role who was not one hundred percent committed to carrying out this act of revenge against the detestable American infidels.

Mustafa turned to face the boys before stepping out of the vehicle. "Remain in the van. I'm just running in to get a few things. We will not be staying here tonight."

Originally, he'd planned on working with the boys here but, he'd recently become suspicious. He thought he'd seen some different cars in the neighborhood and felt more than ever that he was being watched. His house was empty most of the day while he was at work and, when he returned, he always found the tells he had placed where he had left them. Yet, he still felt as if someone had been inside. The latest incident with Akmed had only heightened his uneasy feelings.

He'd arranged to use the home of one of the people who worked with him. They were away for a short vacation and had offered Mustafa their home when he'd told them a story about his house needing to be fumigated and that he would have to stay at a hotel for forty-eight hours. They had quickly offered for him to use their home, relating how they would like to have someone there to prevent a break-in. Mustafa felt Americans were so gullible. You could spin any story to them and win their sympathy. How pathetic, so he had reminded himself to leave some evidentiary clues in their home, so they might be considered suspects. He smiled to himself at the thought.

He went into his house and grabbed the bags he'd packed earlier and placed at the door. He locked his door, ensured the tell was in the proper place and walked back to the van.

It took them about forty-five minutes to head out of Philadelphia and across the Walt Whitman Bridge into New Jersey. They arrived at a one-story bungalow, probably built in the fifties which was surrounded by homes of the same basic look, though some had additions. All seemed to be in modest disrepair, needing paint, new roofs and other cosmetic improvements. He pulled into a driveway after checking a piece of paper and verifying the address. Everyone jumped out, grabbed their bags and headed into the house.

The house's interior was in keeping with the exterior, neat enough, but bespeaking a "make do" attitude. They dropped their bags, looked around and made themselves comfortable in the living room.

"My nephews, I'm so happy to be with you tonight and share with you some exciting news. We have been given the go ahead to conduct an act of heroism against the tyrant that allows our brothers and sisters to starve, to not be educated, to live in deplorable conditions, and to be treated as slaves by other nations. I have been watching each of you for a long time. You have emerged as the leaders of your family of cousins. Tonight, I'm going to tell you why we're here and what we have been called upon to do."

Mustafa for the first time told the four boys in the room about what had happened in Iran. He confided how the boys had been taken from their true families and placed with the people whom they thought were their mothers and fathers. There were soft gasps. All eyes were on him and wide-seeming as saucers. He told the boys that these people who had raised them were not truly man and wife, but that they also had been taken away from their original families and put together by the leaders of their country, leaders who had grown tired of sanctions and being humiliated by the United States and the Western world. These leaders had conceived a grand plan that would take over twenty years to implement. He talked about how the leaders had the patience to take the long term view. "We had been oppressed for thousands of years; twenty more was nothing, if it would allow us to exact the revenge we so desired."

He began to describe the mission. He showed the boys maps of the targets in a city with which they had all become quite familiar due to the field trips Uncle Mustafa had taken them on over the years. The boys understood well the symbolism of the sites they would target. They began to ask questions, not about, why, but rather were concerned, instead, with logistics. Mustafa was quite proud, not only were the boys willing to undertake what needed to be done, but they were immersing themselves in bettering the plans.

However, Kamal, one of the cousins, began to ask questions that disturbed Mustafa.

"Why us? We have not lived in Iran for most of our lives. Why is this our battle?"

Mustafa had anticipated some push back. He knew it was important to answer, but also not to let such matters derail their purpose. He hadn't expected it to come from Kamal. Next to Aziz, Kamal was a strong leader and he was counting on Kamal to play a key role.

"Kamal, you have been blessed to be in a position to take this revenge. Others are not as fortunate as you. Others would give anything to be in your position to exact this revenge, but can't. You must stand up for them."

"I fail to see what this country has done to me. Our families have found success here. We're getting good educations. It seems we might possibly be able to do more if we worked with Americans than trying to destroy them."

"You are young and I appreciate your idealism," Mustafa assured the boy. "However, our leaders have chosen another course. They believe it is the time for revenge and our best opportunity to strike out and inflict great pain. Then, maybe we will talk to the Americans."

"It seems pointless! They will not let us just take their buildings. They will not allow us to destroy their history."

Mustafa's patience was running out. He noticed the others started to show concern and give affirmation to Kamal's words. Mustafa needed to stop this.

"Kamal, please allow me to continue. I have only begun to outline what is being asked of us. I think if you will let me continue, it will become clearer. If not, we can discuss your questions further."

Kamal nodded dutifully. "Yes, Uncle. Please continue."

They had talked through and discussed the plan for almost three hours, when Mustafa decided it was time for a break. They reluctantly broke off the conversation, and each took a turn going to the single bathroom. A couple of the boys went into the kitchen to scavenge for food and Mustafa found a menu on the refrigerator for a local pizza place, which delivered. He called and ordered three large pizzas and several liters of soda. He wanted to reward the boys for their efforts so far. Mustafa was so excited that he believed nothing could cause them to fail.

After the pizzas arrived, Mustafa asked Kamal if they could talk privately. Kamal stood up and walked with Mustafa down the hall, to a bedroom in the back of the house.

"I'm disappointed in you, Kamal. I had thought you would be a strong leader for me; but now, I have my doubts"

"Uncle, I support the cause you want us to fight for, but I'm not in agreement with the tactics. We're in a good position here to bring about change by using the ways of democracy that they have in this country."

"I'll not hear of that. This is Satan's land. We will never work within their system. There is only one way and that is to destroy this country."

"I don't believe we can. We do this and they will just do more harm to Iran and our people. Uncle, we will bring about more death and pain to our families, and do little to this country. They will rebuild. They will come back. I can not support what you ask of us."

"I understand Kamal and I'm disappointed. I respect your decision however, it is no longer possible for you to continue to be with us."

"I understand uncle. I'll leave now. I'll tell no one."

"Yes, you must leave now, and you will never tell anyone!" Mustafa pointed to the door. Kamal turned and began to walk toward it. Mustafa grabbed the boy's face with his left hand, his right hand already snapping open the straight razor. As Kamal made to cry out, Mustafa raked the blade across the boy's throat, cutting him from ear to ear. There was a gurgling sound as Kamal began to clutch at his throat, Mustafa letting the boy flop to the floor, sidestepping to avoid the arterial spray. Blood puddled from the artery onto the carpet. Mustafa did not question the will of Allah that this boy should die. He wiped the razor and his hand clean of blood on the boy's shirt.

Mustafa walked to the door. The mission would be complete before the family who owned the home would return from vacation, so he didn't need to worry about disposing of the body or make any attempt to clean the room.

Mustafa rejoined the group and restarted the discussion. "Kamal will no longer be with us." The others looked back at the closed bedroom door.

Chapter Forty-One

In the morning, after Mustafa had led them in prayers, the boys loaded everything into the van and returned to Mustafa's house. Mustafa had them meet in his basement, so that no directional eavesdropping could capture their conversation. It was time to move from the general overview of the mission and discuss specific roles and responsibilities. He again went to the map of the target area. It was a different map from before. This version had color-coding in different areas of the map. Mustafa explained that the colors corresponded to each one of them and told each boy which color he was assigned.

Aziz's area of responsibility corresponded to the color yellow, the yellow section of the map in the lower center, consisting of three buildings. Aziz knew the area well and he knew what the area meant to the citizens and the history of the United States. He was intrigued with what his Uncle had told them so far and he was trying to figure out what exactly was his mission would be.

Aziz was pleased his Uncle felt he was ready to be a leader. He respected his Uncle greatly. Mustafa had taught Aziz much, more than he felt he ever learned in school. His uncle meant more to him than Akmed did. Aziz could no longer consider Akmed his father, knowing that he was not. He had mixed feeling in regards to Mahasin. She'd been kind to him and he felt she'd loved him and he loved her back. He might always think of her as his mother.

Mustafa had moved down to the yellow colored area of the map and was looking at Aziz.

"Aziz? Are you with us? I know I have covered a lot, but this is important. I'm going to be telling you your exact role."

"Yes, Uncle. I'm sorry. I was just thinking about some things you had said. I'm with you and very much want to hear what you have to say."

"Good. Good. You have a critical role. You and your team, unlike the others who only have one building, will take over and hold these two buildings. It will be a challenge, but critical to our overall success.

You will also need to keep an eye on the perimeter at the back of this building. This is most likely one area in which the police and their SWAT teams will try to retake the building. I'll give you more details on what you will have at your disposal to protect yourselves and your teams. Remember these are historical buildings. They were built solidly, but they aren't fortresses. With them being in the downtown area there are many vantage points for the police to watch you. You must stay away from the windows and in your other building you must use the tarps your team will have to block the large window. If you don't succeed in doing these things you risk the success of the mission."

Aziz nodded throughout the explanation. He understood what would need to happen and what he was responsible for during the mission. It was a huge task, with many risks in the heart of the city. If Mustafa believed in him, then Aziz knew he would be successful.

When each cousin understood his assigned role, Mustafa began to discuss the overall logistics of the mission. He knew it was complicated and if he'd had more time he could have given broader information but, that luxury was gone. At least Allah had blessed him with smart boys. They picked up the information quickly and continued to be engaged, even as he saw the awareness on their faces of what he was asking them to do.

No one flinched, no one-raised objections. Perhaps it was only because of what happened to their cousin but, Mustafa hoped it was more. He wanted these boys, his boys, to be as committed to what they were doing as was he. It was the only way they could be successful.

The boys had maps and diagrams laid out in front of them. The maps had been marked with arrows and listed directions. Each map showed where the boys would be dropped off and how they would proceed to each target, showed and described in detail how they should enter and how they should deploy their cousins. With the maps came a list of the supplies and equipment each would have with them.

"Your cousins will be joining you here in the next hour." Mustafa interrupted the boys' thoughts. "You should be thinking about how you will communicate to them. It will be critical that each of them understand these three things. First they can talk to no one, not even their parents about this. You may tell them their parents know they will be doing this with Uncle Mustafa, but they cannot share any of the details, second, they must completely understand their role by the end of the day. Finally, they must be committed to what we do. No one can hesitate or it will cause disaster. We can only be successful if we all do this together. We're a family and we must work and act like a family when we do this."

All of the boys nodded. While they had a level of fear about what they were being asked to do, their fear of their Uncle was greater. For Aziz it was all coming together, the time spent with their Uncle, the drills, the team competitions, and the "talks" about the evils of The United States. It all made sense, that this wasn't something their Uncle had just decided to do. Aziz could tell from the maps and the instructions that this had been in the works for some time. He wondered how much his father knew? Aziz had seen the boxes in Mustafa's van that had been in the storeroom at his father's shop. His father must have ordered these items and would surely have asked what they were for -- unless he already knew.

His Uncle Mustafa appeared anxious. Aziz took that to mean that they would be underway soon. He was surprised at how Mustafa had dealt with Kamal, since Aziz had liked Kamal. As Aziz looked over his directions and the map itself, he would stop and think of asking Kamal a question or an opinion, only to remember the Kamal was no longer there. He thought Kamal was the smartest of all of them, seeming to always know the answers to the questions Mustafa would ask. Kamal was quick to figure out how to fix things or come up with an alternative which allowed them to be successful. He would have been of great value.

Aziz focused on the other cousins who would be part of his team. For the most part, he felt he'd have the strongest group. His only worry was with a couple of his youngest cousins. It wasn't that their support wouldn't be there, because they would go along with whatever the group was doing. He was more concerned about their ability to keep up with the others and to stay focused when things would get crazy. Aziz had no doubt that things were going to get crazy.

Chapter Forty-Two

✤ ✤ ✤

Jordan returned to the command post the next morning. He'd spent what sleep time he could at a hotel in Center City that they were using to grab rest. He'd slept for almost four and half hours but, more importantly, he'd gotten a good hot breakfast of oatmeal, poached eggs and bacon -- what he called his "breakfast of champions." His special breakfast always picked him up and allowed him to face the good and the bad of the coming day. He was ready for action and wanted to move, but he knew they couldn't because they didn't have enough information on anyone and didn't know when, where or how.

He walked into the post, and was immediately aware of the subdued tone in the room. At breakfast, he'd gotten a copy of the <u>Philadelphia Inquirer</u> and read the articles on the deaths of the two officers. A veteran near retirement and a young female rookie who seemed to have all of the talent and skills to be a great police officer – both were now gone. The city had become a war zone. He knew many of the people with him would know the sergeant who was murdered. Jordan was still nagged by feeling that even though, on the surface, there seemed to be no connection with the numerous cop killings, there had to be a tie. Something bothered him, usually, when cop killings happened in large numbers, there had been a trigger point, such as a trial in which suspects were acquitted even though the public was convinced of their guilt, or at other times, the cause might be a police crackdown on drugs or other criminal activity, which resulted in retaliation killings by those who ran the illicit businesses. However, in Philly, none of that had occurred.

As he entered the main room of the apartment, not many of the agents and officers looked up. Jordan gave a nod to each that did because, he knew what they were feeling. Over the years, he'd lost men, many of whom were friends. It was never easy and, while one would try to rationalize it because of the mission or the service they provided, the death was still a person who was gone. He'd found, at such times, it seemed to be best not to say anything. Words seemed meaningless.

He did want to find Kate and Max as soon as he could, however. He headed down the hallway to the back bedroom they were using as their office. William was there.

"Hey, pretty tough night for these guys."

William turned away from the window and looked at Jordan. "Yeah, most knew the Sergeant. Top-notch guy. They're taking it pretty hard, but they're also professional; so, they're on the job."

"Have you seen Kate or Max?" Jordan asked.

"Here we are," Max said, both women looked as somber as the rest of the group.

"Guys, I've been thinking." Eyes rolled around the room. Whenever Jordan had an idea, it usually meant work for them.

"Okay, let's hear it," Max sighed, never knowing what tangent Jordan would pursue, but well aware that his track record was pretty good in that regard.

"These cops being murdered have me intrigued. There's no reason, no cause for the effect. I want -- I mean, I would like to ask Kate's team to dig into these suspects. It's interesting that they all ended up dead shortly after they committed the murders. I think there might be a link, but I don't think it's going to be found on the surface. I think looking into the families might provide some details."

"Interesting," Max looked over at Kate. "Can you spare a few people to track this down?"

Kate smiled. "If it was anyone else, I would say no, but I think I can free some folks."

"Great." Jordan grabbed William. "Who's in the best shape out there that can work with Kate, but also keep quiet about what we're doing?"

"That would be Pat. He's sharp and he definitely would want to help and knows when to keep his mouth shut."

"Great, William. Will you get him together with Kate?"

William nodded, already starting to leave the room.

"Kate -- thanks. I know you aren't swimming in resources, but I think this might lead to something. How quickly do you think you might have some preliminaries?"

Kate laughed. "Wow, I don't even know what to look for and you're already asking for a report?"

Jordan shrugged, adding, "Let me know as soon as you find anything, huh?"

Chapter Forty-Three

By late morning, the rest of the cousins had arrived at Mustafa's and were grouped into their teams. Aziz, along with the other leaders were going through the plans. Assignments were being given out and Mustafa had told each team he wanted them to brief him and go through their assignments at noon.

Anyone who walked past would have assumed that Mustafa once again had his nieces and nephews over as they played games in the yard. The neighbors knew not to disturb these family events. Any of the neighborhood kids who would try to join would be politely turned away and told this was for family only. Any adults trying to have a conversation with Mustafa would find he wasn't interested in anything but being with his "kids," as he called them. The neighbors admired him for the time and commitment he made to his nieces and nephews, saw the respect the children paid him and felt he was having a strong impact on their upbringing. If they only knew, Mustafa had often thought, the idea amused him.

Mustafa looked around at the various groups. He was encouraged by what he saw. The older boys had stepped into their leadership roles, just like he'd envisioned. They worked well with their cousins, the younger ones showed respect to the leaders, just as he'd instilled in them over the years when they played team sports or went on activities together. Mustafa had always told them, "You listen and respect the one I put in charge of your group, just as you would if it were me." Everyone seemed focused as they went through the activities, just as he'd instructed the older boys the previous night. Every minute, Mustafa was growing more confident in their abilities and in their chance for success. Success did not mean they would live, success only meant the mission would be accomplished.

As he looked around him, Mustafa knew that this would be the last time his so-called "family" would be together. Many -- probably most of the younger ones -- would not survive. Those who did live would no doubt be arrested and spend the rest of their lives in prison -- or, at least a good portion of it in a juvenile facility. If they carried out their mission, not only would it be disruptive and cause great damage both physically and mentally to the Great Satan, but it would also make Mustafa a hero in his own country. He thought often of how his story would be told to recruit and motivate the next group of fighters. He was the pioneer, the trailblazer, from what he recalled of American history. For those who would come after him, it would be different. They wouldn't have the ability to move around and have as much time to plan as he had. The one thing about the Americans was that while they failed to understand the threats before they happened, they very surely did a great deal to make certain the same thing couldn't happen again. Unfortunately for the Americans, people like him and those who recruited him weren't interested in repeat, they knew the best approach was to come up with something new.

Chapter Forty-Four

❊ ❊ ❊

The City of Philadelphia was in shock. Two more of their dedicated police officers had been gunned down. Fortunately, both the gunmen had been identified and, more important to many of the citizens, both killers were deceased. No one really seemed interested in more money spent on trials or paid to house a cop killer. With these latest two officers, the city was again in preparation for a proper farewell.

The ceremony would be held in two days. The Cathedral Basilica of SS. Peter and Paul stood majestically at the intersection of Eighteenth and Benjamin Franklin Parkway and was the Church used for these services, regardless of the faith of the deceased officer. It was customary that Police Departments from around the country send representative officers to the funeral. This could result in hundreds of out of town officers being present.

The logistics were a challenge. With the enormity of the turnout and the subsequent motorcade to the cemetery, it became a major feat merely to move the thousands of people from one location to another. Routes needed to be planned, and, in many cases, roads closed to allow the motorcade to move unabated through the streets. In the case of Sergeant O'Meara and Officer Brown, their funeral service was going to be jointly held, but their burials would be in two separate cemeteries on the opposite sides of Philadelphia. It was a challenge, but there would also be unwavering cooperation between the Philadelphia Police, neighboring communities and the Pennsylvania State Police. The bodies would be brought to the Basilica early in the morning, with the service beginning at ten o'clock and at eleven the two processions would be leaving for their respective cemeteries.

Mustafa read with great interest the articles in the <u>Philadelphia Inquirer</u> about the plans for the Officer's funerals. These would mesh well with his plans. It was clear the man with whom Mustafa had begun to work had done what he'd promised. With the city and the surrounding area focused on the funerals, he would be able to put his plan into motion and use this to his advantage. A smile crossed his face, the expression something which was rare. He would bring great pride to the people of Iran, and start a new life for himself.

Chapter Forty-Five

Mustafa turned his attention back to the teams and put his <u>Philadelphia Inquirer</u> down on the table. He felt certain that, in two days, all would be ready. He'd already informed the parents that the children would not be home for the next several days. Of course, none of the parents protested, for they knew the time had arrived. The children were as ready as they ever would be, the supplies were in place and the final training would soon be complete.

Everything they had done for the past fifteen years was now going to result in an operation certain to make the United States question its security and its role in foreign affairs. While there would be physical damage, it was the psychological damage that Mustafa hoped would be more severe and longer lasting. He would hope that all the people they had become neighbors with, all the customers that utilized their various businesses, their teachers, everyone would no longer trust another person from another country. Mustafa saw discrimination and mistrust as the forces which could cause more harm and destruction than any bomb.

He signaled for the oldest boys, the leaders, to come and join him at the table. They all walked over and sat down. "How is it going with your teams?"

"Mine is ready!" announced Aziz. The others nodded. "However, Uncle, I'm worried about the younger children. Do you really think they will be able to keep up and not cause us problems?"

The others again nodded. "I would agree with Aziz," one of the boys began. "They are willing and want to be with us, but I fear, as we carry out our plans – well, they might be overwhelmed."

"I understand. However, we must all be in this together. You will find, when you are in the middle of this, that you will need every person you have. You don't want to be caught short. Everyone has a role, right?" They all nodded. "If we don't use the youngest, others will have to take over their jobs, plus continue to do their own."

"Yes, Uncle. We understand," Aziz said thoughtfully. "But, is it possible they will get in the way and cause us more harm than good?"

"They have trained as hard as you. You have said they are as motivated. Let's not let their size and age fool us. We may find they are the biggest heroes of the day." Mustafa paused to allow them to think about what he'd said. "Here is what I would suggest. Pair the youngest with an older partner. Have them work together. Make sure the older one understands they are responsible for making sure both of their responsibilities are carried out. This will relieve you having to worry about everyone." The boys looked at each other and nodded in agreement.

"Once again, you come up with a great solution, Uncle." Aziz looked at each of his cousins. "I think that will work well."

"For the remainder of the afternoon, I want you to work with your teams on the plans. When we break for supper at dusk, that will be the end of the day. We will all eat together and then I want everyone to have fun this evening. Understood?"

The boys all nodded their approval as they rose from the table and returned to their teams. Mustafa felt even more confidence in the success they would have in the next two days.

As evening approached, Mustafa's house took on the atmosphere of a party. The kids were ran around, ate pizza and drank soda. Games were being played in the side yard, while several groups were in the front yard and on the porch, with board and card games.

Belle, out on her evening stroll, walked by and couldn't help but notice. "Oh, tonight must be Mustafa's birthday. He's getting a new flat screen TV from his nieces and nephews. I told you about the cute cable guys that were there hooking everything up. He's getting the premium package." As always, Belle was dominating the conversation with her sister, Sylvia, who was visiting from Ohio. "I'll tell you those cable guys were the premium package I want."

"Oh, Belle! You just never stop, do you?"

"Well, I'll tell you this. Mustafa deserves it. He spends so much time with those kids. He's practically raised them. It's nice of them to be so thoughtful to give him all of that. He really deserves it. This neighborhood needs more men like him."

"Everywhere needs more men like him"

"You got that right, Sis." They continued down the rest of the block and then turned right at the next street.

Chapter Forty-Six

Max had taken them out for pizza and a chance to get away from the command center. Max felt the time away might get them recharged and help their mental state. She knew this part of every assignment drove Jordan crazy. He was action oriented and to sit around waiting made him a challenge to manage. She'd found, over time, to get him away from the command center helped in relieving his anxiety. Jordan had reluctantly joined them and she could already see that it was doing him good.

Jordan and William found a pool table in the back of the pizza parlor and jumped on the chance to challenge a couple of the locals to eight ball. Max stood along the wall and watched. Kate had remained at their table talking with Stan. Max found she needed the down time, too, and had left the table when the conversation continued to be shoptalk. She knew Kate and Stan were the consummate hard-core crime fighters and, if they weren't in discussion about the case they were on, then they would rehash an old one.

Max was enjoying watching Jordan and William, when Kate appeared beside her. Kate's coat was already on and Max's was over her arm. "Here. We need to get back. Jordan was right. There does seem to be a connection with these police killings. My team in D.C. is sending us information now. It'll be there by the time we get back. Stan's getting the pizzas to go."

"Of course he is." Max grinned, she knew Stan would never miss a meal. She walked over past William and Jordan to the side of the table where their two opponents stood. "Okay, enough. I can't let this go on. They didn't tell you they were professionals?"

"Lady, what are you talking about?" The larger of the two men responded.

"My friends here are on the tour. They like to come into these neighborhood places and take advantage of the locals. I just can't let it go on anymore. I don't want to cause any trouble. How much did they take you for?"

"Forty bucks so far. But, it ain't fair if they're professionals."

"I totally agree with you." Max turned to look at Jordan and William. "Boys, we need to go and you need to give these men their money back and apologize."

William and Jordan just looked at her dumbfounded. They couldn't believe she was going to make them give the money back.

"Boys, we need to go. We're needed back at the office, pronto."

They both got what she meant. They nodded and threw the money down on the table.

The larger of their two opponents, neither of which would had ever been called small, shouted after them as they left the pool room. "Don't ever show your damn faces around here again or we'll push 'em in for you!"

Jordan grinned at William. "He has no idea, does he?" They both laughed as they walked out of the backroom of the restaurant and practically ran into Stan, carrying three boxes of pizza.

The pizzeria was about twenty minutes away from the command post. Kate told them what little she knew about her team's efforts to search phone and e-mail records and how that data had secured warrants to search financial records. From that information, they were able to identify solid connections which linked all of the suspects in the police murders.

Chapter Forty-Seven

❖ ❖ ❖

They dropped off two of the pizzas in the main room of the command center and took the other one with them to the back. Kate grabbed her laptop and the copies of the documents she'd printed and joined the others.

"Here's what we know. Each of the killers was a two striker. Given a little time, each would have had his third and be looking at life in prison. There is a connection through both phone and e-mails to a contact each had with an as yet unidentified individual. These contacts seem to start approximately six weeks before the suspect murdered the police officer. I have copies of some of the e-mails." Kate passed around a set of documents. "After several of these e-mails, there are phone calls and then a meeting is set. As best we can tell, there seems to be only one face-to-face. After that everything, is done by e-mail."

"These emails aren't specific. How do we know this is connected to the murders?" Jordan paced the room, with the copy of the e-mails in one hand and a slice of pizza in the other. The pepperoni was a little on the greasy side, but the crust was good.

"My team has identified specific words that are common in the e-mails received by each individual. We're still working on it, but we think there were code words for gun, date, location, etc. We think the code key was provided at the face-to-face meeting. We'll have more on that coming in later, but we've seen this type of thing before, mostly with the larger crime families. They'll be coordinating things in various locations and they've found e-mail with a code system to be an efficient way to work."

"Okay, then what was the hook for these guys?" Stan sat in a chair with his hands on the top of his head. Everyone knew this as Stan's body language when he processed information. "Why did they all agree to do this, when every one of them has ended up dead?"

"Financial security for their families, Stan. The financial records we pulled showed large deposits going into accounts held by each of these men or members of their families, all within about thirty days after they died."

"Thirty days?" Max questioned.

"Almost exactly. Our thought is that seems to be the time when people stop paying attention to these families. If it were done right away, they'd be under a lot of media and police scrutiny. But, like everything else, it quickly fades and we move on."

William walked over and grabbed another slice. "Was it substantial? My guess would be that it had to be for them to take this on and then trust the money was going to get to the family."

"We're talking a range between one hundred thousand and one hundred–fifty thousand dollars. We've also seen contact between the first suspect's family and the later ones. We think the organizers allowed contact between the newly recruited and the families to verify that the money did, indeed, get paid."

"Wow! I mean, this is elaborate," William said, shaking his head. I guess there isn't anything money can't buy."

Jordan stopped and put his pizza slice down. "But we still don't know why. Why did this group want to kill cops? It's got to be tied to something else."

"We did run data on major crimes happening within thirty days of an officer's murder. Nothing correlated."

"Maybe the crime hasn't happened yet," Jordan noted.

"Even with the connection, it still seems fairly random. It's been a year since these murders started. There's no rhyme or reason to the timing – at least none that we can find."

Jordan raised his hand. "Look. We can guess all we want. I think they are connected and leading up to something. I'm also thinking it might be tied to Mustafa and his plans."

"Okay, you lost me there." Max looked at Jordan with an expression that told him she wasn't even close to buying what he said.

"We know they've been planning this for quite a while," Jordan explained. "We know -- just with Akmed's business – there was a lot of cash generated and given to Mustafa. We don't know what some of the other family members are doing. So, Mustafa definitely has the bucks to pay out on these hits. They have to be planning something fairly large. Who ever is backing Mustafa has invested a lot of money to train these people and get them into this country. If it's big and they want to create havoc, then why not target the police. It gets everyone in the community unsettled.

People stop trusting, they lose confidence. Then, you pull off some big attack or some disturbance and the whole city might just implode on itself."

"It's a great theory, but we need more than a theory if we want to prevent Mustafa from carrying out his plan." Stan had gotten out of his chair paced the room. "I can't call Washington and mobilize the troops on a theory or hunch."

"I realize that. More importantly, I'm realizing we aren't going to have the time to stop Mustafa. They are too far down the road. We just need to be quick to react when they decide to move forward."

"When do you think that will be?" William's mouth was still full of pizza.

"I think within the next forty-eight to seventy-two hours would be my guess," Jordan responded.

"Where?" Kate asked, with the hope Jordan would have a potential target identified.

"Kate, I wish I knew. We're in an area that's just too target rich. They've got a ton of choices, depending on what they want to do. We won't know until they begin."

Chapter Forty-Eight

❖ ❖ ❖

Sharif Choufani didn't want to get out of bed. He wasn't looking forward to this day. He'd invested the last fifteen years of his life to get to this point because he was passionate about what he did. He knew it was important to his fellow brothers and to the group of people he served. Today would be tough, but at the end of the day he would be able to look back and see the impact he'd made. He would receive congratulations from people he didn't even know and his picture more than likely would be on the television news and in tomorrow's paper. He threw the covers off and walked into the bathroom. He reached into the shower and turned on the hot water. Walking over to the mirror he pulled out his scissors and began to trim his beard. Satisfied after a few minutes he rinsed out the sink and went into the shower. After almost twenty minutes he emerged, dried off, brushed his teeth, combed his hair and then went to the closet. He'd picked out appropriate attire for the day. He dressed and walked into the living room. Noticing the time, he knew he needed to be on his way. Everything meant to happen this day was on a tight and very specific time schedule. Today was a day he couldn't be late. He grabbed his keys and left the house, jumped into his car which he'd parked at the curb in front of his house the night before and headed for his destination.

It took Sharif twenty-five minutes to get there. He found a parking place and when he exited the car, he took a few minutes to look around to see if any other members of the team had arrived. He headed up the steps and opened the door. Once inside, he climbed a second staircase and entered the second door on the right.

"Good Morning Deputy Commissioner." His assistant called out as he entered.

"Hello Alice. Why did I know you would be here before anyone else?"

"It's a big day, sir."

"Yes, it is. I hope we're ready. Do you have the latest itinerary we could review?"

"Right here, sir."

Alice and Deputy Commander Choufani entered his office. Choufani was a fifteen year veteran of the Philadelphia Police Force. He'd started as a patrolman and had quickly moved up the ranks, having been promoted to the Deputy Commander role two years prior. He was in charge of all administrative services for the force. One of those duties was the planning of the funeral for any officer killed in the line of duty. While he hoped it would be a duty he would rarely have to perform, the last year and a half had given him more opportunity than he ever would have cared to have.

This day, he would be burying two more of Philadelphia's finest. No two funerals had been alike, so it wasn't as if he and his team could just pull a file and repeat the steps of the last one. Families had specific requests and there were always needs based on the decedant's religion. Logistics were a challenge, depending on where the funeral home was for the viewing and where the burial would take place. Commander Choufani and his team had to have every detail and contingency planned and coordinated.

While the responsibility rested solely within his command, an officer's death brought out a large number of people who felt they had the right to offer input. Choufani took as his responsibility, as any good leader should, to shield his team from the politics of planning an officer's funeral. He would hear from the officers in the patrol district of the deceased, the Mayor's office would have "suggestions," typically with the attempt to politicize the event to their advantage. The Police Union would also want to be at the table. Since Choufani was a union officer before his promotion into the command ranks, he was usually able to minimize their interference.

This day, he was faced with an different challenge. Two officers who were partners were being remembered on the same day. Two different funeral homes on opposite sides of town had held the viewings. The officer's families, who were surprisingly close, even for partners, had asked to have the service together. While at first Choufani had embraced the idea as one which would streamline the process, he found it actually had led to more significant issues, making this one of the most difficult funerals he'd planned.

The officers' bodies would receive a full escort from the funeral home to the Cathedral Basilica. A full escort involved five police units plus a motorcycle squad for traffic control. In addition, there were on-duty officers who had served with the deceased, wishing to escort their fallen comrade to the Cathedral. This was now times two, which caused a severe depletion in officers on duty, and would be repeated at the end of the service when the two bodies would be taken to separate cemeteries in two processions, leaving the city with a greatly understaffed police force for a good part of the day.

The Commander and his team had created and reviewed every conceivable scenario to avert the shortage in coverage, but had not been able to develop any better solution. Commander Choufani would keep his fingers crossed that the criminal element of the city would be respectful of the day and keep their activities to a minimum.

Chapter Forty-Nine

✤ ✤ ✤

Mustafa had all of the children awake by five a.m. After prayers, he had the older children fix breakfast for the others. He'd purchased eggs, bread and cereal for the children the previous day. He didn't tell them, but he assumed that for most of them it would be their last meal. He gathered the leaders in the garage and they went over the plan one more time. The garage was filled with the backpacks each of the children had packed yesterday. Mustafa instructed each of the team members to ensure they had the packs for their team and to do a final check to make sure they had all of the equipment and supplies they needed.

At that moment, two vans pulled into the driveway. One was the van used to pick up the supplies at Akmed's store and the other was a City of Brotherly Love Company van.

Mustafa asked the boys to gather around him. "I have assigned your teams to one of the vans. As I give you your number, please start putting your team's bags into that van. You do not need to be concerned with the two drivers. You don't need to know their names and they will not know yours. Get everything loaded and then join your teams inside. We will leave in thirty minutes."

Each of the boys nodded to Mustafa as he was handed the number. The boys went to their group of bags and started moving them to the vans. Mustafa motioned for the two drivers to go with him to the back yard.

Once in the back, Mustafa spoke quietly, so they wouldn't be overheard. "Are you ready, my brothers? Today is the day Allah has planned great things for us." Both of the men nodded. "After you drop off the children, you will then come back to the house and pick up the supplies we need from the shed. Then, you will go to work. You must be at work on time. We cannot afford any suspicion. Our mission is critical. We must be successful. Remember the children believe they are the mission, so you must not let them know anything any different. Is that understood?"

"Yes, Mustafa." Both men responded in almost perfect unison.

Mustafa smiled. The day had come. By the end of it, he knew he would bring honor to his country and his family but, he also knew he would provide a wonderful life for himself. He was excited, albeit he realized there was much, much work ahead.

"Go back to your vans and wait for the children."

Chapter Fifty

Jordan and Kate arrived at the command center at the same time. Most of the task force would either be in attendance or assigned to work the funeral. It made Jordan uncomfortable to be so understaffed, but they still needed to gather more credible data in regards to the target or the timetable.

"Anything happening at the store?" Jordan inquired as he entered the room.

"No, just a typical day. Benny just arrived to open. Akmed is already in the store. We know Aziz is still with his Uncle and two vans just arrived at the house and the boys are loading the backpacks into them. All the kids seem to be up."

"So they may be moving?"

"It looks that way; but, we have no indication where or when."

"How about the other two drivers?" Kate inquired.

"We got pictures and sent them to your team to see if we get any hits. They weren't familiar to us."

"Jordan," Kate said as she turned her attention back to him, "we were thinking that if we don't pick up any activity today, it gives us an indication they aren't moving soon. So, we thought it might make sense to move the command post. It's seems Akmed's store has served its purpose. He met Max last night at the Starbucks. It was crowded, so they had a chance to talk. He really doesn't know anything more since Mustafa showed up and took all of his supplies. He hasn't heard from Aziz."

"It probably makes sense. There's no reason to stay here," Jordan agreed. "If they continue to stay at Mustafa's, maybe we could get closer to there?"

"I think we could be more efficient if we just set up at the local office," William offered. "We would be more efficient. All the resources are there and it's easier to move in and out."

Jordan shrugged, indicating that he didn't really care and his mind was on other things. "I think they're going to pull this off before we we get moved. I have a feeling Mustafa's getting them ready to go. Of course, I don't have any idea where! Which really sucks."

They were all over by the window, looking out at the street below. Akmed appeared outside, sweeping his sidewalk and moving several displays out in front of the store.

Max spoke without turning her gaze away from Akmed. "He's ready to come in. He's afraid he's vulnerable, since Mustafa doesn't need him anymore. He believes there is a plan to eliminate him and possibly the other parents, so they can't go to the authorities once the plot is carried out."

"That makes sense. Even if we move from here, we should leave an extraction team to take care of Akmed. We can let him know where they will be. We can have a car around the block that he could either walk to or could get to him in a hurry."

Stan nodded. "Let's put that in place. Max? Can you get to Akmed tonight?"

"Yes, if I put a plant in the kitchen window, he knows to go to Starbucks at two o'clock and at eight o'clock. I'll do it now and can catch him at two."

"Kate and I are going to run over to Mustafa's and check in. I can't sit here all day," Jordan told Stan.

"Okay, but keep in touch."

Chapter Fifty-One

✤ ✤ ✤

DOWNTOWN PHILADELPHIA

Though he'd spent more time here than he would have ever wished, he was always impressed by the Cathedral Basilica of Saints Peter and Paul. Located just blocks from the center of Philadelphia on the Benjamin Franklin Parkway, the Basilica was both imposing while at the same time subtle in its environment, surrounded by modern high-rises and situated amongst Philadelphia's great cultural facilities. Under construction for eighteen years, with completion in 1864, its brownstone façade allowed it to blend in, while at over one hundred feet in height, it drew everyone's gaze. Commander Choufani stepped out of his car and, as he walked up to the cast bronze doors leading into the vestibule, he paused and looked above him at the green patina of the copper dome which rose sixty feet over the top of the Cathedral. He took a deep breath as he entered. Inside, the church had been set up to seat two thousand people. The Commander knew it would be standing room only and arrangements had been made to have audio of the mass broadcast outside for those attending who would not be able to be accommodated inside. Members of the uniformed honor guard were gathered. They saluted Choufani as he approached; he returned the same.

"I want to thank each of you for your service. Unfortunately, it's a service we have had to call upon way to often." He shook each of their hands and moved into the church proper, again his eyes moved up to the eighty foot ceiling and the massive bronze chandeliers. Every surface in the church was either marble or black walnut. It was impressive and he could think of no finer place for a city to say goodbye to its fallen.

He spotted several members of his team in conversation with the representative of the diocese. One of the facets that had made his job easier was the cooperation between the Catholic Archdiocese of Philadelphia and his unit. The Church was always able to accommodate their requests and needs, regardless of the officer's religion. Choufani had planned to do a walk-through with his team prior to the first casket arriving, so he moved over to the group, so they could begin.

Forty-five minutes later, with the walk-through complete and final details being checked, word came that the first hearse would arrive in front of the Basilica in ten minutes. With that announcement, Choufani and his team moved from the planning stage into their operational mode, where everyone had a specific role and place to be positioned. Members of his team were all ready with each family and would lead the escort to the Basilica. Each family would be escorted in behind the casket and taken to their seats. A member of his team, along with a senior officer from the deceased officers' district, would sit with the family during the service and the burial.

Uniformed officers were already arriving. Besides the Philadelphia Officers who were lined up outside, there were representatives from over two hundred and seventy-three police departments and law enforcement agencies, representing all fifty states and six foreign countries. One of the logistical nightmares had been to find parking for all of the cars, which would bring people to the site, and then being able to match the right cars to the correct processional at the end of the service. His team seemed to have it under control.

Fifteen minutes from the time the first hearse and its procession arrived, the front of the Basilica was clear and the second hearse moved slowly down the boulevard. Seeing that it was in the area, Choufani headed inside to ensure all was ready.

Within the next ninety minutes, the city would return to normal and they would move to the two cemeteries.

Chapter Fifty-Two

✤ ✤ ✤

Mustafa made one last pass through the house to ensure everyone was out and nothing was being left behind. He locked the front door and headed to his van. The children were loaded and the vans were at the curb, their engines idling. He opened the driver's door to the lead van and, as he got in, signaled to the other two drivers that he was ready to go.

They headed down the street and the vans stayed together for three blocks. At that point, the last van turned left and headed into a side street, taking a different course. Three blocks later, the second van turned right and followed its own route.

Mustafa remained quiet throughout the trip and only a couple of times did he turn to look at the children. But, he remained quiet. The children were dressed as if they would be attending school or in this case, going on a field trip, with each one wearing a backpack. There was no indication they were about to carry out a terrorist attack on a major U.S. city.

Mustafa reached Third Street and drove through the Society Hill section of Philadelphia, a neighborhood where many homes and businesses had gone through a revitalization, which resulted in professionals moving into the city from the suburbs. Mustafa grinned, hoping that, by the end of the day, many of the residents would regret their decision to leave the quiet and safe suburbs.

He turned left on Walnut Street for two blocks and then turned right onto Fifth Street, he glanced into his rearview mirror and could tell the children still had not recognized where they were headed. Mustafa was not surprised. It was one of the reasons he'd decided to use cargo vans with no side windows rather than a passenger van. While he risked being pulled over by the police for having children riding unsecured, he felt it was a risk he would take, to ensure that the children couldn't figure out where they were.

Between Chestnut and Market Streets, he pulled into a parking space and stopped. He picked up the radio.

"Unit one is in place. Units two and three, what is your status?'

"Unit two, I'm about one minute away." They would park on Sixth Street, between Market and Arch Streets, diagonally across the mall from Mustafa's van.

"Three here. I'm parked." Unit three was also on Sixth, but one block farther away than team two. They were between Arch and Race Streets.

Mustafa smiled. Everyone had made it. He looked to his left, at what lay in front of him -- Independence National Historical Park. Home of Independence Hall, the Liberty Bell and the National Constitution Center, it comprised a three block mall area of historical buildings, modern museums that stood as the birthplace of this nation. What better place to bring destruction and terror?

Grabbing the mike, Mustafa called the others. "We go in fifteen minutes."

Both responded affirmatively. He turned to Aziz. "Are you ready, my son?"

"I am and my team is. We will bring you success, Uncle!"

"I have no doubt of that, my children. You will make me and your parents so proud today." Mustafa looked at them, he knew it would be the last time he would see them. He could tell the young ones had no idea what would become of them. They did not realize it would be their last day alive and by the end of the day, they would be in the paradise promised to all martyrs. Allah would appreciate that it would be the children that would strike this blow to the Americans.

Jordan and Kate parked on the other side of the street, about a half block behind Mustafa's van. They had arrived at Mustafa's house just minutes before the vans left. They knew the other van had parked next to the National Constitution Center on the other side and two blocks from where they were.

No one had gotten out of the vans, so Jordan quickly explored the options. This was a target rich area, with any number of scenarios for what they might try to do or this might not even be the final target, but only a diversion, one which would force all of the limited police resources in Philadelphia this day to converge here while the group in the other van was at the primary target.

Though it was still early, there was already a fairly large crowd on the Mall. It was a school holiday, with pleasant weather so it seemed many families had decided to have an outing. If a couple of the kids moved into the large groups and detonated a bomb it would cause mass casualties and carnage, not to mention the larger crowds that would gather along with first responders, which allowed for a second detonation and a larger fatality count. While Jordan was keenly aware of these types of attacks in the Middle East and Asia, one hadn't occurred in this country, but it drove Jordan crazy that even in a post 9-11 world, Americans largely believed such types of violent acts couldn't happen in the USA. Jordan knew it was only a matter of time and possibly this was the day.

Chapter Fifty-Three

✤ ✤ ✤

BASILICA OF SAINTS
PETER AND PAUL

Commander Choufani had moved to the rear of the Basilica, when the aide to the Archbishop had signaled him that approximately five minutes remained in the service. Choufani sneaked a quick glance at his watch and was relieved to find they were on schedule. The choir would sing the ending Hymn and then a quartet of bagpipers would play as the caskets and then the families filed out of the church.

When he reached the rear of the Basilica, Choufani ducked outside to see if everything were staged for the procession to the cemeteries. This, again, was one of the logistical challenges with two processions headed to two different locations. His team had to ensure the right cars and the right people went with each hearse. He saw the two lines of cars behind the hearses, with discreet signs having been placed to direct people to the correct procession as they departed the church. He nodded at his two coordinators and gave thumbs up. Everything was as good as it could be.

As the great bronze doors opened, the wail of the bagpipes rose, filling the air with their haunting melancholy echoing and re-echoing off the surrounding building. Everyone outside immediately turned toward the doors and stoically looked on as the first casket appeared, the family following in its train. The pallbearers lifted the casket and carried it down the stairs to the waiting hearse. The family was helped to their assigned limousine, then turned and faced back toward the doors. They wanted to pay their respects to Sergeant O'Meara when his casket came out. A nice gesture from the family, Choufani thought.

Choufani felt a tap on his shoulder and he turned around. It was the Commissioner with his hand out. "Commander, you and your team have done another great job today. It was dignified and a beautiful service.

I know we threw some logistical challenges to your team and, once again, they came through with flying colors. Please thank them for me."

"Thank you, sir, and I'll let them know. They'll appreciate it, sir. They put their hearts into every one of these."

The Commissioner nodded and turned away toward his car. Protocol required he attend the burial of the most senior of the officers, which he would do. However, when it was completed, he planned on calling on the other officer's family at their home.

Choufani turned his attention to oversee what transpired as the second casket emerged from the sanctuary, followed by the family. In fewer than five minutes, the processions would leave and head toward their respective cemeteries. Within twenty minutes, they would both be clear of the Philadelphia city limits and, in two hours, the funerals would be concluded and the police department would be back to full strength. Choufani looked up at the cross on top of the Basilica and said a quick prayer.

Chapter Fifty-Four

✤ ✤ ✤

INDEPENDENCE MALL

Kate monitored the special police frequency assigned to the team coordinating the funerals, since Jordan wanted to be aware of the status of the funerals at the Basilica.

"They just loaded the caskets into the hearses. The families are hugging one another and everyone else is heading to their cars with the respective processions. They both should be moving through the city in the next five to ten minutes."

"Okay, let's see if Mustafa and the children make any move. Smart move for you, Kate, to get the frequency for the funeral processions, so we don't have to keep calling for updates." Jordan appreciated Kate's logistical mind. She made a great partner and even in moments like these, he wondered if they would ever have a chance to see if they could be compatible partners in a different sort of relationship.

He continued to study the van, waiting for any movement.

"The side door just opened on the van!" William's voice came over the radio. "It looks like the kids are getting out."

The van Jordan and Kate watched, side door opened as well. The kids bailed out and walked to the curb and into the Mall. The last one was Aziz and when he reached the others, they gathered around him, obviously looking to him for instructions.

The engine of the van started and the backup lamps flashed for a second, with the indication the transmission was put into gear.

Jordan grabbed the radio. "William our van is leaving. What's your status?"

"Looks like ours is going, also. What's your call?"

"I want to keep tabs on the kids. You and I'll stay here and Kate will continue the surveillance on Mustafa. Let's give these kids some space. They haven't done anything -- yet."

The van began to pull away from the curb. Jordan jumped out of the car. As he did he turned to Kate.

"Follow him, but nothing else. If a situation develops, call me or call for backup. He's too dangerous for you to try to take him down by yourself. Got it!"

Kate grabbed the door our of Jordan's hand. "I got it!" she said in a tone that told Jordan his "little-girling" comment was not appreciated.

Jordan made his way across the street and into the Mall. He found a bench about twenty-five feet from where the children had gathered with Aziz. It was an ideal observation post and, with the pedestrian traffic, he didn't stand out.

"Okay, Aziz, show me what you and the kids are up to." He whispered to himself.

In the distance, he could hear the muted sirens of the traffic control police who escorted the funerals. Jordan no longer believed the timing of the activities was just coincidence with the funeral for the two police officers. Mustafa was using it to his benefit. Jordan was sure something would be happen soon.

"Jordan." The radio bud crackled to life in his ear, William calling his name. "I think I have a visual on the third group. I can't be absolutely sure, but I think they are in the next block, standing outside the Constitution Center."

"Keep me posted. My group is standing right inside the Mall. I think they are waiting on something or someone."

"Right, I'm getting the same picture here with this group."

"If something is going to happen," Jordan whispered, "it's going to happen soon. You see anything, you let me know."

"Sure will, partner."

Chapter Fifty-Five

Kate stayed about two blocks behind Mustafa's van. As best she could tell, he was headed back to his house. As Mustafa crossed over Walnut Street, another van turned in from the side street and pulled in behind. Kate couldn't be sure, but her guess was it was another one of the original vans. Two blocks later, when the two vans crossed Spruce Street, they were joined by what Kate assumed to be the third van. It was almost an exact repeat of their routes from the morning. As they continued along Third Street, it became obvious they were in a caravan to Mustafa's house. Kate spoke into her radio. "Jordan, they seem to be going back to the house. Anything happening there?"

"No. They're still standing in their groups. It doesn't seem as if they're going to come together. If this is the mission, it looks like they each have a specific role to play. Kate -- be careful"

There was no response. Jordan knew he had pushed it with her. He never told William or even Max to be cautious. He had to be careful, but he knew why he did it. Kate meant more to him than he wanted to admit.

As they turned onto the street where Mustafa's house was located, Kate pulled back. Stan and Max were moving in place to back her up. She parked at the corner, a block away from Mustafa's. She had a visual of his house and, with the help of a pair of 10X50 Leupold tactical binoculars, could see all three men in the yard as they walked into the house.

Fifteen minutes later, just as the men exited the house, she received a transmission that Max and Stan were on-scene, parked two blocks down on the opposite side of the house. Kate saw that the men wore work uniforms that read "City of Brotherly Love Cleaning Company," Mustafa's place of employment. Were they really headed to work, Kate wondered? It didn't really make sense, to drop the kids off and go to their cleaning jobs. The men headed into the garage and brought out more boxes that they loaded into the vans.

Kate saw Mustafa suddenly turn and look across the street and his facial expression did not look happy. Kate turned the binoculars to see a plump black woman crossing the street. As the woman turned to look for traffic, Kate instantly recognized her.

"Oh shit!" She snarled under her breath. She said into the radio. "We may have a problem, guys."

Chapter Fifty-Six

✤ ✤ ✤

Commander Choufani stood at the height of the steps outside the Basilica. The Captain of the Honor Guard had just closed the rear door of the second hearse and they were marching back to the van that would carry them in the procession. Choufani turned and looked back inside. The Basilica was empty save for a black-cassocked Priest and several similarly attired Altar Servers, clearing the altar after the Mass.

Estimates were that almost five thousand people had attended the Service. The first procession had left almost ten minutes earlier and, by the radio traffic he heard, they were almost to Interstate Ninety-Five. Fifteen minutes later, they would enter Delaware County and would no longer be the direct responsibility of his team.

Choufani turned back just as the second procession began to leave. He stood at attention and saluted as the hearse pulled away. It was a sight that still took his breath away. There was nothing like the procession that followed a fallen officer. Almost as far as he could see down Ben Franklin Parkway was a line of police cars, all with their light bars in operation as they moved quietly forward. It was a tremendous tribute to the brotherhood shared amongst all law enforcement professionals, the turnout of fellow officers to bury one of their own. Choufani knew of no other profession, other than that of his brother fire-fighters, where complete strangers would come together, based solely on the bond of what they do for a job. He remained transfixed as he continued to watch them go by.

A slight tap on his arm brought him back to the reality of the day and his responsibilities.

"We're wrapped up here Commander. Are you ready to head back to the office?" his Lieutenant asked.

"Yes, let's go. I do want to see Father Breslin, before we depart, and thank him for all of his help. But, go ahead and signal dispatch we're done and the other procession has left. Tell them we should be at our office in about twenty minutes."

"Yes, sir," and the Lieutenant grabbed his radio. "Dispatch, this is Command Four. Second procession in route to Bucks County and the Cathedral is clear. Commander is returning to the office with an ETA of twenty minutes. Over."

"Roger that, Command Four. Show second procession in route. Cathedral is clear and Commander's ETA to office twenty minutes. Dispatch Out."

Choufani, the Lieutenant with him, re-entered the Basilica to find Father Breslin, both hoping this would be the last time for them to have to conduct a funeral for a fallen officer.

Chapter Fifty-Seven

※ ※ ※

Jordan kept his eye on the group led by Aziz. As the sirens faded from the first procession, he heard the sounds of the escorts of the second cortege leaving the Basilica. They headed in a different direction from the first and Jordan remembered reading that the officers were being buried in opposite directions from the city.

Whenever he could, Jordan would focus on Aziz. He was impressed by how calm and focused the boy seemed to be. Maybe this was only a field trip. But, if that were the case, why were they still just standing in the same place? He picked up the newspaper, shielding his facial movements as he spoke into his transceiver.

"William. Anything happening with your team?"

"No, they're just staying in the same place. I'm positioned so I can see both groups. Neither one has moved since we got here."

"Yeah same thing here," Jordan responded. "They must be waiting for some signal or a certain time. Can you tell? Do your leaders have radios?"

"Yep, they do. I've seen no adults around them and no one has approached them."

"Okay, let's see what happens," Jordan said, groaning a little as he lowered the newspaper..

Jordan had noticed that while all the children seemed to have radios, they weren't using them -- not even to talk to one another. More than likely, their tasks were going to be independent of one another, with coordination being provided by Mustafa or another adult.

Suddenly Aziz straightened up and grabbed his radio.

"Jordan, my guys are getting a message," William's voice said into his ear.

"Mine, too."

"They're on the move!"

"Same happening here," Jordan acknowledged, "so, let's see where they go."

Jordan watched as Aziz gathered his team and they started across the Mall. Halfway across, they broke into two teams. The one Aziz led continued to move directly across the Mall, while the other team turned and headed down the center of the Mall walkway. Jordan took a diagonal track intersecting the paths of the two groups so he could keep them both in view.

He hopped over a small chain to cut across the grass.

"Excuse me sir. Get off the grass! You think that chain is there for everyone but you?"

Jordan looked back and saw a woman in a green uniform with her finger pointed at him.

"Great, busted by a Park Ranger." Just as he was going to show her his credentials, he noticed Aziz and the oldest boys with the other group had heard the Ranger and were looking at him. If he flashed his credentials, they would know he was following them. He turned back to the Ranger.

"I'm sorry. I was just trying to catch up to my family, before they went into Liberty Hall." Jordan shrugged and put on his best *I'm sorry* face.

"Well, you need to come back here and then walk around. Just like that nice group of school children did."

"You've got to be kidding me!" Jordan said under his breath. He quickly glanced at the two groups and noticed the leaders seemed satisfied that Jordan was just an idiot and they again moved forward. Jordan jogged over to the Ranger. "I'm so sorry. It was really stupid of me."

"Do you have any idea how much we spend to try to get grass to grow? Only to have people like you tramp it down!"

"I'm really sorry. I just want to catch up with my family."

"I'm sure you do. Are they on the tour?"

"Yes."

"Well, then you are out of luck. The tour departs every fifteen minutes and you can't join a tour once it's started. So, you can't go in. So, you might as well just find a seat out here."

"Great. Just great."

Chapter Fifty-Eight

"Mustafa. I want to hear all about it," a loud voice boomed out of nowhere.

Mustafa looked up, then across the street. "Oh, no. Just what I need." The others looked at him.

"My neighbor. She'll talk my ear off, and won't go away. You keep loading the trucks. I'll get rid of her." He walked away from the trucks and intercepted Belle near the end of the driveway. "Hi, Belle! Hey, but, uhh, this is a really bad time. I've got to get to work."

"That's okay. This will only take a minute."

This woman didn't know what a minute was, Mustafa thought.

"I just want to hear about your birthday party and how you're enjoying your new cable hookup?"

"Belle, what are you talking about?"

"Your nieces and nephews. I saw them here the past couple of days."

"Yes, they were here." Mustafa was quickly growing irritated.

"They were celebrating your birthday, right?"

"No. My birthday is six months from now."

"Oh, the cable guy must have had it wrong. Well, they got you a new big screen TV, right?"

"Why would they give me a TV? I don't have cable!"

"Well, you're a great Uncle to them. They wanted to show their appreciation and thank you."

"Belle, you are making no sense. I didn't get a new TV. Now, if you will excuse me, I've got to get to work."

"Well, don't get all snippy! I'm just telling you what the cable guy told me and I'll tell you what, Mustafa, they were one cute group of cable guys. Mmm!"

"Belle, thanks for stopping by. I've got to go. I didn't get a TV and I still don't have cable. You shouldn't listen to those guys when they are at your house. They're just telling you stories so they don't have to go to their next job." Mustafa turned to walk away, hoping she would get the hint.

"But they weren't at my house. They were here at yours. Besides, I only talked to the one outside. The other three were inside working the whole time."

Mustafa stopped dead in his tracks. He quickly turned and, before Belle could react, he was in her face. "They were at my house?"

"Yes. Almost the whole day. They told me you were getting the premium service and it was a big installation job."

"When was this? Belle, how many days ago?"

"It was last week. Either Tuesday or Wednesday. I'm not sure which."

"How many men?"

"Four. Four of the most handsome men in the world."

"Yeah, okay. They were in a Comcast truck?"

"Just like what's always in the neighborhood."

Mustafa was about ready to blow. But he couldn't let on to Belle that something was out of the ordinary. "Well, I guess you spoiled the surprise. Maybe they are giving me the TV this weekend."

"Oh, Mustafa. I'm so sorry! I thought for sure they had already given it to you. I feel so bad."

"Belle, don't worry. This will be between you and me. I'll act as surprised as I can. They won't know the difference, but I've really got to go."

"Okay baby, I'm so sorry! But, one thing? If you have to have them come back, you let me know -- because, I want to be around that day!" Belle headed back down the street.

"Okay, Belle. That's a deal!" Mustafa turned and went back to his two employees. "We've got a problem. The Feds have been here. The place is probably bugged. They're probably watching us right now. There wasn't anything in the house that could have told them what we're going to do. Just stick to the plan. When we leave here, we won't be coming back. We'll use the house in New Jersey for the rendezvous."

The two men nodded.

One of them handed the radio to Mustafa. "It just came over the police scanner. The second procession just cleared the Philadelphia City Limits."

Grabbing the radio, Mustafa keyed the mike, "Leaders you are to proceed. I repeat. You are to proceed." Each leader responded in turn. Mustafa smiled and looked at the other two men. "Let us go and begin. We must move to make sure we're in position before they close down the area." They each got into their respective vans and drove off.

Chapter Fifty-Nine

✤ ✤ ✤

Kate watched as Belle turned and walked away from Mustafa. He looked both irritated and surprised by the conversation. He seemed quite animated as he talked to the two men and, with uncharacteristic hurriedness, they scrambled into their vans and started out of the neighborhood.

"Jordan?" Kate called over the radio as she put her car in gear and followed the vans from an appropriate. "I think we've got a problem."

"Say again, Kate."

"Belle and Mustafa just had a conversation outside of his house and, when it was over, Musfa and his pals left in a big hurry."

"Okay, but who's Belle?"

"She's the woman who talked up Reggie when we were installing the audio and video in Mustafa's house. She's the nosey neighbor, sort of like the neighbor in the old "Bewitched" re-runs."

"You're kidding."

"I wish I was. I think she told him about the cable guys being there and he's figured out it was us. They are high tailing back to you, it looks like."

"All right. This could really throw a wrench into our plans. The children seem to be moving into position for something. Where are Stan and Max?"

"They're right behind me. We've got Mustafa and his guys in sight. They seem to be following their same route from earlier."

"Kate, I think you should go pick up Akmed. If Mustafa's figured out what happened at his house, he might put it together that Akmed talked to us. Stan, Max. can you keep up the surveillance?"

"We've got them -- unless they split up again."

"Okay, but I agree with Kate," Jordan told them. "More than likely, they're going to be coming back here to the Mall."

Kate turned and headed down a side street, to get to Akmed's store. Stan and Max continued along Third Street. Eventually, the vans did the same maneuver as before and turned down various side streets, which left Mustafa's van for Stan and Max to follow.

Mustafa didn't turn where he had before, but continued on. Max glanced at Stan, saying, "Looks like he might be going somewhere else."

"Maybe. But, he could turn at any of the next few streets and still come out at the Mall."

The van finally turned right on Race Street, instead of left, as it would have if it were returning to the Mall. As Stan also turned right, he and Max saw the van turn left into a parking lot. Stan drove past as Max identified the company. "City of Brotherly Love Cleaning Service." Looks like he's a good employee and showed up for work."

Stan pulled a U-turn at the end of the street and slowly headed back. A block before the cleaning service's building, he pulled over. "Well, let's see if he pulls a complete shift."

Chapter Sixty

Mustafa couldn't tell for sure, but felt it was a possibility that whoever was in his house had also watched him and had probably followed him. It hadn't been his plan to come to the office. He'd wanted to head to the target; but, he thought he might be able to throw off his tail by coming to work. They would know this was where he worked and it shouldn't seem odd for him to be there. He also knew that, if they stayed out on Race Street, they would never realize the company had a dock area on Query Street, on the other side of the building. He could walk out the back, jump in one of the other company trucks and be on his way. But first, he needed to make a call.

"Hey, Mustafa! I didn't expect to see you here today. I thought you took the day off to be with you nieces and nephews." the receptionist looked up as he entered the office. She was always nice to Mustafa and, when he'd first started, had helped him around the office.

"I forgot to drop some things off for one of the crews at the Mall. And, my truck is acting up. Could you have Carlos take a look, Judy? And, I'll need to borrow a truck. Is anything available?"

"Well, Mustafa, you are in luck! We just got two new vans in yesterday and they're sitting out back. Carlos just got temporary tags for them, but they don't go to the paint shop until next Monday. Have some keys." She tossed the keys to Mustafa.

He smiled. "Judy, you saved me once again. I'll be back in the next hour or so." Mustafa knew he would never be back to the offices of the City of Brotherly Love Cleaning Service, but how fortunate to get a new van with a temporary tag and no signage on the sides. A plain white van in Philadelphia. How many could there be?

He moved through the building and into the warehouse at the rear. The phone on the back wall wasn't in use, so he walked over and picked up the handset. He dialed the number, hoping the person to whom he needed to talk would answer.

"Hello, South Philly Hardware. How can I help you?" It was the voice he wanted.

"Without saying my name, do you know who this is?" Mustafa asked.

"I do. What do you need?"

"I need you to take care of the problem we discussed. It is time. It must be done quickly! By doing this for me, you will have what you want. Do you understand?"

"Yes. I'll take care of it."

"You are a good man. You deserve this reward for your support of our efforts."

"Thank you," the voice responded. There was the click of the connection severing.

Mustafa hung up the phone. It was good to tie up loose ends as soon as possible. He walked out onto the dock and saw the two vans parked along the fence. Fortunately, Judy had given him the keys to the one in front. He hopped in, adjusted the seat and mirrors, laughing to himself that he was still following the company's guidelines for vehicle safety. He placed the gearshift in Drive and started out the lot. He knew he would arrive at his destination within five minutes and the real work would begin.

Chapter Sixty-One

✤ ✤ ✤

Jordan observed as the teams of children made their way toward the two buildings. One team headed to the building which housed the Liberty Bell. Formerly kept in Independence Hall, a new facility was constructed in 2003, solely to house the Bell and exhibits on its construction and history. Jordan watched as the children entered and queued into the security line.

Jordan turned around. He spotted the other group walking up to the door of Independence Hall, where they were greeted by man in Colonial attire. As Jordan watched, he got the impression the man had been expecting the children. With the Park Ranger still next to him, he asked. "Who is that man talking to those children?"

She glanced over and squinted her eyes. "It's one of the volunteers. It's hard to say from this distance; but, I'm pretty sure it's Sam. He's great with the kids."

"I'm sure he is. Can you get a hold of him on a radio?"

"No, they don't carry radios. Why?"

"Because he can't let those kids in!"

"What are you talking about? They're school kids. We always have kids come in."

"Those aren't school kids. They're terrorists!"

"What are you talking about? Just who are you anyway?"

"How many armed Rangers are on site?"

"I'm not telling you that." She started to pull out her radio to call for assistance. To her, Jordan had moved beyond strange to downright scary.

Jordan took his eyes off the children and turned toward the Ranger. He realized how his comments must have just sounded. He moved his hands to pull out his credentials.

"I wouldn't do that if I were you." The voice was behind him. He turned and saw another Ranger with his hand on his gun.

"I'm a federal agent. I was getting my badge. You have a potential situation here."

"I see that we do, Mr. Federal Agent. Now, why don't you just move your hand back, and then we'll all take a little walk." The man's voice was annoying.

"You don't understand," Jordan began, trying to be patient. "You have four groups of children that have been trained as terrorists, one group entering each building in the Park. You've got a major incident going down."

"Sure we do, buddy. Yeah, the school kids wreak havoc here every day of the week. We can handle them. It's the nuts like you that we have to waste our time on."

"Look, I'm here, my partner up by the visitor's center is watching two other groups. I'm telling you a major incident is going to occur at any moment," Jordan said, his voice extremely well-modulated, he thought.

"Hey look, buddy. I'm the liaison with the Homeland Security Task Force. I haven't been given any alert or, for that matter, any information about a bunch of school kid terrorists targeting Philly." The guy's voice really was irritating.

Jordan was about to get into the Ranger's face, when a man and woman sporting Phillies World Series Champion shirts and ball caps walked up.

"Excuse me, officer? Could you tell me why the Liberty Bell is closed?"

"It's not. You enter right over there," The H.S. Task Force man responded, as he pointed to the long, rectangular building that housed the Bell.

"Yes, we know. We were just there. But, the door is locked."

The Ranger looked toward the building and saw there was a large number of people outside. Several were apparently trying the door, only to find it wouldn't open. He grabbed his radio. "Park Three to LBC One. Over."

There was no reply, only the crackle of static..

"Park Three to LBC One. Confirm center's status. Over."

More static.

"Park Three to Control. Over."

"Go ahead, Park Three. Over."

"Anything going on in the LBC? Over."

"Negative that. Board shows everything normal. Over."

"I copy that – " The Homeland Security man never finished the transmission, for at that moment, there was a shout from a man coming out the doorway of Independence Hall. "There are kids in there with guns!"

He stumbled out of the building and a large red blot was growing on his shirt by the right shoulder. A young Middle Eastern face stuck out through the door briefly, but then quickly closed the door.

The Ranger looked at Jordan. "Who did you say you were again?"

Jordan didn't answer his question, he took over. "You've got four sets of students who have entered each of your major buildings. They are armed with guns and explosives. You need to evacuate the Mall and lock this area down." Jordan reached back for his radio, neither the Ranger nor the H.S. man attempting to stop him.

"Jordan to Command Center. We have a Code One at Independence Park. We need a full Level One Response. I repeat, Level One. I have contact with Rangers on site. We need Philly PD here ASAP."

"We read you Jordan; all units in route."

"William, what's happening up there?"

"They've entered the Constitution Center and the Visitor's Center. It seems they have both buildings under control. A few people got out, but it looks like they've held most people inside."

"Okay, cavalry is on the way. Stay there and keep me posted."

Turning to the park personnel, Jordan asked. "We need a command post. Any ideas?"

"The Greene Federal Building has a back up Homeland Security center we could use."

"Let's go, then," Jordan nodded.

Chapter Sixty-Two

✤ ✤ ✤

SOUTH PHILADELPHIA

Kate pulled into a parking space around the block from Akmed's store. She started down the sidewalk and glanced up at the apartment, which had been their command center. The street was quiet, with few people out this time of day. She looked through the store windows and there seemed to be no customers. She saw Akmed in one of the aisles, as he straightened the merchandise on the shelves. Benny was behind the counter on the phone.

She turned and entered through the front door, which caused the bell attached to the door to ring. She didn't make a quick beeline to Akmed, but attempted to be a customer in search of an item. She knew the hardware store probably didn't have a large number of younger white women who shopped in this store, based on the neighborhood demographics.

Kate turned down the aisle in which she'd seen Akmed. He was no longer there, so she picked up her pace and walked to the end of the aisle. The shelving units were of a height that precluded her seeing over the top, so she had no clue where Akmed might have gone.

Benny said "Thank you" into the phone and Kate heard him shuffle through some items behind the counter. She turned the corner just in time to see Akmed turn down another aisle and watched him walk toward the storeroom. Had he seen her? Did he know why she'd come? Was he trying to get away? Or, did he know why she was there and he was going to grab his things. She continued straight down the aisle, parallel to Akmed. She hoped she could intercept him when the aisle ended and get to him before he reached the storeroom.

"Akmed!" called Benny.

"Benny, what are you doing with that gun?"

"You have betrayed us." Benny shouted.

"What are you talking about?" Akmed stuttered in confusion.

Kate stopped at the end of aisle. She knew Akmed was just around the corner.

"I have been ordered to kill you," Benny proclaimed.

"Ordered to kill me? By who? Who has ordered such a thing?"

"You were supposed to help us. You raised Aziz to be a leader for us. You provided the store and the money. Allah is grateful."

"Benny? Are you part of this? How long have you known?"

"Mustafa befriended me, after you hired me. He showed me the wrongs I had been doing. He showed me the ways of Islam and its righteousness. I believe in what he is doing. I thought you were a believer, also."

"It's crazy, Benny. Innocent people are going to die. Mustafa let my wife die. He is not the man you think he is."

Kate knew time was almost up, and was silently thankful that so many inexperienced people who have the drop on somebody see it as an opportunity to practice their oratory. She could tell by Benny's tone he wasn't going to be swayed by Akmed, and she wouldn't have a clear shot if she came around the corner. She didn't know where Akmed was or Benny for that matter. The one thing she did know was that Benny must not have realized she was in the store. He didn't seem concerned. She needed to get into a better position, where she would have a clear shot at Benny. Slowly, Kate moved away from the end of the aisle, well aware of the anti-theft mirrors which hung from the ceiling. The mirrors allowed the person working at the counter to view the various aisles and watch for shoplifters. Kate stayed low, to avoid Benny spotting her.

She moved across the middle aisle, back to the front of the store. Mercifully, Benny and Akmed continued to talk, but it wouldn't last much longer. Her right hand was on the butt of the Crimson Trace Laser fitted Glock 22. She slipped the pistol out of her holster and moved to the corner directly across from the counter so if Benny hadn't moved, she would have a clear shot. She'd rather sweat information out of him than kill him, but she wasn't a cowboy in an old movie who could just "wing" her target. The more of these people they could capture and interrogate, the better chance they would have of finding other cells.

"Benny! Look at what I've done for you. I gave you a job. I pay you well. You are practically another son to me. Why would you kill me?"

"Akmed, this is not about me and you. This is about something greater than both of us. We can bring honor back to Iran. We can teach the Americans that their liberties mean nothing. Akmed, you must die for your betrayals."

"NO!!"

There was a shot and Akmed fell to the ground. Something metal slid across the floor. Akmed didn't move.

"You're under arrest, you terrorist son of a bitch!" Kate commanded. Her radio was in her left hand, a black gun in her right. "I have a man down and need medical assistance at South Philly Hardware. Suspect apprehended. Officer needs assistance."

Akmed was confused. Kate was there and suddenly, he looked over and she stared back at him.

"Akmed? Are you okay? I mean, you weren't shot or anything. I shot Benny." She held the muzzle of her pistol to Benny's head and pocketed the radio. One-handed, she pulled the apparently unconscious Benny's arms around behind him, locking his wrists together with plastic tapes. "They're Flex-cuffs. Got to be cut off," Kate called over as she dropped on one knee across Benny's calves and cuffed his ankles together. Her gun disappeared under her coat as she took a third and fourth plastic strip and connected these between Benny's ankles and wrists, so he would not be able to stand. "He's not going anywhere, but you and I need to get out of here as quickly as possible. This place will be crawling with cops in a few minutes and, if they find you here, we'll never get you away." She helped Akmed up. They went back to the office and quickly grabbed his bag. As they headed out the back door, they heard the sirens just as the first police units pulled up to the front.

They found Kate's car, tossed Akmed's bag on the back seat and jumped in. As Kate pulled away, all Akmed could say was, "Thank you, Kate. I had no idea about Benny."

"My pleasure Akmed. You're safe now."

Chapter Sixty-Three

❖ ❖ ❖

PHILADELPHIA POLICE
HEADQUARTERS

Commander Choufani was in his office when Lieutenant Hall knocked and entered. "We may have an issue developing, Commander."

"What's going on?" Choufani sat up in his chair. Not only was he in charge of the funerals, but, since the burials were in two different locations, the entire Command structure of the Philadelphia Police Department was divided between the two burial sites. Since Choufani had to remain at the Basilica to wrap things up and needed to coordinate both processions, the Police Commissioner had designated him the Acting Commissioner while he was out of the jurisdiction. Choufani had been hoping for a slow day. It seemed like that was not to be.

"Two officers on foot patrol on Market Street were stopped by a family who reported that several of the buildings at Independence Mall had suddenly been closed. They proceeded down to the Mall and ran into two Park Rangers – one of them the H.S. guy -- as they headed toward the Federal Building. They said they needed to open up the command center and that there was a hostage situation at the Mall, but they didn't have the details. The two officers joined them and called in as they went with the Rangers. We dispatched two more units to the Mall. They should be arriving any moment."

Alice walked in. "We just got a priority one call from the Park Service. This Mall thing is for real. Some group has taken over the Visitor's Center, Independence Hall, the Liberty Bell, and the Constitution Center. They are mobilizing at the Federal Building and they are asking for the Commander in Charge to report there."

"You've got to be kidding me! This is not the day for this." Choufani stood up. "Get my car. Alice, send out a system wide priority call. I need the Senior Operations team in the City to respond to the Command Center.

Activate the SWAT unit and the Homeland Security Task Force and Tactical Teams. Have them mobilize one block west of the Federal Building. Get as many patrol units as you can down there and make sure the Mall is evacuated and the area blocked off. Let's go, Lieutenant."

Choufani and the lieutenant ran down the stairs and out to the street. They were only five minutes from the Federal Building with lights and sirens. As they reached the car they heard the dispatch regarding an officer needing assistance in South Philly.

"Damn, when it rains it pours!" Choufani yelled as he scrambled into the car. He pulled out his cell and called into the dispatch center. "This is Choufani. What's going on with the officer needs help call?" He listened intently as the car sped away from the curb. "A federal agent at a hardware store. What is going on?" He didn't get an answer and hadn't expected one. "How many units are responding?" He got an answer on that. "Okay. Keep me posted. Show us enroute to the Emergency Command Center at the Federal Building." He hung up and looked over at his driver.

"This is one crazy day. Now we've got a Fed at a hardware store that has shot a suspect and is requesting medical aid and assistance. No one has any idea what it's all about."

His cell phone rang. He looked at the caller I.D. It read "PD Dispatch." He clicked the button. "Choufani." He listened intently. "What do you mean no one's there but a man who's been shot and cuffed?" No answer. "They searched the entire building?" There was an answer in the affirmative. "Is there a ranking officer on site yet?" He paused to hear the response. "Okay, when the district commander gets on site and gets up to speed, have him call me. Thank you." He clicked the off button. "I can't believe this. The first officers on the scene observe a man on the floor with his right elbow smashed by a bullet, bleeding of course and unconscious. God, that must hurt. The one officer knows the guy's the store clerk and there's a 9mm Glock on the floor. There's no Fed around, but they find a .40 S&W shell casing on the floor. They searched the whole store and the apartment upstairs – belongs to the owners. Nothing. Not a damn sign of anyone. They don't know what's going on down there."

His phone chirped again. He looked at the screen it was Alice. "Hi, what's going on?" He listened intently and it wasn't good. "Can they get to him? Are the paramedics there? Okay, you call the Command Center. Make sure they're up to speed tell them we'll pull up outside in about two minutes." He added, "And, ahh, Alice? It's going to be a long day -- even longer then we imagined. So, thanks in advance." He clicked off. "We have a man down in front of Independence Hall. No one knows if they can get to him or not. Maybe they can. The initial word is these are kids holding the buildings and no one saw any adults with them. This is getting stranger by the minute."

The car came to a halt behind the Federal Building. As Choufani stepped out, all he could hear in all directions were sirens on vehicles in response to the scene. He knew they would only have about a third of the manpower an operation like this required. He had no idea what the outcome in South Philly would be and how much in resources he would have to dedicate there.

They quickly moved through the lobby of the Federal Building where there was an elevator to take them to the third floor and the Command Center at the center of the building. As they entered the room through the security vestibule, Choufani immediately noticed several people whom he did not recognize, persons who seemed to be in command of the team, the team including several of his officers. He came up beside them and announced. "I'm Deputy Commander Choufani with the Philadelphia Police Department, acting as Commissioner until full command staff is returned to the city. Your turn. Who are all of you?"

Everyone turned to look. Jordan glanced at him, murmured, "Hi," then returned to the computer screen he watched. "Can you get a closer image of the building?" he asked the technician.

"Hold on a second! You don't give commands here!"

Stan stepped between them.

"I'm Stan Kershaw, Acting Director of the FBI. My associates here, Max, Jordan and William, are with various Federal agencies, the initials of which don't really concern us now. What you need to know, Commander, is you have the best and the brightest in handling terrorists and they're right here in this room. So, we can pull the bulls tail about turf for the next forty-five minutes, or we can put that aside and get down to the business at hand. It's your call."

Choufani was taken aback. He knew the name and reputation of Stan Kershaw. When it came to Kershaw, who in law enforcement didn't. He'd heard story after story of Kershaw. The image had always been of a "James Bond" type. Choufani glanced over to one of the local FBI agents he knew.

The agent laughed as he saw Choufani's expression. "Yes, it's really him."

"Okay, sir. I'm sorry, I didn't know," Choufani told Kershaw.

"Yeah, I always get that. They think I should be taller. Here's what we've got, Commander. Four buildings have been taken over by a sleeper terrorist cell. They're holding about one hundred hostages in total. There are some of the perps who are armed. We don't know any numbers on that. They have yet to make contact, so we don't know what the demands are going to be."

"Sounds pretty straight forward for SWAT and the Critical Incident team."

"Well, it does until I tell you the kicker. Your terrorists in those buildings, they range in age from eleven to seventeen." Stan looked straight in Choufani's eyes.

"You've got to be kidding me!" Kids had taken over the buildings and shot a man? "Okay, what else do we know?"

"Jordan. Can you come over and brief the Commander?" Stan waved Jordan over.

Jordan shook the Commander's hand. "I'm Jordan Wright."

"Really?" Choufani asked.

"It's me."

"I've heard a lot about you. My Homeland Security guys think you're the sole reason we don't have more attacks."

"You've got a good group, sir." Jordan led Choufani over to the map of Independence Mall. "We followed four groups into the Mall this morning. We didn't have enough intel to know exactly what they had planned. For all we knew, the kids could've been on a field trip. A man named Mustafa Alfani dropped them off. He's the leader of a group of families who, over the years, emigrated from Iran. One of the parents of one of the boys approached us several days ago. In our interview, we felt he gave us credible information. So we did surveillance of his store in South Philly. It's a hardware store."

"South Philly Hardware?"

"Yes, that's the one."

"We had a call there twenty minutes ago. An officer needing help but, when my team got there, they only found an employee shot and no one else."

"That would be me." The whole room looked over at the door as Kate entered. She walked up to Choufani. "I'm Kate Woolrich. I'm with the Central Security Service, part of the NSA. I was extracting our informant when the suspect was about to kill him. We need to trace the last call the suspect – the guy I shot -- received, because I believe he was given the order to kill just as I entered the store."

"Okay, okay." Choufani needed to draw this conversation back to what he needed to know. "How involved has my department been in this?"

Jordan, Stan and Max all looked at each other and then at Choufani. "Since we came to Philadelphia five days ago, we worked with your terrorism task force."

"Yeah, okay. Let me explain. I'm the administrative commander. I haven't been in Operations for several years, so I tend to fall out of the loop. I'm senior today because of the two officers being buried."

"We know and we have additional information on their deaths we need to share. Payoff in their deaths, along with the other five, are connected to what's happening now." Stan stated. He looked over at Kate and gave her a meaningful eyebrow shrug.

Kate nodded and began to fill Choufani in on what her team had found about the police murders, the suspects and the large payments to the families.

"So they did that just to take over the Mall?" Choufani said, incredulous.

Stan jumped back in. "We don't know for sure. This may be a diversion. They know we'll waste a lot of time trying to figure out a strategy, since kids are involved. They're playing to our emotions. The real target could be elsewhere."

A phone rang in the command center. "It's the phone at the security desk at the Liberty Bell Center." A technician took the receiver in his hand. The lead negotiator for the Incident Command unit looked at Choufani.

Choufani looked at Stan. "Should my guy take the call?"

"I think that's the right move." Stan nodded.

The negotiator moved toward the phone.

"Hello, this is Carl. Who's this?" He waited for a response, got one. "So, hello, Aziz."

There was a grunt.

"How old a young man are you and why don't you tell me what's going on in there?"

Chapter Sixty-Four

✤ ✤ ✤

INDEPENDENCE MALL
ONE HOUR AGO

Aziz lined up the children once they had made it through the entryway of the building housing the Liberty Bell. Since he'd visited the building so many times, he knew the layout well. Off to the side, before the security checkpoint, was a small janitor's closet, to which Mustafa had provided a key. The previous day, when Mustafa was checking in on his crew, he'd placed a box inside that closet, as he had hidden similar boxes in each of the buildings.

Aziz opened the door and inside were two of the handguns from the store room at the hardware store. Aziz took both of them and tucked them into each of his jacket pockets. They were bulky and noticeable, but that would not be a problem for long. Spare magazines for the pistols went into his pants pockets. Also inside the closet were two heavy cables and large padlocks, which would be used to secure the doors. The last of the children moved through the security checkpoint so Aziz stood by the entrance door and pulled the cable from beneath his coat, strung it through the door handles and secured the looped ends into the lock.

"Hey kid! Get away from the door! What do you think you're doing?" The guard who'd just spoken made his away from behind the security desk and walked determinedly toward Aziz.

Aziz pulled out one of the pistols and used it just as he'd been taught. He shot the guard twice. The guard took the bullets in the stomach and fell back to the floor as the visitors inside turned toward the noise.

Aziz went up to his group. "Everyone knows what to do. Stay with your partner and carry out what was instructed. Everything is going to work out." The children paired up and went to various parts of the exhibit. The oldest children approached the adults and families in the facility and guided them to the center of the room. Other children started to emptied their back packs.

Within minutes, they took the PVC pipe and pieced it together to make a frame while others unpacked canvas sheets and attached them to the frames. The frames were stood up at points in the building perimeter and curtained large expanses of glass, so it would preclude anyone being able to see inside. Several of the other children placed electronic devices in various locations around the building and included several next to the Liberty Bell itself.

Aziz addressed the hostages. "We mean you no harm as long as you cooperate with us and do as you are told. We're here to make a statement for our beloved homeland of Iran and our beloved Allah. We brought our fight here to demonstrate that your so-called liberties mean nothing to the rest of the world. We will bring your country to its knees and it will beg forgiveness from our Ayatollah. In a short period of time, your country will respect Iran and the other nations of the Islamic world as the true super powers and the countries which all other nations must respect!" Most in the crowd stared, bewildered and in shock that their planned day to visit the birthplace of the United States had placed them in the middle of this terrorist act.

Aziz walked around, checking on his team's progress. He was pleased with all of the efforts as everyone was doing their part and not one of the children seemed scared or in a panic. Aziz glanced at his watch. In thirty minutes, he would call the number Mustafa had given him and read the note Mustafa had given him to the police officer who would answer. Aziz hadn't read the note, but assumed it was a list of demands.

He motioned two of the other members of his team over to join him. "Please take the guard that I shot and put him outside. When I call to give our demands, I'll allow them to come and take him for medical treatment. He did nothing wrong and we won't treat him like we may treat the others." The two nodded and went over to the lobby where the guard still lay. They picked him up by the shoulders and dragged him to the door. Aziz threw the key to the padlock over to them and they unlocked the door.

"Be careful! Push him out, but don't expose yourselves," Aziz warned. Both nodded and they used the guard's body to open the door and passed him out by moving down his body and shoved him out. As they closed the door, they could hear the man moaning in agony, and they notice there was a trail of blood across the floor. They locked the doors and threw the keys back to Aziz.

"Go back and join the others. Keep an eye on the people. Make sure they do not talk to one another." They nodded as they walked back to the center of the building where the hostages had been made to sit.

Aziz glanced at his watch. Mustafa had been clear that they minimize their use of the radios, since they should expect the police would be able to monitor their communications. The leaders of the teams had developed a code they could use with one another to check the status. They had also designated Aziz as the initiator of any communication, other than in an absolute emergency except to check in at the sixty minute mark after they initially took over the buildings.

"This is One. I'm at the store and have everything we need. How is everyone else?" Aziz released the push to talk switch on his radio.

"This is Two." Aziz knew Two was in Independence Hall. "We had one small accident, but were able to move it outside. Everyone is cooperating and we're all having a good time." Accident was the code word for a wounded hostage.

"Three here." This was the team in the Visitors' Center. "We're in good shape, no accidents, everyone happy." Everyone was their code for the hostages. "Everything is up and running." Aziz let a smile show. This was all good news. Up and running was the code that all of the windows were blocked with the canvas frameworks. Independence Hall didn't have expansive windows and therefore didn't need to block any.

"Hi, this is four. We're also good. Also up and running. Not everyone is happy. Two guests not feeling well, but we're watching closely." This made the smile leave Aziz's face. Not feeling well was code for uncooperative hostages. The concern had always been that if a group of hostages felt they could overpower the children a problem might arise. Team four had the most inexperienced leader, but the largest of the teams.

"Do you have a lot of guests?" Aziz inquired.

"Almost forty." The other leader replied.

"Crap." Aziz said to himself thinking this could get out of hand quickly. He keyed the mike on the radio. "I would suggest you break up the party into different rooms." Aziz hoped they would understand he was telling them to divide the hostages up into smaller groups and separate them throughout the facility. Another choice was to let the potential challengers go, but that could encourage others to do the same thing, thinking it would get them freed. The final alternative was to kill one or two hostages at random, which would force the other hostages to control any of their number who wanted to try anything.

"Four, keep me posted on how your party progresses. Everyone -- we will talk again soon. I have to make another call." Aziz walked toward the reception desk and he sat down and stared at the phone. He wasn't sure who would answer on the other end, but picked up the handset and dialed the number.

It rang.

Chapter Sixty-Five

Mustafa backed his van up to the building and parked by the loading dock. The facility was the most secure facility in Philadelphia, and it still amazed Mustafa how he could just walk in by flashing his picture ID. As he walked up the outside ramp to the enclosed guard station, the guard looked up and waved in recognition to a man he'd seen almost every day for the past three years.

Mustafa pulled the door open as soon as he heard the lock release. He walked in and again flashed the IDs hung around his neck to the guard.

"Hey, Mustafa, how are you doing?"

Mustafa nodded.

"I heard some of the managers talking about your new guys. Sounds like they're doing a great job."

Mustafa smiled, thinking, if this man only knew. "Thank you, Jake. I'll let them know. This is an important customer for us, so I want to make sure the bosses are happy, both yours and mine." Mustafa kept eye contact as he thought to himself that Jake might think differently in about an hour.

Mustafa continued walking down the corridor until he reached the door lettered "Janitorial Services." He put his key in the lock and entered. He found his team waiting for him.

"It is good to see you, Mustafa. We take it all is going as planned?"

"Yes, I believe it is. There is much commotion at the Mall. The children have taken the buildings and the Police are mobilized and I believe I have also taken care of our problem with the Feds."

The three men nodded in relief. Their part of the mission -- the most important part – was about to begin.

"Do you have everything ready? Is everything in place?" Mustafa inquired.

"Yes, we have our carts positioned with everything we need. Nothing seems out of the ordinary today. Everyone we want is in today and working in their typical location. I believe, if Allah wills it so, we're good to go."

"I'm proud of all of you. Today will be a proud day for our country."

Mustafa's phone vibrated in his pocket. "Excuse me. You must all go back to work and undertake our normal activities until I tell you it's time."

Each man shook Mustafa's hand as he left.

"Yes, hello?" Mustafa said into his phone.

"How are things? It sounds like all is going to plan." The man on the other end was his new employer. Mustafa's handlers in Iran were not aware of what Mustafa had planned, since Mustafa had long ago planned not to martyr himself today. He, too, had come to enjoy life in America, but couldn't figure how to get away and disappear from his controllers -- until this man approached him.

"Yes, I believe it is. I'm confident of our success." Mustafa answered.

This man, named Jerome, had uncovered the details of Mustafa's mission and it fit with what Jerome needed. A distraction of what Mustafa's nieces and nephews would do created the perfect diversion. Mustafa had, at first, denied the plans for the Independence Mall takeover and refused to listen.

But, Jerome was persistent. He knew too many of the details and too much about Mustafa. He'd shown Mustafa a way out. Jerome could provide a new identity and a new location to live and enough money so Mustafa could live like the former Shah. He would want for nothing.

"Mustafa, tomorrow is going to be the start of a new day for you. I hope you're excited."

"I am. I'm looking forward to it. There is still much to be done, but the men are ready. The children have been in place for over a half-hour. The Mall is shut down and I'm sure we will be in lock down here in the next ten to fifteen minutes."

"Very good. We'll talk again after you leave and are at the safe house."

"Yes. I'll contact you when we arrive."

"Good, Mustafa. I'm counting on you. Please, do not fail me -- as the Libyans did."

"I'll not." Mustafa said to dead air. He realized Jerome had ended the call. As he went to the door to begin his rounds, he could hear the P.A. system activate.

"May I have your attention, please. May I have your attention. This facility is now in lock down. I repeat, we're now in lock down. All visitors need to be escorted to the visitors' lobby immediately. All tours are suspended and all participants should immediately proceed to the tour exit.

All employees are required to remain in their work area. No one will be permitted to leave or enter the building. Lock down is in effect until we announce all clear."

It was critical for their success that the building went into lock down. Mustafa had been in the building before when a lock down had been declared and had observed that what was supposed to bring organization and security to the facility tended to do the opposite.

He moved along the corridor. Since he was a contractor and his people were all over the building, he enjoyed the ability to move about and not be stopped. He quickly made his way around, to check on the other members of his staff who weren't involved with the plot. He found each of them in their proper position and directed them on what they should do. He then sought out his three accomplices. They had much to do and, while time wasn't the biggest challenge, the quicker they accomplished their task and left the building, the better chance of success.

Chapter Sixty-Six

✤ ✤ ✤

LIBERTY BELL CENTER,
INDEPENDENCE NATIONAL PARK

Aziz spoke into the phone. Mustafa had warned him not to engage in any conversation with who ever answered the phone, just to give the message. He knew he shouldn't have given him his name, but it had happened too fast.

"We have taken over Independence Mall. We have many hostages. We want America to understand that their liberty is meaningless to us and our intent is to destroy the symbols of this liberty, unless our demands are met in the next two hours. The seven political prisoners of Iranian descent who are to go on trial next week must be released from Fort Leavenworth and flown out of the country by private jet. The President of the United States must fully recognize the country of Iran as the national power it is and unfreeze all monetary assets belonging to it. Finally, the United States must denounce Israel and condemn all of it aggressive actions against its neighbors and must immediately insist Israel disarms. When all of these conditions are met, we will leave these facilities. At the end of two hours, if these demands are not met, we will execute hostages. Also, we have two wounded people whom you may come and retrieve in the next ten minutes. They are outside the door at Independence Hall and the Liberty Bell Center."

"Okay, Aziz, let's slow down a minute. How many hostages do you have?

"We have more than enough."

"That's not really helpful." The negotiator looked over to Choufani and Stan.

"It is not important for you to know."

"You understand this is going to take some time. Two hours is not enough time."

"Then hostages will start to be killed and blood will be on your hands."

"Come on, Aziz. You got to help me here."

Aziz hung up. How could Mustafa know the questions they would ask and what their responses would be? Aziz was, once again, impressed by the intelligence of his Uncle. Aziz was also proud of himself and felt he'd done well. He knew Mustafa would be proud.

"Well those are some demands," Stan said as he reviewed the list. Everyone was gathered around the conference table in the center of the room.

"He forgot to ask for lifetime tickets to the Super Bowl, though. The kid was definitely scripted. He knew just what to say. Not too much -- just enough to get their point across." Jordan had made some notes during the conversation.

Choufani was handed a message. "My officers confirm the two bodies outside. SWAT is getting ready to retrieve them, as we speak."

"Let's hope they'll be okay." Jordan always hated when innocents were caught up in these things. "So, he wouldn't tell us how many hostages." Looking over at the Rangers, Jordan asked. "Any idea how many people are usually in these areas at this time of day?"

"It's hard to tell," the Ranger who was the Homeland Security liason responded. "We had more people today because of the school holiday. My guess would be forty to fifty at the Constitution Center, fewer at the Visitors' Center and probably thirty in the LBC. Independence Hall is a little easier, because it's a timed entrance requiring a ticket. There would probably be twenty five people in there."

"How about staff?" Kate inquired.

"The largest staffs are in the Constitution Center and Independence Hall. At this time of day, you probably had fifteen in the Constitution Center, ten at Independence Hall and five to six each at LBC and the Visitor's Center."

"So, we're talking significant numbers. Smart move on their part to have them spread across the buildings. Not too large a number to be handled," Jordan opined.

"The even smarter move is in using kids," Choufani said. "You can take out adults all day and as long as you don't use excessive force, you'll probably be okay. But kids? That's a whole new ballgame." Choufani knew that, when the time came, it was going to be his decision. This wouldn't wait until the Commissioner or any of the other Commanders would return. Action would have to be taken soon. "We aren't going to have the manpower to take down all buildings simultaneously. We might be able to isolate two of the buildings as we take two down. Any thoughts?"

"Well, it seems the leader is in the LBC, so that might be where you need to start." Jordan was tracing over the map with his index finger as he talked. "The Constitution Center has the greatest number of people in it, so I think that should be the other priority. This map works, but it sure would be helpful to me to see the actual layout. Can we get access to the roof?"

"Yes. We have a sniper team up there now. The advantage we get with them having their windows covered is they can't see what we're doing."

"Kate, where's Akmed?" Jordan wondered.

Kate was hesitant to respond.

Stan, saw the potential issue, jumped in. "Jordan, why don't you and Kate go up to the roof and scout it out with the Commander's men and, if you and I could find a quiet place, Commander, I need to brief you on a couple of things that may impact this operation." Stan grabbed Choufani's arm.

Choufani gave him the typical local cop dealing with a Fed look. "I'm all ears. I think there's a conference room over there where we can discuss this."

Stan and Choufani walked into the conference room. Stan shut the door. "The owner of the hardware store is in our custody. He has been our informant and we had to extract him to protect him. Kate couldn't afford to stay in the store and had no idea that Benny, the employee, was under the control of Mustafa. I'm not sure how much help Akmed, the informant, would be to us, but the boy he raised for this mission is the one who was on the phone. Commander, I'm offering you Akmed if you think it might be an asset to your efforts. However, you must understand we made a deal with him and he'll disappear after today."

Choufani looked at Stan. He had no ideas of all the layers that were beneath this incident, nor did he have the time to delve into all of them. The decision Choufani had to make dealt with trusting this legendary Fed and his team or going it alone. "Stan, we've got a big problem here and I think we could benefit from your help and assistance. Let's figure out the best way we can use Akmed, if at all. I want you and your team to have any resources you need. I need your input and advice." Choufani stuck out his hand to shake Stan's. "I have one condition though."

Stan looked at Choufani, not sure what to expect.

"When this is all over, you're going to take me to Barclay's Prime and buy me the biggest steak dinner they have and tell me the whole story."

Stan broke out into a big smile. "You bet, partner. Believe you me it's a dog gone good story. Now, let's go get this taken care of and wrangle up these kids."

Chapter Sixty-Seven

✤ ✤ ✤

CONSTITUTION CENTER-INDEPENDENCE NATIONAL PARK

Jon Halloran scanned the room and located where each of the children was positioned. It was hard for him to believe that a group of kids -- some not even teenagers -- had successfully taken over the Constitution Center. They were well trained and disciplined and demonstrated that this wasn't some last minute effort, but carefully planned. What had transpired was a classic siege strategy to which the kids had quickly adjusted when some of the hostages had resisted. Situations such as this were Halloran's business, but usually from the outside looking in, since he was a Special Ops officer, and reassured himself that, for every plan, there was a counter. He attempted to find the counter that he and his men could exploit as he sat on the floor, hands bound behind him.

Jon and three of his men had just instructed a survival school at McGuire Air Force Base in New Jersey. On the way back to their home base in Virginia, they had decided to spend a day in Philadelphia and visit Independence Park. They had just entered the Constitution Center, en route to the theater for the next show, when the students took over.

At first, Jon and his men had stayed together and could whisper to one another. When the larger group was broken up, Jon had quickly instructed his men to split up and try to be in each group. They found that, once the groups were moved, each one of them could maintain sight of at least one other soldier in another group. They all had been well trained in the art of signaling each other without others being able to tell, so they could maintain communication. They searched for patterns the children might demonstrate that the soldiers could subsequently exploit in order to get the hostages out of the building. They had already determined there were more than enough exits to rapidly evacuate the forty-five hostages. All Jon

Halloran and his men needed to figure out was the best way to get people to follow them. They weren't in uniform, so nothing gave them away as military, but training and experience had taught Halloran and his comrades that people could be reluctant to act quickly when they have been told to sit still and had seen their captors with guns.

As time wore on, the team began to notice the children had lost their discipline. The kids weren't paying as much attention to the hostages and some were even involved with the interactive learning systems found throughout the center. The leader didn't move around as much as he had earlier and was seated at the membership desk. His view was obstructed and would impact his ability to react.

Jon had to weigh when exactly they should move. Conditions had improved their chance for success and he wasn't sure how much longer those conditions would last. In the past, he'd found these things worked in cycles, that the terrorists would slack off for a while, only to tighten up the control. Then, over time it would lessen again. The key was trying to determine when control was at its weakest, prior to returning to strength.

Jon's team constantly gave him input and he began to feel they were close to the point where he needed to act. So, he did a quick survey of the room and felt they were probably in the best situation they could expect. He decided they were at the point of no return, so he signaled his man closest to him that they would move in five minutes and watched as the man relayed the message to the next man closest to him.

Chapter Sixty-Eight

Mustafa moved through the building, until he found the door he needed. The door had a special lock for controlled access, but he had found out by accident the master key he'd been provided opened this door. On several occasions, after he'd first been promoted to this job, he would sneak in after hours. While many parts of this facility operated twenty-four hours a day, this area was on a day schedule only. Security was not aware that Mustafa had access since they would always escort his team into the room for it to be cleaned and stay with them until it was done. To Mustafa, this seemed like a work room, since it was full of tools and metal working equipment. He couldn't understand its importance until he began having conversations with Jerome. Through those conversations, he began to understand that this was the most important room in the entire building and the people who worked in this room were the greatest prize of all.

For months, Mustafa planned on how to get both the critical contents of the room and its occupants out of the secure building with its numerous guard stations, locked doors and cameras at every conceivable point in and outside of the building. Mustafa's work in the building took on a new dimension in regards to how to foil all these systems without raising any alarm. For months, he focused on how to disable the systems and figure out how he could rob the place at night. He fell short. He then thought through a plan in which he would pilfer the things Jerome wanted over time, hoping no one would notice. Again, he couldn't make the plan work.

The more he worked in the facility, the more he begun to understand how it really operated. As he got to know people, rules became less enforced. He was able to walk into the building without the guard physically taking his ID to check its validity. Doors which, in the past, he would have to call to have opened were now unlocked as he approached. The seeds were planted as to how he might be able to do what Jerome wanted him to do -- and right under the all-seeing eyes of security.

His next stroke of genius came to him when there was a lock down drill one day while he was on the premises. He noticed that his role allowed him the ability to continue to move around the building and not get stopped or ordered into a specific area. The only obstacle he could find was the lack of ability to get outside, and possibly back in. The plan ultimately came together when he realized he could use his family's mission to create a diversion.

So he continued to plan and work with the children, but he subtly changed the training, so the children's chance of success diminished and the opportunity for their mission to dissolve into chaos was almost ensured. With bedlam happening across the street, it would more than ensure Mustafa's success in his new mission.

As he walked down the hallway, Mustafa was pleased his men were already at the door, with their carts. They stood in a formation Mustafa had developed, effectively blocking the camera view in the hallway. The camera had been placed to view the door, but also scan down the corridor. Mustafa believed because the door was secured and only a few senior people supposedly had a key, security had assumed the proper precautions had been taken and didn't need to have a backup. While the security team would see Mustafa and his men at the door, the security people's vision would be sufficiently obscured that they couldn't be certain if Mustafa and his men had the proper escort. However, since Mustafa had his key and they would see the door open and the group enter, Mustafa was hoping they would make the assumption, however wrong, that he and his men were indeed under escort.

Mustafa approached the door and inserted his key. There was an ongoing program to change the locks on these secure doors and issue new keys, and, if that had happened since the last time he'd been in the room, his key would no longer work. He turned it and felt the tumblers in the lock turn and heard the subtle click as the lock tongue retracted into the door. He opened the door and waved his men in with their carts.

Inside, the employees looked up and, saw it was the cleaning crew, returned to their work. No one noticed the lack of an escort and they seemed oblivious to the lock down as they continued to focus on their tasks.

"What's going on?" one of the workers shouted as he noticed the four men who had just entered the room donned gas masks.

"Mustafa? What's happening?" another asked as the men dug into their carts and extracted their sub machine guns.

One of Mustafa's crew grabbed a gasket-like rubber tube and stuffed it around the frame of the door sealing, all of gaps. At the same time, the other two crew members retrieved gas grenades, pulled the pins and flung them to the floor, releasing a fentanyl derivative, a gas of the type utilized by the Russian Federal Security Service in counter-terrorist operations.

As if a switch had been pulled which deactivated them, each of the workers collapsed, and fell unconscious to the floor. Mustafa and his crew quickly worked to secure the unconscious six men and one woman who worked in the room. They bound them with Flex-cuffs and placed hoods over their heads. One by one, the seven were lifted into the carts that had been rolled into the room. In the carts were bags of used rags and clothes from the production department and they reeked of oil, grease and other solvents and chemicals used in the various processes underway in the building. They opened the bags and would have gagged from the stench had they not still had on their masks. Mustafa and his men covered the bodies with the rags. There was a chance one or more of the unconscious persons might begin to vomit and choke, but there was no way around that.

Mustafa looked at his watch. It would be fifteen minutes before the air was clear and they could breathe without the masks. Fortunately, the room had a sophisticated filtration system, which rapidly drew the existing air out of the room and replaced it with clean, filtered air, critical to the work done in the room.

In the meantime, he identified the shelves containing the items they would be removing on their second trip to the room. The metal dies were small, but heavy, and surprisingly for something made out of steel, they tended to be somewhat fragile. If any of the dies sustained damage during the operation, they would be unusable and worthless to Jerome – and cost Mustafa a portion of the money he'd been promised.

Mustafa had the men open up two bags they had brought into the room in their carts. These bags contained clean, fresh white cloths. They were of fine material and Mustafa had been told on several occasions that it was one of the most expensive items used in the facility. It had taken months for him to collect enough pieces for this day. He directed each of his men to wrap the selected plates in the clothes and stack them on one of the tables. This would allow the plates to be retrieved more quickly when Mustafa and his men returned.

Mustafa looked at the sensor he'd brought with him, checking air quality. It revealed that the air in the room was breathable. He instructed one of the men to take off his mask and, though the man at first hesitated, he did as told. Mustafa wasn't about to blow the mission because the sensor gave a bad reading. Better to lose one man than the entire team. The man breathed in and out several times and, seeing no ill effects, Mustafa removed his mask and directed the others to do so as well.

"Let's go! Grab your carts and let's head to the exit. When we get to the guard, let me do all the talking. You just stand by your carts and, if necessary, have your guns ready. If he goes to check in any of the carts, we will have to eliminate him. Let me attempt to do it, but if I should fail one of you must be successful. We want to do it without making a lot of noise. You all know how to kill without a gun. That is what you must do."

Every man motioned his agreement. They grabbed their cart and moved toward the door. The carts were heavy with the weight of the bodies.

Mustafa opened the door and they moved out into the hallway. As they moved in single file down the corridor, Mustafa in the lead, the security cameras would see a completely normal image. They had made this a part of their routine, to move down this hallway together at least three times a week. To any of the guards, this activity would resemble their normal behavior and only up close would someone notice the men were straining more than usual to move their heavy carts.

They turned the corner and headed toward the exit. The guard at the door looked at them. Mustafa made eye contact with Johnny. Maybe this was Mustafa's lucky day. Johnny was the guard Mustafa had the best relationship and, every time Johnny saw Mustafa, he would stop to talk. He always had questions about Mustafa's background and what Iran had been like when Mustafa lived there. Mustafa hoped the relationship would pay off in the next few minutes.

"Hey, Mustafa. What are you guys up to?" Johnny called out. He stuck his hand out to shake Mustafa's.

Mustafa grinned and took the hand. "Hey, Johnny. We're just finishing up collecting all the rags that need to go back to be cleaned. We just need to get them out to our trucks."

"Can't really let you go out. You know we're in lock down."

"Yes, we know, but our trucks are right outside. We really aren't leaving the grounds. You can watch us the whole time."

"I know, but we're not supposed to open the door for anything."

"Yeah, well, I guess we could just leave our carts here for now and do it later."

Johnny was about to agree when he obviously caught the odor of the rags, which permeated the small corridor.

"Wow, I never realized how much those things stunk!" Johnny exclaimed and turned his head to try to find fresh air. "Don't you have somewhere else you can leave them?"

"Not really. You know, we're supposed to get them out of the building as soon as we collect them, due to the fire hazard, of just having them in these carts. The only place to safely leave them would be as close to the exit as possible."

"Oh no, you can't keep them here. Let me call and see if they will let you out. Hold on." Johnny walked over to the phone on the wall and punched in a three digit extension. "This is Johnny at the interior dock. I got Mustafa from the cleaning service here needing to remove the soiled rags. His vans are right at the dock. Can I let him out to just load these carts in?" Johnny listened and then cupped his hand over the mouthpiece. He looked at Mustafa. "You're not leaving, right? Just going to load the trucks and come back in."

"That's right," Mustafa nodded.

Johnny repeated it into the phone. "They really stink big time, sir. It's gonna be tough to leave them sitting down here. Okay.. Thank you." Johnny hung up the phone and turned back to Mustafa and his group. "They said I can let you out, but only to load the van. None of the vans can leave and you all have to come back in when you're done. Got it?"

"Not a problem, Johnny. We've got more work to do before we can call it a day, anyway. Thanks for helping us." Mustafa moved toward the door.

Johnny held up his hand. Mustafa froze, thinking Johnny was going to look through the carts. Mustafa could see each of his men tense.

"I've got to call the guard shack and let them know you're going to be coming out. They'd freak if you just walked out the door now." Johnny picked up the phone and dialed a different three digit extension. "Hey, Phil. I'm going to be opening the door. Mustafa and his team are coming out to load carts of rags into their vans, but no one is leaving. They come right back in. I cleared it with upstairs. Okay. Thanks. They'll be coming out now." Johnny hung up the phone and nodded to Mustafa. He pressed a button and Mustafa could hear the sound of the door unlock.

"Thanks, Johnny." Mustafa signaled his men to move through the doorway. They quickly loaded the carts into two of the vans. Within a matter of five minutes, they were back inside and headed to various parts of the building to get the additional carts they would need. In fifteen minutes, the guards would rotate and a different one would be seated at the console, monitoring the camera in the hallway next to the room they would re-enter. From the guard's perspective, it would be assumed this was the cleaning crew going in to clean. The guard would have no idea this was their second visit.

Chapter Sixty-Nine

Jordan and Kate stepped onto the roof of the Federal Building and walked over to where the sniper team was posted. They flipped their IDs to the sniper's spotter, the man's eyes had followed them since they stepped out of the doorway.

"Any movement in any of the buildings?" Jordan knelt down next to the sniper. "I'm Jordan, this is Kate. We've been in the command center, but wanted to get a look around."

"No, sir. Nothing is moving out there," the attractive blond informed them. "They haven't even been in the tower of Independence Hall. Doesn't make a lot of sense to me. If I were in their shoes, that would be the first place I would have someone. You've got a bird's eye view of the whole Mall. Nothing could move without you seeing it. Like I said, sir, doesn't make much sense, given some of the other things they've done."

Jordan stood up and walked over to Kate, who stood at the low wall which surrounded the edge of the roof. She looked out over the Mall area.

"I can't believe you've never been here before. The birth place of our country, every American should have to come here." Jordan stared directly into Kate's eyes. This was the first time they had been somewhat alone. He felt the urge to take her into his arms, but knew that wouldn't be well received by the sniper team on the roof with them.

"So, tell me again what each of these buildings are?" Kate asked Jordan, turning away as she felt his eyes on her.

"Well, if you look to your right, the building at the Southern end is Independence Hall. That's where they signed the Declaration of Independence and created the Constitution. The building in the next block heading north -- the rectangular one -- is the Liberty Bell Center. They moved the Liberty Bell into there in 2003. That's where Aziz is with his group. In the next block, you have the Visitors' Center. Right in front of us is the Constitution Center. It opened on July 4th 2003. It's got a great interactive media show at the beginning. Maybe I'll take you to see it sometime."

Kate gave him a look. "I'm still waiting for the dinner you promised me."

"Come on. A little something came up, right?"

"I'm just saying, I'm looking forward to some follow through."

"Okay, I get it."

"So, smart man, what's the big building over there?" Kate was pointing with one hand while she held her binoculars up to her eyes with the other, to the Northeast of their location, past the Constitution Center. It was a massive structure filling up the entire block on all sides. It was a plain concrete structure with minimal windows. It seemed extremely out of place, next to the stately buildings on the Mall.

"That would be the US Mint."

"Kind of ugly, isn't it?"

"Well, I think it's designed more for function than beauty."

"They make all the money there?"

"Just the coins are done at the Mints. The bills are done in D.C. and Fort Worth."

"You're always a wealth of knowledge," Kate proclaimed with a smile.

"Yes. Yes. My mind is full of useless information."

Kate continued to scan the Mint building. "Jordan. Look at those vans. To the left of the Mint, in the loading dock area."

Jordan picked up his 10X50s and scanned, the spot where Kate pointed. He saw a plain white van. "I see a van with no markings. Is that the one you're talking about?"

"Keep moving to your left." Kate didn't move her head and waited for Jordan to see what she'd found.

Jordan scanned to the left and saw two more vans. Each had a magnetic sign attached to their door. The signs read, "City of Brotherly Love Cleaning Service." Jordan lowered his binoculars. "Shit! You think those are the same vans?"

"Could be. You never know with white vans."

"Yeah, but Mustafa's was painted with the name, not a magnetic sign."

"Right. But, remember, Mustafa dropped that van off at his office. Maybe he got another van and drove it here. The first one with no markings looks new, anyway."

"It is. I can see the temporary tag in the rear door window!" Jordan lowered the binoculars, letting them hang on their strap around his neck.

"Hey?" he asked the sniper team. "You guys have anyone over by the mint?"

"I'm not sure. I know they're in lockdown," the blonde answered. "We didn't put a sniper over there because we found, in the past, the building just isn't built in a way that would give us a good position."

"Jordan, look at this." Kate called.

Jordan turned back and brought his glasses up. "I don't see anything."

"Look behind the vans, at the open door."

"I don't believe it. Speak of the devil. What is he doing? You can't tell me he dropped these kids off and went to work."

"No, I don't think so. Remember what that building is. Could it be part of the plan?"

"Well, I can't believe they could get out of the Mint with carts full of coins without being stopped."

"No way!" The spotter interjected. "I've got a brother with the Federal Protection Service. We laugh about them going into lockdown, because that place is so secure all the time. If they're bringing something out, it's probably been checked and searched two, maybe three times."

"Thanks," Jordan told the spotter. "That's helpful. I think we should go pay a visit to the Mint."

Kate and Jordan moved away from the edge of the roof, toward the stairway access door.

"Are you going to stop by the Command Center and tell Stan?"

"I don't want to waste time. We need to find out what's going on over there and quickly. They may be loading up and going. They know they can't go back to Mustafa's house, so they're going somewhere else."

Jordan reached out to grab the doorknob.

"What the hell!" The spotter called out. Grabbing his radio, he keyed the mike. "We've got people moving out of the Constitution Center. They're exiting through several doors on the west side of the building. Tac One, are you seeing this? Over."

Jordan and Kate ran over to the side of the roof by the sniper team. Though the building was in the same block they were, they each grabbed their binoculars.

"I've got multiple targets at the door." The sniper called out.

"Confirm." The spotter acknowledged.

"Careful, they aren't kids at the doors. They may be Good Sams!" Jordan yelled out, "Sams" referring to Samaritans who might have helped facilitate the escape. Jordan continued to scan from door to door, focusing on the men holding the doors helping others to escape.

Police officers on the street were coming forward with guns drawn, herding the hostages out of harm's way but keeping them together. One lesson learned over the years was how terrorists had used mass releases of hostages as a way to facilitate their own escapes. They would run out with the rest of the crowd and quickly disappear. It became S.O.P. for Police to keep everyone together and release no one until identities were verified.

"Those guys at the door are trained. I think they're Special Ops," Jordan said.

"Are you providing confirmation, sir?" The sniper queried.

"Not at this point. It's just a hunch. Wait! Yes, confirmation! I know one of them. Definitely Special Ops." Jordan eyes were focused on Jon Halloren, a former colleague from previous missions.

"We have confirmation the men at the door are Special Ops," the spotter said into his radio. "I repeat. Confirmation men at door are Special Ops. Stand down when hostages secure."

"Jon, you son of a gun. You turn up in the strangest places," Jordan said under his breath.

"You know him?" Kate was by his side as both were watching the men being escorted away from the building by the police.

"Yeah, we've done some ops together in the past. If you were ever in a hostage situation, he's the guy you want to have in the room with you. He's top notch."

"Do you want to go down and talk with him?"

"I do, but I still think we need to get to the Mint. We'll call Max on our way down. Tell her what we saw and where we're going. Max and William both know Jon."

Chapter Seventy

❖ ❖ ❖

"Max, this is Jordan. Do you read?" Jordan called over their frequency.

"Go ahead, Jordan."

"Are you aware of what's going on at the Constitution Center? The hostages are coming out."

"Yes. We watched it up here."

"Did you see who brought them out?"

"Sure did. We're having him and his team brought up here. Are you still on the roof?"

"Negative. Kate and I are en route to the Mint. We saw Mustafa there and are going to go over and investigate. Could you call over and let them know we're coming?"

"Sure will. Keep us posted."

"Commander, do we have a line to the Mint from here?" Max asked.

"I believe we can call directly to their security center."

Stan walked over to Choufani. "It might expedite things, Sharif, if you made the call. I'd have to go through the crap about who I am and why I'm here. You can cut through that if you wouldn't mind."

"Not a problem. Lieutenant Hall, can you connect me to the security center in the Mint?"

The Lieutenant walked over to the phone and looked at the master list for the number.

"If I might suggest," Stan said to Choufani, "let's not tell them about Mustafa. If you would just tell them two agents are coming over and want to check some things, do you think that could get them in? I want to make sure we don't tip Mustafa off. I really want to catch him. My guess is the Mall is the diversion and the Mint is the target."

"Okay, I can do that. But I want to move some of my units closer as back up. Then, if something does start to go down, we can be on top of it."

"Sounds like a plan."

"I've got them on the line, Commander. It's a Captain Patterson, sir." The Lieutenant handed the phone to Choufani.

"Jim, Sharif Choufani here. Look, I've got two agents coming over there just to check things out. Could you have someone meet them and take them around?" Choufani was listening to the reply. "I realize you are on lock down, but we're facing something unique here on the Mall and we just want to cover all of our bases." Choufani again was listening. "Thanks, Jim. It's an Agent Jordan Wright and Agent Kate Woolrich. Two of the best and they're on loan to us from the Feds, but we've turned them into Philadelphians." Choufani laughed and hung up the phone. He looked at Stan. "They're in. Patterson will meet them at the main entrance. Remember that steak dinner you're buying me?"

Stan nodded.

"I think you owe me another."

"Not a problem. My pleasure." Stan slapped Choufani on the back, startling him. "I'll let Jordan know."

Chapter Seventy-One

✠ ✠ ✠

"I have a problem. I have a problem! Aziz! I need help! Help me!"

Aziz heard the voice over his radio. At first, he wasn't sure whose it was. Why had someone broken the rules and used Aziz's name? He keyed his radio. "This is one. Who is this?

"Aziz, this is Parijan. Our hostages are leaving. They are running out the door. What do we do?"

Aziz couldn't believe what he was hearing. He knew Parijan was a member of the team at the Constitution Center, but, where was the leader, Soroush, number four on their call signs. He knew Parijan wouldn't know the codes, so Aziz had to respond and find out what exactly had happened. "Okay Parijan, first tell me what happened to Soroush."

"There were men here, amongst the hostages. One of them said he needed to go to the bathroom. We were taking him, but as we walked by the desk where Soroush was seated, this man jumped and grabbed Soroush and hurt him. Soroush is unconscious. He may be dead!"

Aziz sighed. This was not good. To Aziz, it sounded like Soroush had gotten sloppy. "Parijan, tell me what happened next."

"More men got up from the group. Two of them charged Naseem and knocked him out. After that, they yelled at the other hostages to move and they ran to the emergency exit doors. Before we could do anything they were gone. They're all gone Aziz! What do we do?"

Only Naseem and Soroush had guns and it sounded like the men who had attacked them got the guns. With all the hostages gone, it would only be a matter of minutes before the SWAT team would try to breech the building. There was little Aziz could do for his cousins at this point. Perhaps he could use the distraction to his advantage. He just needed to think. "Parijan, take everyone and go to the center of the building, away from any of the doors, and barricade yourselves in a room with no windows, if possible. We will try to come get you later. You have nothing to fear."

"Yes, Aziz. That is what we will do."

Aziz knew that he could never go rescue them. There wasn't any more he could do, but he hoped by them doing what he asked it would delay the

SWAT team in their effort to take control of the building. Aziz needed to determine his own action.

"Number one, this is three."

"Go ahead three." Three was the leader in the Visitors' Center, the building adjacent to the Constitution Center. Aziz was guessing they had seen what was taking place next door.

"What are we going to do, one? This is bad. My team saw the hostages leave. They know the police will enter there soon. What's our plan? What are you going to do?"

The last thing Aziz needed now was for another one of his leaders and their team to be in a panic. This had gone from bad to worse, faster than he'd anticipated.

"Three, nothing has changed. Stay on task. Team four made some mistakes. Keep your team focused. Take nothing for granted."

"Yes one, but this wasn't supposed to happen. Mustafa said we would be in control and the enemies of Islam would try nothing."

"They haven't tried anything. Team four messed up. Make sure you team doesn't do the same. One, out." Aziz couldn't waste time with this conversation. He had to figure out his next steps. Mustafa was to have called forty minutes ago and he still hadn't. Aziz wasn't sure what that meant, but it was unlike Mustafa to not do something he said he would. Aziz walked to the far end of the building, facing north. He moved the canvas out of the way, so he could look down the Mall. He could see the eastern part of the Constitution Center that wasn't blocked by the Visitor's Center, which was located directly between them. He didn't like what he saw.

Aziz could see police units had surrounded the entrance. The police would move in a matter of minutes to capture the team and the team wouldn't be able to hold out for long. The men who initiated the escape had more than likely told the police that they didn't believe there were any more weapons, and since Soroush and Naseem knew how to arm the explosives, they had decided only to arm them at a later point to ensure none of them went off prematurely. He really hoped Mustafa would call since he needed his advice. They had never planned for this happening.

"One! One! This is three. We've got a problem."

What could it be now, Aziz wondered as he turned away from the window?

Chapter Seventy-Two

Mustafa and his team were back at the secured door, just as they had been earlier. He assumed the guards had rotated and someone else would monitor the camera as he inserted his key and opened the door. They quickly moved inside and packed the cloth wrapped dies they had earlier pulled off the shelf. In the Engraver's room of the U.S. Mint, a team of men and women designed, carved and manufactured the dies that stamped the coinage for the United States Monetary system. With these dies and the ability to purchase the right metals, one could duplicate the coins used everyday. Flooding the market with excess coins could have a devastating effect on the economy.

The attempt had been made in the past to either counterfeit or steal the printing plates for the paper currency used in The United States. But, with the advent of the new designs for the major bills, it had become almost impossible to pull off credible bill duplication in the numbers necessary to cause a problem.

Coinage in the United States had not dramatically changed in years. It was such a standard and people were so used to it, even efforts to introduce new coins -- such as the Sacagawea dollar coin -- had failed to be adopted by the American public. Merchants didn't inspect counterfeit coins, as they did with currency. When Jerome first told Mustafa what he wanted, Mustafa had laughed and thought Jerome was crazy. After he heard the entire plan, Mustafa found Jerome a genius since according to Jerome, there were many places in the world where he could set up shop and mint coins without any interference. He'd also figured out an ingenious way to get the coins back into the U.S. Everything was focused on dirty bombs and drugs at ports of entry.

Mustafa would be a rich man by the end of the day. He just needed to deliver the dies and the engravers to Jerome and the Cayman Islands bank account he'd opened would be filled. It would be enough to last a life time when he included the money he'd held back from the Iranians when he'd decided to switch masters. Life would be good.

"Everything is packed, Mustafa. We're ready to go when you are."

The shelves were nearly empty and the carts were even heavier. After they placed the various dies in the carts, the men had opened up more bags of dirty rags to throw over the top and fill the carts.

Mustafa inspected the room carefully, to ensure they hadn't left anything. He looked at each of the carts and made sure nothing was visible that would give them away. "Okay, the plan is the same. We'll move toward the back door. Hopefully, we can get through the guard. It may still be Johnny. Those guards don't rotate as often but, this time though, when we go out the door, you will head toward the vans. I'll stay on the dock. When you have everything loaded, I'll take care of the guard and open the gate. We will have to move quickly and get out. Everyone has their route, so make sure you follow it. No mistakes, no changes and you must not stop anywhere."

They all muttered in the affirmative to Mustafa.

"Let's go."

He opened the door and the men moved their carts out to the corridor. They didn't encounter anyone and as they rounded the last corner, Mustafa saw that Johnny was still at his post.

"Hi, Johnny! This is our last load. Okay for us to go out, like last time?"

"I don't know, Mustafa; I didn't know you had another trip to make. We're still in lock down."

"I understand. We can leave them here and get them later, if you want us to. I just don't want you to have to deal with the odor."

"I know. I know. It's just that a couple of Federal Agents just showed up and wanted to look around. I don't want them to come by while I've let you out. You know what I mean."

"I see." Mustafa tried to keep his composure. What did it mean that agents had come there? Maybe nothing, but it would be best for Mustafa and his men to get out immediately. "We'd just be a minute."

"I don't know, Mustafa. If it was up to me, I'd let you."

"Well, what if we just rolled the carts out and put them on the dock. We won't load the vans."

"Hey, that's an idea. That will only take a minute, won't it?"

"Sure. We'll be out and back in before you know it."

Johnny grabbed the phone and called out to the guard shack. "They've got more carts to bring out." Johnny hung up the phone. "Okay, but be quick about it."

"Thanks, Johnny."

Johnny opened the door. Mustafa walked out and guided the men, as if he were going to show them where to place the carts. When they were out and Johnny closed the security door, Mustafa pointed his men to the vans. "Be quick."

The other guard walked out the doorway of the shack. "How are you, Mustafa? Looks like the SWAT team just went into the Constitution Center. This might all be over soon."

Mustafa almost lost his composure. He looked out across the Mall and saw the police had moved in and around the building on the Mall. He didn't know what could have happened and how it had happened so quickly. "Did they go in and get the hostages?"

"No, the hostages came out about fifteen minutes ago. It looks like they escaped."

"Really?"

"Yep, now they're just going in to get whoever was holding them. Maybe I'll get home for supper."

"Yes, maybe you will." Mustafa glanced over at his men. The last of the carts was being rolled into the vans. "Well, that should about do it." Mustafa reached into his jacket for the small stun gun, drew it, fired, hitting the guard's neck and worked the trigger.

"What the ...," the guard gasped as he fell into a crumpled heap. His body convulsed with each pull of the trigger.

Mustafa didn't even wait for him to hit the ground as he stuck his hand inside the guard booth and hit the button to open the gate. The vans had already started to move forward. He turned and leaped off the dock and ran to his van. One of the men had already started it. He threw it into drive and quickly moved through the gate, as it began to close. As he headed out, Mustafa took one last look at the Constitution Center, only to see the SWAT Team emerge with the children.

Chapter Seventy-Three

Chaos reigned in the Independence Mall Visitor's Center. It wasn't the hostages who created the havoc, but the hostage takers. They had witnessed what had happened in the building next to them -- the hostages escape and when the SWAT Teams had entered the building -- panic had set in among the children.

Everyone spoke at once. "What are we going to do?"

"It's only a matter of time before they come here!"

"We need to leave now. This wasn't the plan."

The leader, who had the radio call sign "Three," walked over to the group of children. He wasn't sure what had happened either, but he wasn't about to allow his team to panic and create more problems.

"I need all of you to listen to me! This is not over. I don't know what happened at the Constitution Center. They made mistakes and they are now paying for them. Let's make sure we don't make the same mistakes. We still have control of the other three buildings. Aziz is still leading us. We will succeed."

"We don't agree, Feroz. The situation is changing," one of the boys challenged. "Look at the power they have. They aren't afraid of us, as Mustafa told us they would be. They don't care that we're children. They only see us as terrorists."

"I don't agree," Feroz interrupted. "They made mistakes. They let their hostages get away. We still have ours."

"But what's to stop them from doing the same thing? We only have two guns. The male hostages are bigger than most of us. Lucky for us they didn't see what happened." Omid interjected, the oldest female in the group.

"We're better organized. If we stick together, we will be fine. Uncle Mustafa told us what we need to do. We stick to the plan, until Aziz or Mustafa tells us differently." Feroz countered

"I don't agree. If we stay we will die or be captured. I think we should leave now." Nouri joined the conversation.

"How would we do that?" Feroz demanded. "If we walk outside, we will be captured. They will know we're kids. We can't just walk out."

"We can go out through the underground parking garage. Remember, we saw it on the plans where we first were told of the mission. We can go down there and as the hostages leave, we can use the distraction to run out of the garage and away. Once they have the hostages, they might not worry about finding us." Nouri pointed to the door leading to the garage.

"I doubt that. They will keep looking until they find us," Feroz advised.

"Either way, we're captured. Going to the garage gives us a chance." Omid pleaded.

Feroz had had enough of this. "I'm in charge. We stay here and complete what we have been trained to do."

One of the older boys came up to Feroz. "Maybe you shouldn't be in charge any longer. I think one of us should take over." Sanjar stood face to face against Feroz.

"That's not the plan!"

"We need a new plan." Sanjar countered.

"Yeah, let's vote on it." Nouri moved over and stood by Sanjar.

Feroz was beside himself. "We aren't going to vote on anything. We do what I say we do."

"Not anymore." The voice came from behind Feroz. It was Payam, Feroz's second in command. "Things have changed, my cousin. We need a new plan. I believe we should leave. I'll take those that want to go with me. If you wish to stay, you can remain with anyone else who wants to stay. I don't think many will."

"I can't believe you would do this to me! We have been through so much!" Feroz insisted. "We can still succeed!"

"No, we won't be successful. Where is Uncle Mustafa? Ask Aziz if he has heard from him. I suspect he hasn't. We have been left here," Payam declared.

"No. No! Uncle would not do that! He has too much invested in this. He wants it to succeed."

"He dropped us off. That was never part of the plan. He never told us he would leave us. He hasn't come back. He's done something else." By this point, all of the children had gathered around Feroz and Payam. Those that didn't understand what had happened either quickly figured it out or quietly asked one of the older children. "Who wants to leave with me?"

Payam turned and put his arm up in the air to signal others who wanted to leave with him to do the same.

Only Feroz and two others didn't raise a hand.

"I'm going, Feroz, and these cousins seem to want to come with me. Everyone who's going with me go over by the door." He turned and pointed to an access door that was marked "PARKING."

"This is a mistake, Payam." Feroz grabbed his radio. "One! One! This is three. We've got a problem."

"This is One. What's the problem, three."

"Most of my team wishes to leave.'

Aziz couldn't believe it. What was going on? "Three, they can't leave. They must stay until we're directed to leave."

"I've told them. But they are ready to leave. There will only be three of us left. I don't think I can keep them here."

"You must!"

"We're leaving now, Aziz!" Payam had grabbed the radio from Aziz. "This is over. We're heading out." Payam threw the radio down. It broke into pieces, the batteries skittered across the floor.

Payam returned to the group. He opened the door and the group moved down the stairway and into the garage.

Feroz stared at the broken radio. The second radio had stopped working about an hour ago. He had no way to communicate with Aziz. He knew the only way to save himself and the other two who had stayed with him was to end this. He walked over to the main entrance door and undid the chains. He opened the door slightly and gestured for the hostages to leave. He knew what he had to do. He grabbed his gun and walked to the center of the building.

Chapter Seventy-Four

✤ ✤ ✤

"I can't believe a bunch of kids did this. Who would have ever thought?" Jon Halleron, his team with him in the Command Center, told Stan and Max.

"I know we couldn't believe it when one of the fathers first told us the story. It's been in planning since the oldest kids were infants." Max related what they knew to give Jon and his team the context of the situation. In most hostage incident, one didn't have the opportunity to have someone on the inside that was trained to understand terrorist behavior. "Iran definitely decided to take the long term view."

"However, I'll tell you, for the amount of training it seems they had and their indoctrination, they didn't exhibit the level of discipline I would have expected. Matter of fact, based on what you just told us, I would say they were sloppy. It's possible you can exploit that element with the remaining teams," Jon suggested.

Stan had called Jon's commanding officer and apprised him of the situation. Stan got the reply he'd hoped for and Jon's team was ordered to assist in any way possible. Choufani's group had of secured the proper gear for the team, along with credentials which would allow them access throughout the Federal Building and all of the secured sites that surrounded the Mall.

"The Constitution Center is secure," one of the officers in the Command Center reported. "They have seven in custody, all kids. They'll be bringing them out in ten minutes."

"Great news!" Choufani walked over to where the officer was seated. "Tell the team great work."

"Will do, sir."

"One down, three to go," Choufani stated as he walked over to where Stan and the Special Ops team were talking.

"Once they sensed resistance, everything just broke down. The Leaders were easy to identify and take out. We only saw two guns and two radios.

When we had the two armed kids out of commission, the rest just stood around. The evacuation was easy." Jon wrappedg up his briefing.

"How do you think they would respond in a SWAT Team breach?"

"If you didn't have the leaders identified prior to the breach, you could have some problems. I'm not convinced they wouldn't shoot a hostage. There was no effort to communicate, so no bonds were being built."

"But, I don't think they're expecting a breech," one of Jon's men chimed in. "I think they've been led to believe that, because they're kids, the police won't try to come in. You know, don't want pictures of the big bad SWAT Team taking out thirteen-year- olds. I think they're betting on that. All you might have to do is let them think you are coming in and it might cause the breakdown in their structure. It fell apart immediately when we began our action. Frankly, we could have just walked out and not had any resistance from the kids."

"That's an interesting theory. If we thought that might work, maybe we could use uniformed officers instead of SWAT." Choufani mulled over what he had heard and thought out loud. The more he got to know Stan and his team, the more he was glad they were on site.

"It could work," Jon agreed. "I think any show of authority would work. Your risk is low with only two guns. We got a quick look at the explosives and, at least from where we were, I don't believe they had been armed yet. The kids may have been waiting for a signal."

"So, someone is directing this from outside. Aziz isn't in charge?" Another of Jon's men mused.

"Commander, we have something happening at the entrance to the Visitor's Center."

Choufani and the group walked back over to the monitors. "Can you bring it up here?"

"Yes, sir. Coming over now."

The screen flickered. The screen was split in thirds, three cameras showed the front and two side angles of the entrance. The door had been pushed slightly open, and left just enough room for someone to walk through. Nothing happened, just the door open but, in the next instant, the door flew open wide and people started poured out. Radios came alive, various personnel relayed what they saw.

"Looks like the hostages are getting out. Make sure we have people there to direct them to safety." Choufani commanded.

"Yes, sir. Units are moving in from the East and North."

"Sir, we've got something happening in the Parking Garage." The screen flickered and divided into fourths, adding a screen that showed the inside of a parking facility.

"Where is this?" Stan looked at Choufani.

"This is directly underneath the Visitor's Center."

The screen showed an individual who moved out of a doorway and cautiously moved into the garage, bent over, they used the cars as cover.

"Do we have anyone down there?"

"Yes, sir. We had a tactical team in the stairwell leading up to the Center. It's the same stairwell they are coming down. Our team was able to overhear a discussion about some of the kids leaving and that they were going to go through the garage. Our people moved out and redeployed to the garage."

"Good. How many men?"

"It's a team of three."

"Okay. Let's get some help over there as quickly as we can. Are they able to communicate?"

"Yes, sir."

"Tell them to take a position that will deny the children exit from the garage."

"Yes, sir."

"Sir?" Another officer looked at Choufani. "We have a report of gunfire coming from the Visitor's Center."

"Shit! Are there still hostages in there?"

"We aren't sure, but there can't be many. The hostages had stopped coming out and then there was a shot."

"Just one?"

"Yes, sir, single discharge." The Officer looked back at his screen. "Commander, look at the entrance."

A white piece of fabric was being waved from the doorway. "Tell our guys to approach with caution," Choufani directed. The tech repeated the order. Two Officers approached the door. Even with no audio, it was clear the Officers were demanding that whoever was waving the "flag" should exit the Center and come out onto the Mall. Two kids -- one probably eleven and the other perhaps fifteen -- walked out. They fell to the ground. The Officers ran up and patted both of them down and placed

handcuffs on them. Another team approached the doorway, and then proceeded inside.

Within a minute, word came on the radio. "We have one person inside
with a gunshot wound to the head. Looks like a suicide."

"Tell them to secure the building and particularly the access doors to
the garage. I don't want those kids to go back upstairs. As soon as that's
done, I want all of our resources deployed to the south of the Mall. We
need to end this and end it now." Choufani knew this could go two ways
and one way was really bad. "Stan I need your advice."

Chapter Seventy-Five

❖ ❖ ❖

"Captain Patterson, I'm Jordan Wright and this is Kate Woolrich. Thank you for allowing us to enter during your lock down and take a look around."

"Not a problem. When Commander Choufani needs something, I try to help," Patterson remarked, perfunctorily as he examined their credentials. "He and I worked some cases together a long time ago." Kate and Jordan shook hands with Patterson as he returned their I.D. "What exactly can I do for you?"

"Let me be straight with you," Jordan started.

"Straight's good," Patterson replied quickly.

Jordan was glad it came with a smile. "With all the activity on the Mall we just wanted to ensure the Mint wasn't a target. There are a lot of things that don't add up with what's going on over there. So, in looking around to see what could also be a target, you guys kind of stick out."

"Yeah, I'm sure we do," Patterson responded still giving Jordan and Kate the once over. "I can tell you this. We went into lock down within thirty minutes of when things started to happen on the Mall. Since that time, no one has gone in or out of the Mint."

Kate jumped in. "I'm not sure that's correct Captain."

Patterson went rigid, as he showed his displeasure with having his security questioned. He glared at Kate. "Come again?"

"We observed some men outside of the Mint in the loading dock area. They were placing large carts into vans."

"Then they couldn't have been in the Mint. They might have gotten caught out there when we went into lockdown."

"One of these men may be involved in what is happening on the Mall. We just wanted to see if you knew him or were aware of what they were doing at the Mint," Jordan interjected, to keep the conversation moving. He knew Kate would want to argue the point of who got outside.

"Do you have a name?"

"We do. Mustafa Alfani."

"He's the supervisor of the contract cleaning crew." Patterson interrupted. "He's worked here for four or five years. Everyone likes him and he keeps his people on their toes. Are you sure he might be involved?"

"We've had him under surveillance for the past week. He's absolutely connected. He may even be the mastermind. Do you know where we can find him?" Jordan queried.

"He's got an office here, but he's usually on the floor checking on his team. He's allowed to move around during the lockdown. I can call and have my guards find him."

"No, let's not alert anyone yet -- if you don't mind. Let's start at his office."

"Follow me." Patterson led them down the hallway. They turned right and entered a corridor with glass windows on both sides. The corridor was raised above a work floor which housed several large machines. Even with the thickness of the glass, the noise still penetrated and caused the floor to vibrate.

"This is the room where we produce the blanks on which the coins will later be stamped. These big machines take the sheets of metal -- whether nickel, copper or a combination -- and stamp out the right size. That's called a planchet. In other rooms, the planchets are heated to make them more malleable and then the go through a die machine that stamps the proper markings and symbols."

"Wow! This is incredible." Jordan looked around, out both sides of the window. "Hey, can I come back some day and get a tour?"

"Sure, but let's see how today goes first."

Kate was not as engrossed as Jordan. She turned to Patterson. "Is there anything done here that's not done at the other Mints."

"Well, let's see. We make all of the Purple Hearts and Bronze Stars here and nowhere else."

"I see." Kate was hoping there might be something that would make sense. She didn't think it was feasible Mustafa and his guys were going to make off with a lot of coins.

They continued to walk down the hall and -- suddenly -- Patterson stopped in his tracks. "There is something we do here and no where else. I should have thought of this sooner."

"What!" Kate and Jordan said the word almost in unison.

"This way!" Patterson turned and started a long-stride walk down another hallway. "The engravers -- it could be the engravers."

Jordan and Kate looked at each other. Neither had any idea to what Patterson was referring.

"We have the engravers. No one else does." He looked at Jordan and Kate and picked up on their perplexed look. "The dies that stamp the coins begin by being carved by hand. We have seven engravers here. They do all of the engraving and manufacturing of the dies. It's all done here. There are only seven because we've only found seven who can do it. It's intricate. It takes skills beyond engraving. They're masters!"

"Where are they?"

"They have a secured room in the rear of the Mint. Only five people have keys and access. Anyone else would need an escort."

"What about Mustafa?"

"He couldn't go in without one of my people. He would have to be escorted. The escort is supposed to stay with whoever enters until he or she leaves."

They rounded a corner and Patterson stopped in front of a wide steel door. He reached for his loop of keys. Hurriedly, he quickly sorted through them and brought one up to the lock, inserted and turned it. The click of the cylinders sound like the ticking of a grandfather clock.. Patterson pushed the door open.

No one was inside.

"Oh, my God!!!"

"They're gone?" Jordan already knew the answer as he quickly surveyed the room, all of its equipment and work stations.

Patterson had a shocked look on his face, one of impending doom "Yes, but that's not all. Most of the dies are gone, also." He went to the phone and dialed a three digit number. "This is Patterson. We've had a breach in the Engravers area. We need to find Mustafa and his cleaning crew. They may be armed and dangerous." He hung up the phone.

Jordan grabbed him and Kate. "We need to get out to the loading dock as quickly as we can."

"This way!" Patterson led them out the door and to the right. They maneuvered through a series of hallways, turned a corner and found a guard by an exit door.

Jordan was well turned around and didn't have a good sense of direction after the race through corridor after corridor, but he felt the door ahead must lead to the dock area.

Patterson focused on the guard. "Johnny, have you seen the cleaning crew? Did they get outside?"

Johnny hesitated, but the look on his face told them the answer.

"How long ago?" Patterson demanded.

"It was just to take their carts out, sir. Their coming right back in."

"Open the door, now," Patterson's shouted, his commanding tone further paralyzed the guard.

Kate saw the keys hanging on the guard's belt and grabbed them off. She tossed them to Patterson.

"Thanks." He mumbled as he fished out the right key. He kicked the door open and drew his pistol. He could see the outside guard incapacitated on the ground. He moved outside, followed by Jordan and Kate, Kate's Glock in both hands. They looked to their left and caught a glimpse of Mustafa as he jumped into the van. He was out the gate before any of them could take a clear shot.

"We need a car!" Jordan shouted.

"Mine's right there!" Patterson pointed over to a navy Crown Victoria. The three sprinted to it and jumped in. They were out the gate within twenty seconds of Mustafa, but it had given him enough time to elude them.

"Where would they go if you needed to get away quick?" Jordan asked, looking directly at Patterson.

"I know what I would do." He punched the accelerator and they headed north. They made a quick left and a block later a sharp right. Patterson pushed the accelerator to the floor and the car jumped up the ramp to the Ben Franklin Bridge.

"Both of you are Feds, right?" Patterson asked as he pushed the car up the bridge and changed lanes to pass slower cars.

"Yeah, why do you ask?" Jordan responded. He had his right hand planted securely on the dash as a brace against the inevitable crash he anticipated with Patterson's driving.

"Once we get on the other side of this bridge, we're in New Jersey. I don't want these guys not getting convicted because of a jurisdiction error."

"Not to worry! Our jurisdiction's got jurisdiction. Hey, Kate, call the command center and talk with Max and Stan. Tell 'em what's going on."

"I'm on it." Kate was thankful for the distraction since she'd been looking straight ahead and waited for Patterson's luck to run out as they hit something. She attempted to dial in the ever shifting car. On her third attempt, she completed the number.

Patterson turned to Jordan. "If we don't find them quick, we're going to have a real problem."

"How do you mean?" Jordan didn't take his eyes off the road and traffic ahead. He'd thought about closing his eyes, but decided he wanted to see what they would hit before they hit it.

"This road about two miles after the tolls splits off into about five different main roads. At that point they could have headed anywhere."

"Where's the toll booth?" Jordan asked, just as the booth appeared straight ahead. The toll lanes were old and narrow and there was no way Patterson was going to get through them at the speed at which he traveled. Jordan braced himself, with the anticipation of the application of the brakes at any second. It never happened.

"Holy, shit!" Jordan shouted as they rocketed toward the booths.

"Relax! We've got plenty of room." Patterson hit his siren to announce his approach. One lane of the ten lane toll plaza was open and Patterson aimed for it. There was only one problem. It was for traffic headed the opposite direction.

Jordan couldn't believe what was about to happen. He couldn't open his mouth to say a word. He just stared ahead, with the knowledge the end was coming. "Saint. Francis, protect us!" was his only thought.

Patterson pulled the car left, then recovered right. They were directly in line with the lane. The red light flashing above warned the lane was not to be entered and the wooden gate was down. Patterson pushed the accelerator to the floor and the Interceptor engine responded with a burst of power. They shot through the lane. As they cleared it both Patterson and Jordan saw the furniture delivery truck that bore down on them. Jordan finally closed his eyes.

Patterson yanked the steering wheel hard to the right, causing the Ford to fishtail back over into the proper driving lanes as the air horns on the truck blew their anger.

"Yeah, baby!" Patterson let out as they headed down I-676.

Jordan opened his eyes. The road directly in front of them was clear and the traffic ahead was headed in the same direction. Jordan looked at Patterson. He was ready to give him a piece of his mind, when he was interrupted.

"Here's what Max had to say." Kate spoke from the floor of the backseat. "The hostages are out of the Visitor's Center. They have most of the kids in the underground parking garage and they are in the process of bringing them out. One of the terrorists -- they think the leader for that team -- killed himself and two others surrendered. From what they have heard from the hostages, the kids had an argument and most of them decided to leave, once they saw what happened at the Constitution Center. Jon and his team gave some great information on how the kids worked. Stan and Choufani agreed to have Akmed call Aziz at the Liberty Bell Center and see if he can't persuade him to end the incident. Max and William are headed out to catch up with us. They are also notifying New Jersey State Police."

"Kate," Jordan said quietly.

"Yes, Jordan?"

"Did you just see what this mad man did at the toll plaza?"

"No, I was on the floor. Why? What happened?"

Jordan looked at Patterson. Patterson had a wide smile on his face.

"Oh, you wouldn't believe it if I told you. Anything else?"

"Yes. Patterson's men confirm the engravers are not at the Mint. The inventory will be complete in about fifteen minutes, but you were right, Captain, a significant number of dies are gone."

"Let's just keep looking for a white van. We need to find them." The smile had left Patterson's face. He was back to business.

Chapter Seventy-Six

They continued to search in the area where Interstate Highways 676 and 295 converged. Max and William had arrived in the area five minutes ago, so they divided the area between them. But, time was not on their side. As each minute passed, Mustafa put more miles between himself and his pursuers.

Jordan felt Mustafa and his men weren't purposelessly running, but more than likely moving to a predetermined location. He had bet the plan Mustafa had done so far included backup locations in case their primary destination had been compromised. Jordan figured Belle had said something to Mustafa, which made him feel he couldn't go back to his home. Jordan bet Mustafa had a backup somewhere in the immediate vicinity of the search area, since it was an excellent location with several major north-south roads, allowing for numerous escape options.

"Hey, stop! There's one in there!" Kate yelled from the back seat.

Patterson slammed on the brakes as he pulled to the curb.

"What are you talking about?" Jordan turned to look at her in the backseat.

"At the Wawa. There's a City of Brotherly Love van parked on the side of the building."

"Are you certain?" Jordan surveyed the parking lot of the regional convenience store found throughout the Philadelphia area.

"I stared at the vans long enough when they were parked at Mustafa's. I'd know them anywhere."

Patterson had already spun the car around. There was an empty lot across the street from the convenience store where, indeed, a van was parked.

"Let's just hope its one of the ones we need to find," Jordan observed as all three of them focused their attention on the van.

"That may be our guy coming out now." A good-sized man of apparent Middle Eastern descent walked out of the market with a large soft drink cup and the straw up to his mouth. The other hand held a bag which had the shape of a hoagie.

"I guess moving all those dies and engravers causes you to work up an appetite. What do you think, Kate? You saw these guys the longest. Is that one of them?"

Kate had retrieved a miniature pair of binoculars out of her bag. Not the best, but good enough to get a slightly better view of the man. "Yep, that's one of them."

Jordan grabbed the radio. "Max, we've got one of the men and a van at the Wawa at six-o-two Blackhorse Pike. He's just getting ready to leave."

"We'll move toward you. Keep us posted."

"10-4"

Patterson pulled away as the van turned out of the parking lot and onto the road going northeast. Patterson, Jordan and Kate stayed three car lengths back on the heavily trafficked road.

Twenty minutes later, Patterson pulled the car to the curb in a modest but decaying residential neighborhood as the van pulled into the driveway of a home in the next block. Max and William positioned themselves a block to the other side of the house, while additional units would cover the back.

Chapter Seventy-Seven

Choufani looked hard at Stan. "Are you sure that's our best option? I'm not sure I completely buy the father's story -- so far, anyway."

"I think it's the best we've got. Give me some slack on this. I think it could work."

Choufani nodded, exhaled loudly, "You haven't let me down yet."

Stan grinned, walked to the door and opened it. "Akmed? Can you join us, please?"

Akmed tentatively entered the room, quickly glancing back and forth between Stan and Choufani. He took the seat that was offered.

"Akmed, I've played it straight with you since the beginning. I haven't lied to you or promised you anything I haven't delivered." Stan was bent over the table and looked directly at Akmed, their faces less than a yard apart.

Akmed nodded in agreement.

"Now we need your help. Aziz and his group are the only holdouts. We can end this two ways. First way is to go in with our tactical squads. It will be quick and decisive, but I got to tell you I don't like Aziz's chances in that scenario. Here's what I want to do. I want to get you and your son on the phone and give you a chance to talk him out of taking this any further."

Akmed's head slumped down and his body began to shake. "I wish I could help. I want my son safe, but I don't think he will talk to me. That man he had to call uncle has taken him away from me." His voice sounded strained, as he choked back tears. "I just don't know if Aziz isn't too far gone."

Stan came around the table and put his arm on Akmed's shoulder as Choufani sat down beside Akmed.

"Look, ahh, it's worth a try, huh? He may be finding out that his uncle led them down the garden path and isn't even with them. We think Aziz is vulnerable and you might be able to use that vulnerability to re-establish a relationship. Can you at least try?"

Akmed was quiet for several minutes before he raised his head up, brushed a tear from his cheek and spoke. "For the honor of my wife, I must do this. I will talk to Aziz."

Stan and Choufani glanced at one another and Choufani quickly exited the room. Stan turned back to Akmed. "You will do your wife and yourself proud, Akmed. I have a feeling this will work. It will take us a couple of minutes to set up and then we make the call."

Akmed nodded. If he could get his son back, then all would not be lost. Akmed found his mind filled with images of Aziz as a little boy, growing toward strong manhood, folding the woman he'd thought was his mother into his arms to give her a hug. How she had loved Aziz.

A technician entered the room – Akmed didn't know how long he'd been lost in memories. He installed the phone and fitted Akmed with the headset. Stan and Akmed were alone in the room.

"When you hit the red button on the phone, it will call the phone at the Liberty Bell Center where Aziz and his group are located. Every time we've called, he's answered; so, I anticipate he'll be picking up the phone on this call, too. We're ready whenever you are."

Akmed took a deep breath and slowly and audibly exhaled, as if he were in a yoga lesson. He'd seen it on television. He looked at Stan and then pressed the button.

He waited. He could hear the phone ringing on the other end.

"Yes. What do you want?"

It was Aziz. Akmed momentarily couldn't respond. Words would not form in his mouth; his throat went completely dry. He was sure Stan could hear his heart pounding. Hanging up seemed like the best option.

Stan patted him on the shoulder and whispered, "You can do this."

Akmed straightened up in his chair. "Aziz, it is me -- your father. We need to talk, you and I."

The reply came quickly. "I have nothing to say to you. You raised me for this mission and I must complete it."

"Aziz, listen to me. This mission is not what was planned. Your Uncle has misled you and the others. You cannot be successful today."

"I don't believe you. We will prevail and our demands will be met."

"Aziz – son. Listen to me. When was the last time you spoke to Mustafa?"

There was silence from the other end.

"Please, Aziz. Answer my question?"

"When he told us to begin taking the buildings and hostages," Aziz blurted out.

"And nothing since?"

"No."

"Was that the plan?"

"He was supposed to call every hour." The words seemed to race from the boy.

"And, he hasn't?"

"No. We haven't heard anything from him. We've had questions he could have answered. We've had things happen we hadn't planned for. He hasn't helped us at all." Aziz was sounding more like the teenager he was and not the terrorist he attempted to be.

"Okay. Okay. It's all right, Aziz. I'm here to help you. I can give you the direction you need. Your Uncle misled you. He misled me and the other families. He even tried to have Bennie kill me in the store, today."

"What father? What did you say? Bennie tried to kill you?.."

"Yes, at the direction of Mustafa. Mustafa is not what he seems. He is running from the police as we speak. He won't be helping you today, Aziz, so please allow me to help you."

"I don't know who I can trust. I couldn't even trust my own cousins today!"

"Trust me. For the sake of your mother, give me a chance? Give us a chance?"

"Father, what is going to happen to me?"

Akmed wasn't sure how to respond. He looked at Stan.

Stan reached over and hit the mute button. "Akmed, you have to understand. I mean, yeah, he's a kid, but he's been involved in a crime and people have gotten hurt. But, given the circumstances and what we know has happened, if we can get him to surrender, I'll be able to go to bat for him with the prosecutors, to make sure they have the full story and understand."

Akmed returned to the call. "Aziz, listen. Bad things have happened today, but they were not your fault. There will be some punishment; but, eventually, we will be together. We will have each other. Does that mean anything to you."

Again there was silence – and it was followed by the sounds of sobbing.

"Mother would be so ashamed of me for what I have done." Aziz said, his voice little over a whisper.

"Your mother will be proud if you can make all of this end right now. She loves you Aziz. I love you --.son."

"Yes, father, I know. I, ahh, I love you. Tell me what I need to do? I want to go home."

"Bless you, my son. I am so proud of you. I am going to let you talk to a man named Stan. He has been of tremendous help to me, Aziz. He will tell you what you need to do. I will see you soon." Akmed gave the headset to Stan and fell back in his chair, his eyes filling with tears.

Akmed didn't have any grasp of time. It could have been ten, twenty minutes or a half hour or longer that Akmed found himself standing outside the Liberty Bell Center. Uniformed Philadelphia policemen were leading the children out and Aziz was brought over – no handcuffs – and Akmed was able to hug his son and the words "I love you" spilled from each of them as they held one another. Then Aziz was led away to a waiting car by two Federal agents.

Stan put his arm around Akmed's shoulder and they turned and walked in the opposite direction.

"You'll be able to see him tomorrow." That was all Stan could think to say.

Chapter Seventy-Eight

✤ ✤ ✤

CHERRY HILL, NEW JERSEY

Jerome pressed "End" on his cell phone and laid it in the console between the seats in the front of the car. A glance at his visage in the rearview mirror and the look of satisfaction was obvious. Mustafa had both surprised and impressed him. When they first created this plan and Mustafa discussed his role, Jerome, without telling Mustafa, had given it less than a fifty percent chance of success. But, Mustafa had informed him that he not only had the dies, but was also successful in getting the engravers out of the Mint. The seven people who were the only ones who knew how to create and engrave the markings for all U.S. coinage were now under his control. This was better than he ever imagined.

It was wise, occasionally, to reflect on one's past in order to move with surety to one's future, one's destiny. Jerome Fernandez-Medina was born in London of an American mother and Mexican father. His father was a senior diplomat, serving as an Ambassador in the capitals of Europe. Jerome spent the first sixteen years of his life living in Embassies, with only infrequent visits to Mexico. When his family did return permanently, Jerome was appalled by the poverty -- and the concentration of wealth. While his family enjoyed privilege and affluence, Jerome felt they didn't do enough to heal the relentlessly growing rift between those who had and those who did not, a schism which would someday engulf his country.

He found kindred spirits in his cousins; they decided the political process was too corrupt and slow moving to ever affect change. Their approach was to join the other side, the criminal side. They targeted the central states of Mexico, Veracruz and its large expanse of land along the Gulf of Mexico, Guerrero and Oaxaca, which bordered on the Pacific, and Puebla, which provided an additional connection between Veracruz and Guerrero. Strategically, this gave them the ability to move various goods, both legal and illegal, from one port to the other. These States also were home to many of Mexico's most famous resorts and soon, Jerome and his cousins controlled many of them. With the cash flow, they were able to invest in other not so legal businesses and as these businesses turned large profits, they were able to launder the money back through the resorts. Different in approach from the other crime families was their sponsorship of job training and social welfare programs, to help the poor in the States they controlled. While it developed skills in the population they could use for both their legal and illegal enterprises, it also built loyalty and allegiances among the people.

As their dominance grew, they observed a larger problem that was impacting Mexico's ability to grow as a country. It was Mexico's neighbor to the north. They came to believe the policies and politics of the United States were directly responsible for a whole host of their country's problems.

Jerome took the lead, to bring the battle to the interior of their enemy. Since he spoke flawless English and his features were more Anglo than Mexican, it was easy for him to move in the political and social circles of the United States. With dual citizenship, he had no problems traveling back and forth and, through his family, he had numerous high level contacts from which he could readily glean information.

While many of their contemporaries were enjoying the profits from flooding the U.S. with drugs, Jerome felt there were other efforts which would bring about greater results. The answer for Jerome and his cousins was to bring about economic catastrophe.

Jerome's plan was to utilize the great number of people who moved between the U.S. and Mexico, both legally and illegally, to flood the country with U.S. coinage. With the dies from the mint and the imprinting machines he'd been able to obtain, they could put an enormous amount of money into the system in a short period of time. The beauty of the plan was that, from a technical standpoint, it wouldn't be counterfeit and, until the Mint could change all of their dies, it would be months -- more than likely years -- before America could change out all of the coinage. It seemed far-fetched when they first started, but now Jerome realized that, in less than seventy-two hours, he would be sending money back to the U.S.A. -- in his efforts to bring the country to its knees.

He cut the wheel and avoided a maroon Mustang which had ignored a stop sign. Jerome resisted giving the driver the finger.

Picking up his phone, he speed dialed. It wasn't as easy with the driving gloves as if he had been bare-handed; but, gloves were a necessity. The call was picked up on the second ring. "Please be ready to go in a half-hour. We will be heading south as I discussed." He disconnected. He had the address to which he was headed in the anonymously rented car's navigation system and it showed he should arrive in ten minutes. He hoped Mustafa would have everything ready. He wanted to be quickly on his way, since any time waiting around was time for the authorities to catch up with them.

After a series of turns the navigation system had advised he make, he found himself pulling up to a small ranch house with three white vans in front. Jerome was happy to see that white magnetic pieces had been placed over the signage painted on two of the vans, so they couldn't be identified. He would be leaving in a van that was in the garage, one that he'd left there the previous evening, abandoning the rental car. He had never touched it with his bare hands, nor combed his hair nor worn anything while driving it but commonly available Levi jeans and knit shirts from J.C. Penney.

Slowly, Jerome stepped out of his car, looked around to see if anything seemed out of place. The neighborhood was quiet, with a considerable number of cars parked on the street as well as in the driveways. But, nothing showed signs of not fitting. He walked to the side door of the house and quietly knocked.

Mustafa appeared and let Jerome in. They had only met in person twice before.

Jerome held out his hand. "You have done a great job. As I promised, you will be rewarded."

"Thank you. It worked better than I planned." Mustafa didn't want to jeopardize his payoff and future by telling Jerome about the incident as they left the Mint. He'd watched the neighborhood since they arrived and hadn't seen anything which led him to believe they had been followed or were being watched.

"Where are they?" Jerome inquired.

"The engravers?" Mustafa wasn't sure if he was talking about them or his accomplices.

Jerome nodded.

"They are in the basement. In the soundproof room we built."

"Very good. When I leave, you are to eliminate them."

"I'm sorry?" Mustafa couldn't believe what he just heard. Jerome wanted him to kill the engravers. He could have done that at the Mint. Why build the room? Mustafa was confused.

"I need you to take care of them. They are no use to us alive. If it's a problem, I'm sure one of your associates would be more than happy to take care of it and I'll split your payment with them." Jerome didn't have time for this.

"No, no. I'll take care of it. I just wanted to make sure I heard you correctly."

"Good! Then it will be done."

"Yes. Consider it done."

"Alright! Is my van loaded?"

"No, I thought you wanted us to wait until you arrived." Mustafa was starting to worry. He had thought Jerome wanted him to wait until he got to the house.

"No, but it won't take us long."

He walked into the living room. "Let's go," he announced. "We need to load the van in the garage." Mustafa led the men out the side door. He instructed one of the men to open up the van in the driveway while the rest entered the garage. They immediately began transferring the bags containing the dies into the other van. When they were finished emptying the first van, it was traded out with the other van on the street.

As they were unloading the second van, Jerome stopped cold. He could only stare toward the front of the cab.

Mustafa saw what he was doing, but didn't understand. "Is everything okay?"

"No. Come here Mustafa!" Jerome ordered.

Mustafa walked over to the back of the van where Jerome was standing, Jerome still staring toward the front. "Did you instruct your men to come right here and not stop?"

"Yes. Of course. I told them not to stop for anything." Mustafa still didn't understand what was bothering Jerome.

"Do you see it?" Jerome asked, the tone of his voice rising. He raised his hand and pointed.

Mustafa followed the pointed finger and finally saw what had drawn Jerome's attention. In the cup holder on the console sat a paper soda cup. The condensation on the outside of the cup proved it was recently used and still held the remnants of a drink.

Jerome turned and walked to the back of the garage. "Mustafa, who was driving that van?"

"It was this man." Mustafa pointed to one of them.

Jerome had instructed from the beginning that they would never use these men's names. Jerome walked right up to him. He was inches from the man's face. The man held his eyes down.

"Look at me!" Jerome demanded. "Did you stop on your way here?"

"Yes. I was thirsty. It was only for a minute."

"Were you told not to stop? Not to stop for anything?"

"Yes."

"You choose to disobey. I cannot tolerate someone not following orders."

"It won't happen again. I'm sorry." The man still averted his eyes, but he was clearly pleading.

"You are right. It will not happen again! Let this be a lesson to all of you." Jerome looked at the other men. "Let's finish moving the bags. I need to get out of here."

The men turned to return to the van outside to unload the rest of the bags. Jerome reached to his waistband, a Walther PPK .380 coming into his hand. From his jacket pocket, he took a suppressor, screwed it to the threaded barrel which protruded past the front of the slide. Jerome raised his silenced automatic and fired two rounds into the back of the thirsty man's head. The man slumped to the concrete, blood and brain spattered against the side of the garage. The other men stopped and stared in shock, each speckled with red and gray bits of the murdered man's skull and brain. When they looked at Jerome, he hoped his expression told them all they needed to know was that they were to get back to work.

In ten minutes, the van was loaded. The last van in the driveway was moved out into the street.

"Mustafa, send the men inside. I need to talk with you." Jerome turned and walked to the van as he spoke.

Mustafa gestured for the men to go into the house. "I'll be with you in a minute." When they entered the house, Jerome walked up to Mustafa. "They have served their purpose. It is best to eliminate them. They can only cause us harm if they are captured. You can keep their share of the money."

"I think they now know better than to talk," Mustafa said as he looked down at the body in the garage. "But, I understand your point. Consider it done."

"Use this. I have another." Jerome handed Mustafa the gun he'd used to kill the man in the garage. He had never touched the gun bare-handed, nor any of the cartridges without wearing gloves. "This way, when they find the bodies, it will look as if one killer did all of them." He handed Mustafa three loaded magazines. "Use it also to kill the engravers, too."

Mustafa nodded and took the gun and ammunition.

"You have done well my friend. I look forward to seeing you in a couple of weeks." As part of Mustafa's reward, Jerome was providing him passage to Mexico and a villa in which to live.

"Thank you. I'll see you soon." Mustafa waved as Jerome jumped in the van. He slowly moved out of the driveway and turned left onto the street.

Mustafa closed the garage and walked into the house. The remaining two men were in the living room, watching TV. Mustafa raised the gun and shot the man who was across the room in the recliner. Two shots through the forehead with the second shot startling Mustafa for the silencer no longer seemed to be muffling the shots. It startled the other man, who tried to get up off the sofa.

He wasn't fast enough.

Mustafa regained his composure, turned and fired off two more shots, both creating loud reports from the gun, but finding their target and dropping him on the floor. Mustafa moved back to the kitchen. He changed the magazine. Then he would go down in the basement and kill the engravers.

Chapter Seventy-Nine

✤ ✤ ✤

"There's a van leaving the house." William radioed from his vantage point in the back yard. He'd arrived a few minutes earlier and had joined Jordan.

"He's coming our way. It looks like it's the new arrival." Max was slumping down in her seat so she wouldn't be seen as the van passed, but was still trying to get a good look at the driver. "Stan and I will follow." Stan had arrived on scene right after the loading of the vans had begun.

Jordan and William watched Mustafa walk back into the house, carrying a gun with a suppressor and what looked like extra magazines. "Let's get ready. Looks like maybe something's about to go down." Jordan whispered to William.

As Mustafa entered the house, Jordan and William moved closer, but still stayed in the shadows of the back yard. They heard a noise, not sure of the sound. They exchanged glances just as more of the same sounds were heard. Definitely shots being fired. They raced toward the side door. "Shots fired inside!" William called over the radio.

Jordan was looking in the door as Mustafa came back into the kitchen with the gun. Jordan saw him drop the magazine out of the gun and he looked at William and mouthed. "Let's go!"

Jordan bounded through the door with William right behind.

"Drop the gun!" Jordan commanded. "Federal Agents! Don't move!"

Mustafa was startled but his reflexes forced him to keep the gun and finished jamming a new mag in as he sprinted from the room in a low crouch. Jordan fired a double tap, but his bullets lodged in the cabinet as Mustafa spun around the corner. Jordan pointed for William to go around through the living room as Jordan followed Mustafa. Mustafa couldn't go far.

Jordan turned the corner into a dark room -- the dining room -- and scanned the room, trying to detect any movement or shape. Slowly, he passed through.

"Stop right there, man! And, put the gun down!" He heard William command.

Jordan hurried around the corner. Mustafa was pinned against the front door like a butterfly in a collection, shifting the muzzle of his gun from Jordan to William and back.

"Give it up, Mustafa. There's no way out of here." The screech of car tires out front confirmed Patterson and Kate had arrived. Jordan could see Mustafa realized others had reached the house.

"Just put the gun down. It's over, Mustafa," Jordan directed, gesturing for Mustafa to place his gun on the floor.

Mustafa couldn't believe this was happening. Had Jerome set him up? Maybe these weren't Federal Agents, but Jerome's men? Then he realized that, either way, the outcome would be the same. He wasn't going to Mexico and the life about which he had dreamed was never going to be more than that -- a dream. He knew it was over, so he began to slowly bend down and started to place his gun on the floor. But, at the last instant, he brought it up to his open mouth and pulled the trigger.

"Shit!" Jordan snarled, closing his eyes and turning his face as the room filled with a red mist when the back of Mustafa's head exploded and there was blood and brain all over the door and anything near it.

William keyed his mike. "All clear in here, suspect down. Enter through the side."

Jordan walked over and crouched beside the body. "Warn them this gun is hot."

They'd leave it for evidence techs, he knew, but it was never a bad idea to warn someone about playing it safe. "God, what a hell of a mess. Hope he didn't have something or we might get it too. Don't touch your eyes or nose until we can clean up." He looked up at William. "We need to see who else is here. The engravers must be somewhere. Tell Kate to search the vans with Patterson before they come in." William radioed to Kate as he and Jordan walked back into the kitchen and searched for a door to the basement.

As they moved down the stairway, they found an abnormally clean basement with no junk or piles of anything. At the far end was a well built wall with a steel door, secured by a massive padlock. Jordan walked over to the door. Like so many people, Mustafa had chosen convenience over a higher level of security. He'd hung the keys on the wall next to the door. Jordan took them down and stared at the lock. It didn't look to be booby-trapped, so he held his breath and inserted the key into the padlock and it fell open.

With one hand, Jordan took the lock from the hasp, with the other his gun from his holster. William took one side of the door, his pistol in both hands. .

William tapped Jordan on the shoulder and held up his index finger, indicating Jordan should hold. William was listening to his radio. He leaned into Jordan. "Kate said the vans are clean."

Jordan nodded and proceeded to open the door. As it opened, light entered the darkened room, illuminating several people inside. Jordan threw the door open all the way and went through from left to right, scanning the room as William came in behind him, right to left. Neither saw any threat. A quick count revealed seven people, one female and six males.

"I assume you are the engravers from the Mint?"

"They sure are!" Jordan looked behind him to see Patterson standing there with Kate. He had a big grin on his face as he entered the room. The recognition was mutual and the hostages applauded.

Jordan smiled at Kate. She walked up to him. "Great work today, cowboy!"

Jordan smiled. "We've still got some work to do. The dies are gone. I've gotta get that rotten terrorist bastard's blood off me."

Chapter Eighty

Stan and Max did their best to keep the van in sight. The van was navy blue and the night was moonless. It had been easier when they were on the main roads with street lights, but those roads were behind them and they found themselves on side streets and rural roads with little traffic and no street lighting. The man in the van had gotten a good head start and they had to let him get several blocks down the street when he left the house before they could turn around and pursue.

The driver seemed to know his way or was using a navigation system, since his turns were fluid, without any hesitation. Stan and Max had gotten caught behind a car which had stopped at an intersection when the traffic light had just turned yellow. Stan had almost rear ended the car stopped

Max noticed the van turning right farther down the road, so as soon as the light turned green, Stan veered around the car, passing it in the intersection and causing several other drivers to honk their horns, shout their anger or give them the finger.

They turned right and found themselves on Ark Road. No taillights of the van or of any vehicle were visible in front of them. Stan drove about a mile and a half and then pulled over to the side of the road.

"What do you think Max? I haven't a clue where he might have gone?"

"I know. He could have gone anywhere or known we were following and pulled off and hid. Damn! We were so close."

They both looked at each other as a low rumble began to vibrate the car. It increased in intensity rattling the plastic interior of the car.

"What the hell is that?" Stan shouted.

"We're not on railroad tracks, are we?" Max called out as both she and Stan looked out the windows to assure themselves a train wasn't bearing down on them.

There were bright lights flooding the driver's side of the car, reminding Stan of the train signal scene in "Close Encounters Of The Third Kind." And the noise became deafening. It wasn't a UFO it was a small business jet, streaking into the night sky. As it cleared the car, the glass still vibrating,

Stan and Max looked at each, realizing full well that the aircraft almost certainly carried their suspect and whatever he'd had in the van.

Stan threw the car in gear. "Let's find the damn airport."

A quarter mile down was a side road. Stan turned left and quickly came upon the entrance to the South Jersey Regional Airport. Stan and Max ran from their car and into the office, startling the sole person behind the counter.

Stan flashed his badge. "The plane that just took off, where's it going?"

"Uh, let me look at the flight plan." The man grabbed a pile of papers and sorted through them. "Headed to Hartford."

"Can you make me a copy? You get many jets taking off here?"

"Nope. Runway's kind of short and he almost didn't make it. I'm not sure what they had in that plane, but it must have been awful heavy. He had to sit at the end of the runway and rev the engines with the brake on. You know. Kind of like a catapult? And, he still almost didn't get up."

Looking at the documents, something didn't seem right to Stan the amateur pilot. "Look at this. Seems like a lot of fuel to fly to Hartford? I figured he wasn't going there. This confirms it."

The man looked at it. "Wow, you're right. He could get a lot farther. Matter of fact, he likely would still be too heavy to land in Hartford. I better call them and let them know."

"You can do that, but my guess is they aren't headed to Hartford, son. You have a direct line to the FAA?"

"Yep, but it's for emergencies only."

"Guess what this is, buddy," Stan said and he tapped his badge with his finger. It took only a few moments to alert the FAA and Stan found Kate outside. "I've got the FAA tracking the flight. Their flight plan was filed for Cincinnati, but they're heading south. They've got more than enough fuel to get anywhere in Florida. Fortunately, they don't have enough fuel and the plane doesn't have the ability to fly anywhere outside the U.S. Maybe Cuba, though. Damn. Did you find anything?"

Max shrugged. "The van is a rental and it's clean inside. We'll get Crime Scene out here, but my guess is they won't find anything. William called. They found the engravers and they're all right."

"Well, that's the best news. I've got people going to FAA in D.C. to monitor the flight. We'll see where they go."

Chapter Eighty-One

As each minute went by, Jerome was becoming more assured of his success. He thought back to the take off with the pilot screaming his head off and cursing Jerome about the weight of the bags and he wasn't sure they were going to clear the trees. They needed the small jet to get in and out of the airport, but they were going to push the machine to its operational limits both in weight and distance. The pilot had pulled back on the yoke with his knuckles white and the climb out was steep. Jerome could no longer look out ahead of the craft, but rather looked down, not sure they would make it. But they had.

After two hours in flight, they had just descended into the Miami area and had clearance at the Tamiami airport, even though they had no intention of setting down there. They would descend to below five hundred feet and buzz the airport, then head out over Homestead, Florida, and into the Gulf. They would stay below one thousand feet – below scanning altitude for most of the radar in the area -- until they reached their final destination.

Jerome loved Key West. His only regret was that today's visit would be short. He enjoyed coming to the island and just being able to blend in with all the zaniness and irreverence that characterized the place. He owned a house a few blocks off Duval Street, but he wouldn't be visiting it today. The trick would be getting in and out of the airport without drawing too much attention.

Even trickier was landing without permission at a commercial airport. Fortunately, they would be landing when no commercial flights were scheduled and what they had been told was a slow time for the airport. Also, as was the case with so many of the citizens of the Conch Republic, a few dollars in cash could cause them to look the other way at the right time. Today, Jerome had the two air traffic controllers along with the airport manager on his payroll. Even if someone had figured out what he was doing, Jerome felt it would be hard for them to get to the airport in time to stop him.

After another thirty-five minutes the pilot looked back through the open cockpit door of the Lear 100. "We're getting ready to land. I'm making my approach."

Jerome flashed thumbs up and tightened his seatbelt. There was a long runway, so the landing shouldn't be a problem. He never really liked flying, particularly in a smaller plane. The pilot banked hard to port, positioning the plane for landing. Jordan heard the gear come out and lock into place. He gripped his armrests tightly and glanced out of the window as they descended, looking to see if he saw anything out of the normal. The airport appeared as it always did, so he faced forward, just as the rear wheels touched the runway. The weight of the plane was carrying them quickly down the runway. He heard the engines go into reverse thrust and felt the plane braking. The plane came to a stop about five hundred feet from the end of the runway, and quickly taxied off but, instead of heading toward the terminals, like every other plane, they headed instead to the far end of the airfield.

As they approached the rendezvous, the plane slowed and the engines became silent. For the first time, Jerome could hear the unmistakable sound of an approaching helicopter. He looked at this watch. Right on time, he thought to himself. The plan was working flawlessly. The plane stopped. Jerome looked out the window to ensure no one was coming out to the plane. It was dark and there was no sign of any vehicle headlights. He unbuckled and rose from his seat. The pilot emerged from the cockpit and opened the forward cabin door and dropped the stairway. Jerome began passing bags over to him and he lowered them slowly to the tarmac. The helicopter was now directly overhead and flying with no navigation lights. As it descended, it came to rest on the tarmac about ten yards from the jet, two men jumped out and ran over to help move the bags to the chopper.

In less than ten minutes, all of the bags were transferred and Jerome jumped into the helicopter. It lifted off slowly, turned to the south and headed out over the water.

The pilot and the other two men jumped in the plane and headed toward the runway. In less than two minutes, they were airborne and headed in a westerly direction. Each would be receiving a handsome pay day for the few hours of work. The pilot had purchased some beer and snacks while he waited for Jerome in New Jersey. Airborne outside of U.S. boundaries, the pilot turned on the autopilot and headed to the back to have a drink with his friends. He'd met Jerome through an acquaintance and when Jerome had laid out his plan and asked if he was interested and could he get a team together, he had jumped at the chance. The money he made today, even after his expenses, was more than he made in two years of flying charters. Even though he might get his pilot's license suspended, it was worth it.

He grabbed a beer and toasted his buddies. They had clearance to land in Mexico in about two hours. The reduced weight factor would get them on the ground without having to run on vapor.

"Hey! What's this?" one of his friends called out as he returned from using the onboard head. He held up a large Halliburton attaché case, one of the aluminum models that seemed to be the latest fashion accessory for international executives.

"The guy who was on the plane must have left it," the other man who had been on the helicopter said as he took another long pull on his beer. "I guess it's ours now."

The pilot looked at the case and knew it was something you wouldn't leave behind and suddenly realized he wasn't going to get to spend the money he had earned...

There were numerous reports that night from several ships and planes in the area of a bright fireball being observed in the sky. Neither wreckage nor bodies was ever recovered.

Chapter Eighty-Two

Less than thirty minutes from the airport, the helicopter set down on the deck of a freighter heading west, toward Mexico with a load of products from various European companies, all purchased by and for the enterprises Jerome's family controlled. The crew quickly offloaded the bags from the aircraft and placed them in two empty shipping containers that the manifest would show were part of a shipment of BMW auto parts for numerous dealerships in Mexico. Any sort of external scan would reveal a container full of small metal parts and the inspection wouldn't go any further.

When empty, the helicopter was pushed off the side of the ship, which Jerome considered just part of the cost of doing business. In two days, he would be back in his home with his family. The Fernandez-Medina family had just entered a new business -- minting U.S. coins --and he was looking forward to wreaking havoc on the U.S. He'd instructed the family's financial advisors to begin to liquidate all of their U.S. holdings, except for some personal real estate assets, so there would be nothing to forfeit or seize if they were ever suspected of perpetrating this fraud.

He wouldn't make money on this venture, but that wasn't what it was about. He wanted to right the wrongs his people and his country had suffered. The economic success of America had come at the expense of the Mexican people, with the United States looking to Mexico as a source for cheap products and even cheaper labor. The United States did not respect the culture and history of his beloved country so, he'd called this "Project Alamo," after the Mission in San Antonio where the pivotal battle for Texas was fought in 1836. When the Mexicans finally won the thirteen day siege, their victory turned into a rallying cry for Texans, which soon ended in the defeat of the Mexican army outside of modern day Houston.

Jerome wanted revenge for everything that had happened since that time to his country. Bringing the U.S. to its economic knees would be a defeat from which the Gringos might never recover.

He received word on board that the sheets of metal needed to produce the coins had arrived and were dispersed among the three locations where the coin production would take place. Everything was coming together.

Chapter Eighty-Three

FBI FIELD OFFICE-PHILADELPHIA

"We've got a lead." Stan came bounding into the office. "The pilot of the helicopter was a DEA informant and he had a tracking beacon on his helicopter. They were able to track his route and then cross reference the shipping traffic. They have it narrowed down to three ships."

"Great. What do we know about the ships?" Jordan was looking over Stan's shoulder, reading the documents.

"One's a cruise ship; so, I think we can eliminate it." Stan turned to the next sheet of paper. "The other two are commercial ships. One's a freighter out of Holland, heading to Mexico. The third one is a tanker, empty, heading to Venezuela to pick up a load of crude for a refinery outside of New Orleans."

Jordan, Kate and Stan looked at each other. It was a crap shoot. You could land a helicopter on either one.

Kate looked up from the papers Stan had put on the desk. "Can we get some satellite photos?"

"On order. Told 'em to hold the anchovies. They'll be here in fifteen minutes."

"What happened to the chopper? It didn't fly back, right?" Jordan continued to shuffle through the papers as he asked the question.

"We think it was pushed off the side. Two other ships reported debris in the water and described what could be rotor blades bobbing in the water."

"Wow! Someone's got some big bucks on this if they can just push a helicopter off the deck," Kate whistled. "We're playing with some big boys, here."

Jordan looked up. "Send Max, William and Jon's team to Mexico. I think that's our ship," he said, pointing to the paper that described the vessel and its contents.

"What's your thinking there, Jordan?" Stan asked, looking at Jordan.

"My gut," Jordan replied. "They've got bags of metal dies. I'm not sure how you get them off a tanker. The crew would have to carry them off and, even though it's Venezuela, I don't see how you do it without raising suspicion. On a freighter, you could put the stuff in a shipping container. That gets hauled off the ship with the others. You arrange a pick up and you take it wherever you want. That sounds hard to do here but, in Mexico, my guess would be it's a piece of cake. Since money seems to be no object, who knows how many people are getting paid off to make this happen?"

"We've got some Mexican Federales that owe us a favor. I'll get them in the loop," Stan nodded.

Chapter Eighty-Four

❖ ❖ ❖

MEXICO

Max, William and the Special Ops team arrived via a C-17 at one o'clock in the morning at the Mexican Air Force base. Arriving almost at the same time were Stan, Kate and Jordan. Upon landing, they were met by General Domingo Estrada, the commandant of the federal militia in Vera Cruz. General Estrada and Stan had worked together for twenty years and Max could tell from the moment they met that the relationship Stan had with this man was carrying over as they were greeted like old friends and promised that anything needed would be available to them.

They arrived at the Port ninety minutes before the ship was to dock. As they'd driven, the General had gone over a map of the port and his suggestions for securing the ship, the crew and the vessel's content.

They confirmed with the General that the crew count was eleven and that Dutch Customs Officials, who had supervised the loading and debarkation of the ship, had verified this and the fact that it had made no stops since leaving the Netherlands.

As soon as the ship docked, the General and his team boarded the vessel and removed the crew. Max and William then boarded to search for the dies and when completed, they would interview the crew. During this time, the crew would be quarantined at the Port, the General assured them. Jordan and Kate would reconnoiter the shipyard to ascertain who might be staging to pick up the load of dies.

William and Max stood behind a bank of cargo containers as the freighter – enormous seeming from so close -- was brought into the slip by two large tugs. Jon's team remained in the vans in order to avoid arousing suspicion. The docking procedure itself consumed almost thirty minutes and not until the ship was tied up did the General and his men approach. Two squads, each led by an officer, raced up the gangplank, weapons at high port. Within five minutes time, the crew began walking down the gangplank. Ten men walked down and were escorted away by Mexican troops.

An officer standing with Max and William motioned for them to board the ship. At the top of the gangplank, they were greeted by General Estrada and the vessel's Captain. At this point, Jon and his men moved out of the vans and up the gangplank, joining Max and William on the ship.

The Captain seemed extremely nervous and Estrada made a subtle gesture to Max that he'd picked up on it also. They moved away from the rail, crossing the main deck, passing the bridge, where several of General Estrada's men were reviewing documents spread out on the table. The Captain led them down into the main hold of the ship. It was filled from top to bottom with shipping containers.

"Where do we even begin?" William let out a sigh.

One of the Estrada's officers appeared with two sheets of paper and spoke with the General in Spanish.

"My Major has found some inconsistencies with the container count, Captain. The number listed on the manifest at the Port in the Netherlands shows two fewer containers than the paper work you were going to present here. Why is that, Captain?"

The Captain looked down at the floor. "I did not want to do this. I had no choice. The owners ordered me to carry two empty containers and have enough room on the deck so a helicopter could land. I did as I was told."

Max didn't think it would be so easy. "So where are the two containers you brought on empty?"

The Captain pointed to two containers on top of the stack.

"Are you certain?" Estrada pressed. "If we open them and they are not what we are looking for, it will go badly for you."

"If you are looking for heavy bags, that is what is in there."

Max and William nodded.

"Major," Estrada said, turning away, "get the harbor master to order someone he can trust to operate one of the on-board cranes, to put those two containers on the dock. And, make sure they are secured until we can be there for them to be opened. No one else gets close to them. Claro?"

"Si, General."

"Call the base and have them dispatch a large flatbed truck to the docks immediately, to haul the contents of these containers to the base." Estrada turned to Max. "I assume you will want them loaded on your plane."

"Yes, General. That would be perfect."

"We will go now and interview the crew," Estrada said, nodding.

It took about ten minutes to get off the ship and walk to where the crew was being held. Estrada, Max and William walked into a large cinder block building and down a corridor to a secured door with two of the General's soldier's standing guard outside. They saluted as they opened the door for the group to enter.

William noticed first. "There are only nine here."

Max and the General looked at him, somewhat perplexed at his comment. Then it registered. One of the crew was missing.

"Sergeant! Where is the other crew member?" Estrada demanded.

"In the bathroom, sir!"

"Is anyone with him?"

"Yes, sir! Corporal Ortega."

William ran to the restroom door. He turned the handle, but the door would not budge. It wasn't locked, but something was keeping it from opening. General Estrada waved several of his men over. With two of the men aiding him, throwing their shoulders against the door, William pushed it open. What had wedged the door was the body of Corporal Ortega, his throat slit and a crimson pool beside him. A window with a steel screen had been ripped open from the outside, providing an escape route.

William turned away, but turned back when he heard a shout from outside, a female voice ordering someone to stop. The command was in English. It was Kate. As he started to move to the window, his body recoiled with the sound of two shots being fired. He grabbed his side arm and fumbled in his pocket for a small mirror he always carried. He pushed himself up against the exterior wall and positioned the mirror to give him a view point of outside. It was an alleyway and he could see two men running toward a large parking area. He quickly maneuvered to the other way and again used the mirror to survey. That's when he say Kate prone on the ground not moving.

He swung around to exit through the window and turned quickly to Max. "Kate's down, we need medical, NOW!" He dove out the window and to Kate's side.

Quickly, two men appeared with their medical satchels They worked feverously to assess Kate's wounds.

One of the American medics approached Stan. She's got a bad leg wound. It's not life threatening, but if we want to save the leg we need to get her out of here as soon as possible. The closest hospital we know where she can be treated is Scripps Memorial in San Diego.

Stan didn't hesitate. "Take my plane and get her there!" he turned to the General. "Can you get them escorted back to the base and get priority clearance for the plane to get to San Diego?"

Estrada grabbed Stan by the shoulders. "Consider it done my friend."

Stan nodded and looked at Max. "You go with them and use my name every way you can to move things and if that doesn't work, call me."

Max turned without a word and followed the stretcher with Kate to the waiting Ambulance.

William walked over and joined Stan. A quick look from Stan told him they were now back to the matter at hand. "My guess is there's a dead crew member on the ship along with the helicopter pilot. Our man escaped. I think we need to get the dies to the plane and get out of here. I trust the General, but I don't know how much control he really has here. We should go."

Stan walked over to the General. "Sir, we need to get those containers to the airport at once. I don't think there is any further need for us to remain here."

Before Estrada could say anything, they were joined by Jon. A little breathless sounding – he'd evidently run from the ship – Jon informed them, "We've found two bodies. One's the pilot and the other is a crewman. Looks like our suspect killed the sailor and dressed in his clothes to disembark with the crew.

The General's disappointment that all had not gone as planned was evident in his face. "Yes. The truck will be here in five minutes. It shouldn't take more than ten minutes to load the truck and I'll have you escorted back. You understand, I'll need to stay here?"

"Yes, General. We appreciate all you have done for us. I'm sorry about the corporal."

"Thank you," Estrada nodded.

At that moment Jordan came around the corner. He ran up to Stan. "What happened here?"

Stan looked at him and didn't respond.

"Stan?"

"Kate's been shot. She's going to be all right, but her leg is real tore up. We're getting her to San Diego. The man who shot her got away and we think he was on the ship. We lost him."

"Maybe not. General can we get video of the cars leaving through the gate?"

"Sure that shouldn't be a problem. But I don't know how it will help. Once out of the gate they could go in many directions. We would never find them."

"Possibly, but I have a hunch. As I was moving around the shipyard I found a Mercedes 500 AMG in the employee parking lot with it's engine idling. Seemed to stick out amongst all the old beaters I imagine the dock workers are driving. I put a locater beacon on it. As I was heading back here I noticed it was gone."

"Good thinking son." Stan slapped him on the back. They jogged over to the main building to view the tapes. Sure enough the cameras caught the Mercedes flying out of the parking lot minutes after Kate had been shot.

At Stan's request, Estrada dispatched a helicopter to pick them and locate the vehicle.

Chapter Eighty-Five

✤ ✤ ✤

GATED ESTATE
IN CENTRAL MEXICO

Jerome had traveled the one hundred miles from the port and was now safe in the confines of his walled and heavily guarded estate. He was tired, depressed and angry, having come so close to success, only to be on the run.

As they had docked, he'd noticed the abnormally high level of attention being paid to the ship. It wasn't long before he'd spotted the army units attempting to stay out of sight. He searched the vessel for the helicopter pilot and found him in his cabin. Effortlessly, Jerome snapped the man's neck having caught the pilot completely by surprise.

Jerome regretted killing him. The man had been a loyal employee for many years and had always done what was asked of him without question. As he gathered up the pilot's personal items, he found his cell phone. He scrolled through the numbers and two attracted his attention. One was in Miami and the other in Washington, D.C. He could think of no reason why the pilot would have numbers on speed dial for those locations. Jerome pocketed the phone to check the numbers later, when affairs were not so pressing. He dragged the body to an electrical cabinet near the engine room and stuffed the pilot inside. He went to the trash room and threw the man's bag into the furnace.

Coming out of the trash room, Jerome spotted a sailor similar to his own height and build. Jerome walked up to him and, as the man turned, Jerome smashed the heel of his palm against the base of the man's nose, instantly breaking it and driving the ethmoid bone on a trajectory into the man's brain, killing him instantly. He dragged the body back to the trash room, stripped it and changed into the fellow's clothes and then he stuffed the man into a large trash container.

As Jerome left the compartment, a call came over the P.A. for all of the crew to report topside. The men on this ship knew who he was and knew not to say anything when they saw him dressed as they were, or to mention that one of the men was missing.

Jerome walked off the ship with the others and, as they were escorted to a nearby building, he made eye contact with one of his people who had been there waiting for him. They immediately knew the plan had changed and they had to get Jerome out of the Port.

Upon entering the room, Jerome saw his opportunity and asked to go to the restroom. The soldier assigned to go with him sensed no danger and Jerome quickly disarmed him and used the corporal's own knife to slit the man's throat. He went to the window and his own man was at the back of the building. Seeing Jerome his confederate located tools and quickly had the metal barrier off the window and Jerome climbed out.

"Stop right there!" Jerome heard the command and it took him a second to realize it was in English. This couldn't be good. He nudged his man in a knowing way and they both turned and fired. Jerome's shot caught the women in the leg while the other shattered the women's arm forcing her to drop her gun. Hurriedly, they made their way to a waiting vehicle and left. They could view all of the activity aboard the ship and Jerome knew something had gone wrong. How had they known? He needed to find out.

He grabbed the cell phone and pressed the code for the number in Miami. It started to ring and was quickly answered.

"Roberto, this is Mike Hall where are you? We lost your signal. Have you met up with the contacts at the shipyards? They know you are with us."

Jerome didn't respond.

"Roberto,.... Roberto. Oh shit!" The line went dead.

Jerome immediately hung up. How could he have been such a fool? "Trust no one," he'd murmured.

Throughout the entire journey to his house, his mind focused on his revenge. By the time he reached his home, a new plan was already formed.

Jerome gave a nod to the man who'd driven him and put his hand on the knob of his front door and turned it. He opened the door and walked into the foyer.

"Daddy! Daddy! You're home. I missed you!" Jerome's son ran up and jumped into his arms. "Did you bring me anything from your trip?"

"I did, my son, but it got lost. I'll bring you two things next time."

His wife and daughter came down the stairs.

He was home. But only for as long as it took for him to plan his next assault on America.

Chapter Eighty-Six

✤ ✤ ✤

On a hill with a vast vista that covered central Mexico, Jordan raised up from viewing the man with his family with the Oberwerks long range binoculars provided by General Estrada. The locater on the car had led them to this area and the large palatial estate they were now viewing.

"Who is he General?" Jordan asked, staring intently at the General, his expression communicating Jordan's "don't give me any bull shit," attitude.

"He's a powerful leader of this region's most powerful families. They control business in this area, both legal and illegal. The people love him. We know he's bad. We know that was his ship and his cargo. But there is no way my country is going to do anything to help you obtain his arrest. I am sorry."

"That's not good enough General." Jordan stepped toward the General wanting to get right in his face. "He shot an agent. He stole from the US government. What more do you need. More importantly I've seen him before. Stan remember the cell we had under surveillance in upstate New York. That's the man Kate and I saw go into the house right before it blew up. We need to take him down. Now!"

Stan stepped in between the two, giving Jordan a small shove to move him away.

"Excuse my friend here Estrada, but it is hard for us to leave without this man."

"Stan, I know, I know. I would turn him over to you in a minute. But I would never be allowed. Frankly, I'm probably endangering my career even bringing you out here."

"I understand. Jordan take your last look. We need to move out and get home." Stan patted the General on the shoulder.

Jordan walked back over to the chopper and pulled out the scoped sniper rifle. He hoped the son of a bitch was in the same room. He wouldn't be afforded the time to search for him. He moved quickly back to where he had stood and quickly aimed.

The crack of the rifle report echoed throughout the valley.

Stan whirled around. "Son what have you done?"

Estrada walked up and grabbed the rifle. "You have made a grave error in killing this man. Stan, I may have to keep him here."

Jordan laughed. "The bastard's not dead. Take a look he's probably still on the floor, but I didn't hit him. But I'm sure I scared the shit out of him. He needed to know we know who he is. I've made my point."

Jerome heard the slug penetrate into the wall before he heard the glass of the window disintegrate in pulverized glass. His instinct drove him to the floor. His guards stormed the room with guns drawn.

"El Hefe" the guard shook Jerome as he lifted him off the floor, glass shards falling off his back and hitting the floor.

Jerome shook his head. "We have made some new enemies, different from ones we have had in the past. Our tactics will change but our plans do not." He brushed himself off and went to the window. As the wind blew in from the window, only the thumping sound of a helicopter leaving by flying low enough to be blocked from view by the surrounding hillside was heard.

"It's not a good idea for you to stand there." The guard came over and attempted to put himself between his boss and the open window.

"They have made their point and they are gone. If they had wanted me dead, you would of found me that way."

Epilogue

After the debrief with Stan, Kate and Jordan went to get a beer. Kate had arrived that morning from California after she recovered from extensive surgery and rehabilitation and only had minimal need for a cane.

The beers were cold and felt good going down. They had walked over to the Ritz-Carlton, across from City Hall, in downtown Philadelphia. The hotel was in a converted bank building and the decorator had retained the elegance of the original bank. Huge, white marble columns outlined the center of the lobby, with a matching marble floor. It was elegant, but comfortable. The lobby was crowded with business men and women in conversation. Kate and Jordan retreated to the bar, back in the corner, Jordan's favorite watering hole. It had actually been the vault for the bank and the safe door still remained at the entrance.

"Quite a mission, huh?" Jordan said with a shitty grin on his face.

"Oh, I don't know. It's not everyday you get an all expense paid trip to California."

"I could think of a better way to get there." Jordan laughed.

"Yeah, you're right. You know I still don't get the kids?" Kate became serious.

"What do you mean?"

"That they could be so persuaded, so indoctrinated to do what they did and not question it." She shrugged.

Jordan looked perplexed for a minute. "Oh right. You missed this part. About a week after the attack a couple came back from vacation and found a 15 year old boy in their house with his throat slashed and blood all over. The house had been a scene of a party gone bad or that's what the cops thought. Turns out they both worked at City of Brotherly Love cleaners and had given Mohammed key to the house to use while they were gone. The kid turned out to be one of the other boys in training, killed during a meeting of the teenage leaders.

"You're kidding." Kate shifted in her seat, still dealing with the discomfort in her healing leg. "How do you know this?"

"Aziz and Akmed have been very helpful in taking us through the history of this group. It goes back almost thirty years after they released the American hostages."

"Really, that long, how do they do that?"

"It's cultural. We think one hundred years is a really long time. Our enemies think of it like it's tomorrow. That's why they are always going to be a challenge to us. They think so differently. For them they've been fighting this war since the birth of Christ."

"Unbelievable." Kate nodded her head.

"So what's going to happen to the families?"

"Several of the parents have disappeared. It seems they had an escape plan if things didn't work out. The children who were arrested will stand trial. It will be interesting to see how the jury reacts."

"What about Akmed and Aziz?" Kate inquired.

"Well, they have both been very helpful. The information they provided has helped in uncovering two other cells that had not yet been activated. They still have to go to trial, but I think they'll get lighter sentences and then Stan has arranged for them to go into witness protection.

They both sat there and looked at each other for a few minutes, processing the conversation.

"So, Kate, what are you going to do with your time off?" Jordan inquired.

"I'm not sure. Maybe hit some of the antiques shops north of here."

"Really? That's interesting. Want some company?"

"Company would be nice." They smiled at each other.

"If we leave now, we'll beat traffic." Jordan said, already knowing the answer.

"Let's go." Kate jumped up from the table and headed for the door. Jordan fumbled for money in his pocket and pulled out a twenty dollar bill and threw it on the table.

"Do you want your change?" the bartender called after him.

"No. I had enough with change this week. You can keep it."

They made chit-chat as they drove to Jordan's house, then they made dinner together and dined on the porch.

"This is really a great place." Kate observed. "If it were mine, I'm not sure I would ever leave."

"I know what you mean. It's the place that keeps me sane." Jordan was looking out over the vista, staring at the hills in the distance. "I'm glad you're here, Kate."

"Thanks for letting me come back. I'm gonna turn in. We've got a big day of shopping tomorrow." She got up from her chair and moved toward the door.

"Yes, a big day. See you tomorrow."

Jordan remained on the porch for another hour before he headed inside, went to his room and changed. Once again, he went back down the hall and, once again, found himself outside her door. He hesitated and started to walk back. He stopped, stepped back and went to her door.

He knocked.

From the Author

❖ ❖ ❖

I hope you have enjoyed reading Enemy Among Us. While I want my readers to be entertained by my writing and characters, my intent is to stimulate your thinking. There is much that goes on in our world on a daily basis and it's important we pay attention to it. The people who wish to destroy our way of life are fanatics. Their hatred is strong and their moral compass corrupt. They do take a long term view in their war on us. Their planning takes years and they constantly train. They rarely repeat the same type of attack, knowing that we are reactionary and will mobilize our resources on what has happened not on what could happen. Be diligent and be safe.

My next book will be out in 2011. It is the story of a new Russian Czar who wished to reunite the nations of the former Soviet Union. He acquires one of the lost coins of Judas which he feels will give him the power to carry out his mission. The gang is back lead by Jordan Wright with Father Marco and Gerhard playing larger roles. I hope you will consider reading it.

After thanking you for reading my work, I must thank my family and friends. It isn't always fun being around an author, but my family is my strength. My wife Mary is my greatest supporter and is my strength. My three children Lauren, Jordan and Annemarie are my inspiration. Finally my ever growing faith in our Lord inspires me to pursue my dreams.

All the best to all of you.

Randy

Connect with me on:

Website: http://www.randyreardon.com
Facebook: http://www.facebook.com/pages/Randy-Reardon-Author-of-Thrillers"

CPSIA information can be obtained at www.ICGtesting.com
Printed in the USA
LVOW081320181212

312237LV00002B/101/P

9 781456 508289